Odyssey

Down Under

Volume Six

JAMES GARDNER

NEWMAN SPRINGS PUBLISHING
320 Broad Street
Red Bank, NJ 07701

First originally published by Newman Springs Publishing 2024

ISBN 979-8-89308-251-7 (Paperback)
ISBN 979-8-89308-252-4 (Digital)

Printed in the United States of America

Author's Note

Dear reader,

I wish to tell you about my dog, Cocoa, who came into my life as a young dog. A chocolate Lab who was very exceptional in all his ways, Cocoa spent twelve years with me as we grew into old dogs together. When I first laid pen to paper to write my first book, Cocoa lay patiently by my side as I wrote, only raising his head now and then to see if it was time to stop writing for a while. Having spent twelve wonderful years together, I knew we were just two old men going through life, both getting a little grayer and both walking a little more unsteady, but our love for each other never faltered. He was a perfect companion in a lonely life, essentially a comfort dog. As I watched the gray continue to increase on his muzzle and around his eyes, I knew time was dwindling down. I worried that if I went first, how would he cope, being so devoted to me? Yet how would I cope if I lost him?

One night, he wanted out, but he did not do his usual comeback. I went to search and found him lying in the leaves by the edge of the woods, in frost-laden leaves. To stay the night, he would have frozen to death. I knew what he was doing now. He wanted to distance himself from me because he was going to die. I said, "Old friend, you are not going to do this to me! If you are to die, you die with me!" It was a long vigil that night, and in the morning, he was getting worse. That morning, on January 24th, my best friend died in my arms! Grief set in, and I thought I would never write again. You see, I always had Cocoa involved in my stories. But now, struggling to write again, I will write for Cocoa; he will again be written about and travel with me in our imaginary world to exotic places. Be together again with others as far as the imagination will take us on these mythical journeys. You see, I have to do this, to keep Cocoa alive in my heart and my mind.

I just wanted you to know this.

Back to Japan

Return to the Land of The Rising Sun

I woke up to the sound of light rain pattering down on the thatched roof. A soft breeze was blowing inside through the openings and smelled so fresh and clean. For a moment, I thought, *Where am I?* Then Cocoa raised his head to look at me. He laid his head on the edge of the bed and pushed at me through the covers as he had done for many years. His eyes sparkled and his tail wagged with a thump-thump! I turned to see Lei sleeping beside me. Breathing slowly, peacefully, she looked like an angel, then reality set in—I was in Samoa! Cocoa was with me, and Leilani was by my side. It made me feel so happy inside. Cocoa let out his little greeting, "Rroooow!" Lei opened her beautiful eyes and smiled. Was I in heaven? I thought so for a moment, then said to myself, "Almost, next to it!"

I rolled out of bed, and all in one motion, Lei was arising and Cocoa wanted out. I said, "Okay, boy. Go!" He could open the door himself and go out but needed me to let him back in. Lei stretched and reached for the bed covers to help me make the bed. The help was wonderful! Her first words were, "What's the plan of the day, honey?" Old terminology from my navy days. Every day the plan of the day was announced, as well as the uniform of the day!

I looked at her and said, "Plan of the day: nothing! Rest and relax! Uniform of the day," as I looked at her sheepishly, "as you are."

She grinned and said, "James, you get angry early!" We both laughed.

Boy, did I love this woman! A kiss and a hug, and I said, "I'll get breakfast for you. Make the coffee. You all noticed I bought Kona

3

Coffee at the market—Kona Coffee straight from Hawaii! Best in the world!"

Just then, Cocoa wanted in—he was not going to miss out on anything! I walked to the door and pushed it open, still talking, "We will have bacon or sausage and eggs with homemade wheat bread, toasted, tropical fruit, and Kona coffee. Lots of it!"

Lei frowned a little and said, "I don't remember you getting eggs?"

I said, "Well, yesterday, I heard a couple of Guinea hens cackling in the bush! I sneaked in, found their nest, and retrieved the eggs!"

Lei just stared at me, then went silent. After a long pause, she remarked, "James, just hold the eggs for me. I don't think I want eggs today!"

I laughed. "I was teasing, sweetie. The eggs came from the market—real chicken eggs!" We both laughed, and breakfast was underway. Two eggs for me, two eggs for Lei, and one egg for Cocoa! I had spoiled him. He didn't want dog food; he wanted people food. So I would have to take people food and mix it in with dog food.

After breakfast, Lei and I shared cleanup. The rain had stopped and turned into a sunny, balmy day with the cool breeze coming in from the sea. "Hammock time," I yelled, and Cocoa rushed for the door! This was a nothing day for us—to do whatever we wanted. Lei and I stretched out and Cocoa took position underneath, half out, so he could roll his head back and keep an eye on us. I went into one of my deep thoughts and was quiet.

After a while, Lei looked over and said, "What's wrong, honey?"

I was quiet for a moment and said, "Oh, I don't know, honey. Sometimes I get scared, baby."

Lei asked, "What are you scared about?"

I said, "Aw, I don't know. Sometimes I think how all this is so beautiful, and I have you and all, and maybe it would end! I don't think I could handle the loss!"

Lei thought for a moment then replied, "Let me tell you something, *Jamie*," and she rolled over on me and kissed me hard. "It's never going to end for you and me, baby! I love you too much, and we will always keep what we have!"

I paused. "Lei, you just called me Jamie! That was a secret name between my Anita and me one time! Who have you been talking to?"

Lei crawled onto me and said, "You don't worry about who I talk to! We women have our ways! You just love me, and believe in me! I love you!"

I said, "Is that like the Indian thing that Hawk talks about?" She moved on me closer, Cocoa looked back. I thought this might get serious, so I picked up my phone and reached off the hammock to lay it on the ground. Just as it touched the ground, it vibrated—a ring. I yelled, jumped, and thought I was snakebit!

Lei said, "Answer your phone, dear!"

I looked at the number, knew who it was, and answered, "What's your problem, Captain?"

Captain Mobley was chuckling on the other end. "What's up, mate!" he asked with a chuckle.

I said, "You will never know, Captain!"

He said, "I'm not interrupting your day, am I?"

I replied, "No, go on!"

He said, "If I asked you and Lei to come with me on another cruise, would you go?"

"What if I said no?"

There was a long quiet pause, then he responded, "Then I guess I wouldn't go either!"

I chuckled. "Just teasing, Captain. You know, if the *Sheila II* is going out, we would go too."

I heard relief on the other end. "Wow, that scared me!"

"I have some questions on that, Captain. When, where, and would Helm be able to go with his new wife, baby, and all?"

"Yes, Helm has already committed. He has a good wife. She knows the sea is in his blood, and when the call comes, he goes. But yes, he does respect her, and if a situation arose, he would pull out!"

"So Captain, do you have a game plan?"

"Not yet, mate, working on it. I want to go back to the Land of The Rising Sun! See most all of it this time! Take Ying Yang along to interpret for us!"

"Does he know yet?"

The captain chuckled. "No, but he will go."

(Now Ying Yang was a good friend of Captain Mobley. His name was Darrel Ying. He was the child of a Japanese mother and a Chinese father, thus named Darrel Ying. A successful power business-man in Japan, Ying Yang was the nickname Captain Mobley gleefully put on him. Darrel takes it all in good grace. In fact, when Darrel produced his teriyaki sauce, he called it Ying Yang's Teriyaki Sauce.)

"This call is for preliminary work," remarked the captain. "We have some planning to do, James. Setting course, contacting Ying, outfitting the *Sheila II*, orienting the crew, and hopefully giving you time to bone up on Japanese history."

"Darrell will help you with that for a log! I'll check back."

He chuckled. "Well, James, I hope you don't get mad. I put my little stick in and stirred things up. Not in a bad way, you see, just a little help! Contacted Hawk and Curt. They will be ready to bring you to Sydney when things are in place. They are also going to take care of Cocoa while you are gone!"

I said, "No problem with that, but what if they have tourist flights scheduled?"

"No problem there! They are both excited to have Cocoa for a while and not have him go to a babysitter. They even have a seat behind the pilots reserved just for Cocoa," then he roared with laughter.

"I'll get back, mate!"

I hung up and looked at Lei; she just rolled her eyes and said, "I guess I better get my 'ditty bag' ready to go." Cocoa just laid back his ears.

We settled down, then Lei took the phone from my hand and laid it on the ground. She rolled toward me with her head on my shoulder. She scooted close. She ran her fingers through my hair, which really relaxed me. She laid her head on my chest; soon I felt her relax, and she was breathing deep and soft. She was totally asleep. I heard Cocoa sigh and looked down as he laid his head down between his front paws, his eyes blinked shut. He was in dreamland. I lay silent, feeling the balmy breeze blow softly across us.

My eyes became heavy. I was half dreaming. I said to myself, "I don't really want to sail the seas to Japan. I'd rather have Leilani fly me to the moon!" I drifted off. Much later, I felt Cocoa softly nudge my hand to awaken me. That was his way, all through our years together. Nudge me gently in the morning to get me up. Darkness was starting to fall upon us, and the breeze was still constant off the sea. I said, "Right, old boy, time for us to get up!" Lei then stirred. I said, "Come on, baby, we need to get up and let me fix your supper." She rolled out with a big smile and embraced me. We started for the house, and I said, "Come on, 'Buck,' in we go," and Cocoa was up and following.

Inside, Lei said, "We don't need to do a lot, especially you! You have spoiled me all day!"

"So let's have some good coffee and a bowl of fruit."

When the coffeepot made its last blurb, Lei poured the coffee. She asked, "Where do you want to have your coffee, honey?"

I said, "On the moon! Fly me to the moon!"

She stopped, looked at me for a moment or two, and then asked, "On the moon?"

I said, "Yeah, just me and you!"

She came to me, put her arms around me, and said, "James, sometimes you say the strangest things!"

I said, "Yeah, because I love you!"

Lei put our coffee in place then turned and asked, "Would you like some fruit?"

I said, "Is it passion fruit?"

She burst out laughing and said, "What's with you?"

I said, "Nothing other than I love you so very much."

She then came into my arms and embraced me with a big kiss. So we sat down and enjoyed our "Kona" coffee, the best in the world, and ate our fruit. It was just a tropical fruit mix, but it could have been passion fruit! Cocoa was sitting by me, taking it all in.

As I finished, I handed the bowl to him and asked, "Little passion fruit, old boy?" Cocoa just turned his head away and lay down.

Lei burst out laughing. "I don't know what to think about you two!"

I said, "Well, it's just two minds working together!"

Lei said, "I love it!" and Cocoa went over to her and laid his head on her knee. When we went to bed that night, with Lei finally asleep and Cocoa taking a turn on her side of the bed, I thought, *Am I able to write a ship's log about our travels to Japan? Or will it turn into a love story?*

After breakfast, the phone started ringing in the yard by the hammock. I rushed out but missed the call. I didn't mind; last night, the phone was the farthest thing on my mind! I looked at the number; it was Captain Mobley. I punched the number, and his response was immediate. "Hello, mate! How are things going?"

"Good, Captain, and you?"

"Just great, James, good to hear from you. I have been making plans!"

"You at Captain Cook's dock on board *Sheila II*?"

"No, mate, been working from the outback station. Got things in order here! Still need to round up the crew and have a field day on the *Sheila II*. Get everything shipshape! Looks like three weeks to a month, so you have plenty of time. All you and Lei need to do is grab your ditty bag and come on when Curt and Hawk pick you up! Cocoa too! He has a reserved seat behind the pilot. He will be fine. He has been in air travel before when you went back to retrieve him from the farm! I have contacted Darrell Ying! He will meet us on schedule, South Island in Japan. A place called Kagoshima." Then he laughed. "I can spell it but it's a little hard to pronounce!" Then he roared with laughter! Yes, old Captain Mobley was back in fine form! He went on. "Darrell picked the Ronda view! There is a nice, protected bay off the Pacific leading inland to the town. Very picturesque and quiet. I'll contact you in plenty of time. Okay, James, warm up your pen! Now give that pretty island girl of yours a hug for me and old Cocoa, a pat on the head!" Then he again roared with laughter.

"No problem, Captain. I'll hug them both!"

The day of departure arrived quickly. Curt and Hawk pulled up in their jeep to take us down to the docked plane. Curt dropped the tailgate to board Cocoa. Cocoa just looked at it! Lei said, "Oh no! Cocoa rides with me, up front!" So Lei climbed in and pressed over to me real hard, which I didn't mind a bit, and Cocoa jumped in beside her real close. He turned his head and gave Lei a lick on the cheek.

"Well," I said, "he never gave me a lick on the cheek!"

Lei giggled, and I could swear Cocoa was laughing! We arrived at the dock, and there sat, rocking gently in the water, the de Havilland Pontoon Plane, all shiny teal blue and white. The walkboard was in place. Hawk was the first to assist us. Cocoa boarded without a pause. Hawk patted his seat, and Cocoa jumped on. Curt in with the gangway, the engine starts with a smooth purr. We taxied for the bay. Hawk shoved the fuel levers forward, and we were skipping across the water and lifting smoothly into the air. I looked at Cocoa; he was watching out, not a care in the world—if there was a wind, his ears would be flapping! We smoothed out for the flight to Sydney. Cocoa napped; he got up again to watch us land. A seasoned traveler!

When we disembarked, Curt assisted with the gangway quickly enough to get us off. Lei hugged Cocoa and told him she loved him and wanted to be a good boy. I hugged him with love and told him we would be back in a little bit. Be a good dog! I stepped off the plane, and Lei was at the door, tears streaming down her face, then I lost it big time! I grabbed her up, my tears flowing, and hung on tight! Curt was loaded and on, and the plane was speeding across the bay in a quick departure! There was nothing to say! Our hearts were already bonded together; we regained composure, and the Aboriginal folks in the market watched with sad eyes as we walked toward the ship.

The crew was all on board; it was like an old home week when we walked on! Hugs, kisses, and handshakes all around! It was like our services in Samoa when we came in—hugs and handshakes all around, no matter who you are or what color. It is a good thing! The captain welcomed us aboard! Of course, "Cookie" would come up with one of his quips. I was glad he wasn't going to bang his pot!

When quiet prevailed, he remarked, "I have heard the old legend in the sailors' world that a woman aboard stoves an ill wind! But that," he declared, "is rubbish and a downright myth!"

When Leilani walked aboard, I felt the *Sheila II* lift her keel upward another foot of water! They all cheered! That earned "Cookie" a second hug! Lei then asked him if, on this cruise, she could help in the kitchen. Cookie remarked, "No, ma'am, in the first place, it's a *galley*, not a kitchen. In the second place, you are like the Queen of Samoa to me, so *kick back* and enjoy the ride!" Everyone cheered again.

The captain said, "Well, the gang's all here. We may as well get underway!"

Quickly, arrangements took place to *cast off* and *get underway*.

When we moved away from the dock and headed for the bay, one of the crew pulled out a "boatswain's whistle" that he brought from his enlistment. He *piped* us down as we were moving into the harbor. It was so moving and a surprise that, again, tears were in my eyes! Leaving Sydney Harbor in full sail on a blue and sunny day, with calm water, was a sight to see! I will have to put this in my log! The journey has begun! We are off to the Land of the Rising Sun, where life is now beautiful, and legends of the Sumerian warriors still live on.

As we moved north into the night and passed over the Equator, things quieted down. The work of getting underway was behind us, and we were sailing steadily on course. Everyone seemed quiet, and I imagined it was because of the venture we were now on. We had touched Japan once on our journey to the Aleutian Islands. We pulled into the beautiful bay of Osaka and viewed a brief splendor of one small part of Japan. The stop was mainly because Captain Mobley wanted to see his old friend Darrell Ying, a wealthy man with great holdings around Osaka, and an international businessman himself! We were treated like royalty there; maybe this is why they returned there. Not for the captain to be treated special but to achieve the goal he always wanted: to see all the islands of Japan! The captain and

Mr. Ying had conversed. Darrell Ying was just as excited and said he would meet us at Kagoshima, located at the southernmost point of the Japanese Islands. It was up a beautiful, protected bay, between the Sea of China and the Pacific. He would be on board for the whole tour, our guide and spokesman, which would be wonderful since we did not know the language or the culture. I was impressed with the first meeting with Mr. Ying and looked forward to being with him again. The captain had readied the extra stateroom, you might say, on deck for Darrell Ying's quarters. I had briefed Leilani all about him and our journey there, and she was all excited about this venture as well.

As we sailed along in the quiet, the captain seemed *wound up*. "James!" he said, "Are you ready for a big log?" And he laughed.

"Well, Captain, I have been struggling with this one. It's clear out of my league, you know! I'm hoping Mr. Ying will be able to feed us a narrative."

"Oh James, I know you have a story there somewhere!"

"Yes, Captain, but this becomes more of a history than a story!"

The captain chuckled. "Okay, mate, give me a little history lesson, then we will get on with what we don't know and what we will see and feel when we get there! We have only touched the part where Darrel Ying lives. We have a good feel for that. How would you say the rest of Japan compares with the rest of the South Pacific islands we have seen?"

I studied this a moment, while Lei looked at me anxiously. I took her hand and smiled. "Well, Captain, Japan is north of the Equator, so it can be seasonal but tropical. It can have winter and summer in reverse to Australia and the Pacific islands. It can even have severe cold and snow, ice, in the higher elevations." I winked at Lei, and she pulled in close to me. "Wow, that ought to spike my thoughts! I would also say that, like the Pacific islands, its formation came about by volcanic eruptions, then followed by exotic plant life and animals of different species. It became a beautiful paradise also, in its own right, but plant life could differ from the Pacific islands. There are trees, plants, and flowers not found in other parts of the world. Islanders did not come up here in great canoes. It was inhabited differently. Now all I can say, Captain, is we will have to go into a long history lesson to give you more insight and also into topography and customs to explain why Japan is like it is!"

The captain said, "Mate! Sounds like you are on a roll! We have got all night, lay it on me!"

"Okay, Captain. but not to bore you. I'll keep it brief and then we go into just how it is in Japan. I guess hoping when Darrel comes aboard, he will round this all out with his stories about people and customs. Maybe a little more about the environment."

"Well, James, I know they are highly industrialized, but I don't need to know all that. Just down to how they lived and also how they live now!"

"I was hoping you would say that, Captain, because I don't want to go there either. Also, my log will not be laden with war stories or atrocities that occurred during our war years. If it's ancient history like the Samurai warriors, it would be of interest to me!"

"Sounds great, mate, start with the beginnings!"

"Now, Captain, I have a lot of wind, so how far do you want to go?"

"All the way, mate! All the way!" And he roared with laughter!

"Well," I said, "If you want to get some shut-eye during the day and take watch at night, we can get through this. After all, we don't need story time with the crew on this. They will have the log." Lei yawned.

The captain said, "Good plan, mate! I'll put Helm on watch, with crew help, for a few nights, and we will have a go!"

Lei rolled her eyes. I looked at her. She said, "Don't worry, honey. I will be up with you! I would not miss this for the world!"

So down we came, and we three stumbled into breakfast, with looks from all. After breakfast, the plan was put in place, and we three went to bed! Helm was happy to be in control of the ship all day, and the crew couldn't care less. That night after supper, the captain relieved Helm, and we started in. "Well, Captain, if the sea doesn't get rough, or King Neptune rises up out of the sea, we are ready to go on!"

Lei gave me a quizzical look and remarked, "King Neptune?"

I said, "Well, sweetie, that's another story in itself. I'll tell you later!"

The captain chuckled. "I'd like to be in on that one!"

"Here we go! History lesson 101. Keep in mind that all this starts with the Japanese Islands, primitive and uninhabited. We are going way back in history, pre-twelfth century, and covering many centuries of ruling forces and wars moving toward pre–World War II. We cannot begin to tell the history of Japan unless we include Korea and China. Both have influenced the establishment of Japan with their customs, knowledge, and practices. In the eighth century, Asian people migrated from Korea and China to the Islands of Japan. A centralized government was set up. The government was similar to the Tang Dynasty in China.

"The government evolved as Japan became populated and there was an economic increase. Soon, Mogul incursions changed the government and economics of the land. Japan became a dictatorship, which lasted centuries. In time, the government evolved into a Confucianism government, similar to China. Then Moguls gained power and ruled. Then another factor pushed them out and took overrule. Then came, in time, a State of Korea and Japan. Korea was pushing a unification plan. So many dominant factors evolved in and out of Japan's government that either helped or hindered progression. Then in the twelfth century, Kublai Khan smashed a great fleet to conquer Japan. There were many victories, but a great sea storm came up and destroyed most of his ships. A second attempt was made, and with powerful forces to penetrate the Japanese defense, a great typhoon struck!

"In the twelfth century, four million peasants were gathered up to dig a canal through the mountains, which would allow the transport of goods from the north. This extremely stressed the economy of the population. Then to add to the woes, a great drought set in. So after the Chinese stirred up the Red Turban Rebellion. All this happened at a time when the silk trade was in full swing! All this was going on about the same time as the pursuit of the silk trade when the Italian explorer Marco Polo visited China. He spent seventeen years in China and stayed on to serve Emperor Kublai Khan as a government official.

"In 1868, we see the transformation of the Enlightened Rule. The process of becoming an industrialized nation moved ahead and positioned Japan to become strong in the industrialized world. By 1860, Japan had endured twenty years of isolation under the governing powers. An alliance of Samurai sought to mobilize Japan. The Samurai challenged the government, took control, and moved Japan into modernization. The army and navy were built up into strong forces. And some of the Samurai became officers in the military. Their sense of discipline created and produced the most powerful force in Asia.

"So this brings us to the close of our history lesson, Captain. To move on would be to rattle the sabers of war, and we do not want to go there! Now we understand what shaped Japan after years of poor government and abuse. Now we will move on to the beauty of the land, the interest of the country, and the people."

The sun was peeking over the horizon and casting a red glow on the sails; I was glad. I had never had such a long talk. Helm was coming for the wheel, and we would head for a good breakfast with Cookie, then *kick back* in our quarters for a good rest.

We arose by late afternoon, rested, and ready for a good meal from Cookie. After supper, Captain Mobley grimaced. "Well, James, are you ready for the night shift?" Then to Lei, he said, "How about you, Lei, are you going to bear another *all-nighter*, or are you bidding out?"

Lei said, "I'm in, Captain. I don't want to miss any of James's continuing stories! Besides, I want to stay close to him!"

The captain chuckled. "I can see that. That is good!" As we went up to the wheel, Helm was on watch. The captain frowned. "Helm, have you been here all day?"

"No, sir," Helm replied. "We rotated through the crew." That seemed to please the captain. Helm was a strong leader and had no problem enforcing what was correct. So the Captain took the wheel and with a grin, nodded to me. This man sure did like the stories.

"So, Captain, let's go back for a little more geography since we are going to make a *good go* of the islands this trip.

"What is interesting, is Japan's name is derived from *Nippon*, meaning 'sun's origin' because the Japanese believe that the sun rises first in Japan. Japan is also known as the Land of the Rising Sun. Japan consists of four thousand mountainous islands. They seem to lie in a bow shape. The four major islands, or the largest, are the heart of Japan, where all industrial and productivity takes place, and also dense population. The highest mountain is Fuji, snowcapped, and the longest river is two hundred twenty-eight miles, and the largest lake, Biwa, is on Honshu. To the north, the largest island, Hokkaido, experiences harsh winters, and the mountains are harsh and volcanic. But yes, one may say that these islands are very beautiful with their seasons, mountains, and lush trees and grass.

"One may be fortunate to see wildlife moving through and browsing on the lush grasses. There are sixty-seven volcanoes, and some are active and some potentially active. And yes, Mount Fuji, Japan's highest peak, is also active. Most of Japan's mountains are too steep for development, which explains the dense development and population along the coastal areas. Because of volcanic eruptions, the Japanese had to design and build their homes to compensate for this activity. Early on, they built houses of paper which kept them cool in the summer but not in the winter. The paper house is now nonexistent.

"Earthquakes are another form of destructive nature that the Japanese had to endure. The shifting of the ocean floor could create a massive quake, sending a great tsunami, or tremendous wave ashore, causing massive destruction." I paused, thinking to myself. The captain and Lei looked at me in anticipation. I then said, "Captain, another facet of history came to mind. I talked about people coming to the shores of Japan from China, Korea, and possibly Malaysia. There is more to the story! You see, these people crossed into the islands of Japan by crossing the Tsushima Straits into Kuzuki. When they entered the islands of Japan, they found an aboriginal type of people: swarthy skin, hairy, round eyes, Caucasian-like. This indicated that they had come from the islands of the Pacific. This all adds to the mystery of the first people to inhabit the islands of Japan." I looked at the captain. Sometimes mysteries go deep!

The captain stood for a moment; he looked a little perplexed. Lei looked from him to me. "James, is that all you have to say about the history?"

"Well, Captain, it's like this: I could have bored you with a history lesson, and it's not an entertaining structure for our trip log. We need the new and exciting, not the old and antique histories. I brought you down to the era of Japan's industrial growth and the rattling of sabers for war! I didn't want to get into that! Let me conclude history, Captain, by putting it this way.

"As for history, what I've shared with you so far, let's put a wrap on it this way: as for the history of Japan, history can go back as far as 400 BC. An ever-changing culture of government declines in quality sometimes. One interesting note is that as governments progressed, they were somewhat based on Buddhism. The main capital of Japan at that time was named Kyoto and consisted of several places to be combined under rule. Later in history, it became known, as we know it today, Tokyo! I would like to leave more, if needed, for Dr. Ying when he comes aboard. He is going to be a real asset to us. He knows the country, customs, and language! I understand also that we are in for a treat because they say that Japan is beautiful with black islands, some snowcapped, drifting down through lush green tropical forests to the shores of an emerald sea! I also want to learn from Darrell Ying what he can share about the time of the Samurai warriors!"

"Gotcha, James," the captain replied. "We will let old Ying Yang fill us in on some more! But stand by if you want to include more."

"I will do that, Captain, I will do that." I paused a moment and then said, "Please, Captain, don't call Mr. Ying 'Ying Yang' when he comes aboard." The captain just roared with laughter. Then Lei and the captain looked at me seriously.

"James, Lei, and I have noticed that you are a little *lost* and can't seem to retain your usual humor. Are you okay, mate? It kind of worries us a little." Lei nodded.

"Just a little tired, I guess, Captain. I have Cocoa on my mind lately, maybe?"

The captain said, "We will fix that! Helm, get on the radio and see if you can raise that 'Indian Boy'!"

The radio crackled, and in quick response, Hawk came on the line. "Hi, Captain, what's on your mind?"

The captain asked, "What's your location, mate?"

Hawk laughed. "About due west of you, Captain, in the Pacific."

I could hear Curt reading instructions. The captain chuckled. "What are you two up to, mate? Got a full load of folks going up to Hawaii? Is Cocoa telling dog stories? James is standing by and wants to know how his old dog is doing!"

"Well, Captain, the passengers are all asleep, so Cocoa is presently looking over Curt's shoulder! Doesn't want him to hit any of those *bump marks* in the sky," then laughed. "Now he is intently looking at me, hearing you and James talking over the phone. He wants to know what's going on. Though with the captain, *their ships.*"

"So my old buddy is hanging tough!"

"You betcha," said Hawk. "You know old dog! He can hang with the best!"

"Okay, mate. You hang tough also. We were just concerned."

"Don't worry, Captain. The old dog takes good care of us! You and James hang tough also. Captain, we're going to the islands where you gotta! Over and out!"

I felt relieved. The captain just smiled, and Lei hugged me. I guessed from where we were, it wouldn't be long before our journey to Japan began. After Cookie's gourmet supper, the captain, Lei, and I relieved Helm from the wheel. No story time tonight, just *kick back* and have a little rest and a little chitchat. So things were calm for a while and the three of us could reminisce about days gone by, which turned into story time again! But a little lighter than history and culture!

In the morning, we headed for a good breakfast with Helm manning the wheel, freeing the captain up for a spell. As we started to head for the galley, Helm spoke, "Captain, my calculations say we will be approaching the small islands of Japan by midmorning!"

"Good go," said the captain to Helm. After a leisurely gourmet breakfast and lingering over several cups of the special Kona coffee, we headed back on deck. The helm was comfortable to stay on wheel watch. The captain relieved him for breakfast, and before we knew it, he was back to take the wheel! You see, Helm had a romance with the sea, and it was always second nature for him to lend a hand wherever needed.

It wasn't long before the small islands off Japan's larger islands came into sight. First, volcanic peaks rise from the sea. A little closer, and the tropical foliage began to glow in the early morning sunlight! Spectacular! Must I repeat myself again and quote "Land of the Rising Sun"? The captain now took the wheel and asked Helm to stand by. The captain remarked, "I will set course around the west side of the small islands and be sure of safe waters. As you recall folks, the opposite side of the islands were World War II beachheads, for a few, remember Ilea-Sakishima, Okinawa, and Tara. Not to get into the wars as James said, but reminders of the many lives who fought and died there. James shared with me that his big brother was involved in many Pacific establishments of beachheads. James was happy when his big brother came home. James would not share war stories with me, but only told me the monkey story!" Then he chuckled to himself.

Lei jumped up and begged, "I want to hear the monkey story!" The captain glanced over to me for approval, and I nodded my head yes.

The captain continued, "On one island, big brother's platoon established a beachhead, and then tents were set up for temporary barracks. The Japanese were still active on the island, thus that was why they were there, to push back, destroy the enemy, and secure the island. I see James getting nervous, so back to the monkey story! Well, it seems that the monkey population was still active in the jungle! So one day, Tim and his buddies took a net and fruit in a jar and ventured into the jungle! In a clearing, they set down the jar and retreated into hiding to wait! It was a while before the monkeys would venture out.

"Out of curiosity, they moved around the jar, peering in and jumping back. Finally, one took the nerve to investigate, looking everything over. He found the top. He slowly reached in for the fruit.

The men came out of hiding, running with the net. The monkey would not let go of the prized fruit, so he was running, dragging the jar. The net was thrown, and the monkey was caught.

"Back at camp, Tim made a leash and collar. The monkey was vicious and hissed, trying to bite anything within reach. After a few days, the monkey calmed down and each day became tamer. Tim then tied him to the cot. He became a guard dog and would let no one come close to the cot but Tim. He was taming down really well when night came the monkey got under the covers with Tim. Finally, Tim let him loose, and he followed Tim around like a dog. They shared everything, even meals.

"One time, James's mother found out where Tim was located, in a secret type of way. She got busy and baked one of her delicious fruit cakes and packed it with a securely sealed jar of peaches. It finally found its way to the island by mail call. Tim's buddies were all ecstatic! A package from home! They wanted to share. Of course, the monkey was right in the middle of it too. Unwrapped, he gave it to his friends to share, but they were not getting any peaches. That was for him and his monkey.

"So in a thank-you letter to home, he wrote, 'Mom, got the package. You made a platoon happy, and me and my monkey happy. No fridge, so Monkey and I decided we better eat them. I poured them out into my mess kit. I would dip one out, and the monkey would take a turn and pick one out, watching me!' So when his mom got the letter, being a reserved woman, she wasn't too happy about the monkey eating out of the same pan! So many happy days were spent together with Tim and his monkey.

"But you know, all good things seem to come to an end, sometimes in a bad way. One day, general quarters were sounded. The Japanese were making an advance toward the camp. All the boys ran for their tanks. You see, Tim was in the Tank Destroyer Division and the driver and leader of his tank crew. Tim started the tank and began to move when the spotter shouted, 'Tim! Stop, the monkey!' The little monkey was not going to let his master go. He ran and jumped on the tank tread. Tim tried a quick stop, but it was too late. The monkey went under the tank tread. They had to go on. After the

Japanese were engaged, many lost their lives and were driven back. Back at base, the monkey was found, and the whole platoon held a military funeral for him before he was buried. You see, the monkey had become part of the boys."

I had tears running down my cheeks, and Lei was in a full *sob* when I took her in my arms and gently comforted her. The captain's eyes were misty. He said, "James, I am so sorry! I did not know that it would end like this. Forgive me!"

I said, "No problem, my captain, just a well moment."

I got Lei settled down and hung on to her. The captain said, "James, I really am sorry, but you know what? James, you have stories to share. You have stories that need to be told!" I shook my head. "James, can I tell just one more? You know, the one about the chow line?"

I looked as Lei stared at me. "It's okay, honey. It's not in a bad way!"

Then the captain remarked, to the others who were gathering to see what was going on, "James has told me many stories that have never been put into his log. Good stories my mate has! And sometimes stories need to be told lest we forget!

"Well, we were back on the same island. Brother Tim was in the chow line. He tells James that at 5:00 p.m. every day, as regular as clockwork and barring no call to arms, chow down was standard. The platoons all lined up at the mess tent. Rough tables were set up inside. The boys were always hungry, no matter what. They noticed that the chow line was getting longer and taking more time to move. As they looked around at everyone they knew, there were strangers lined up within the ranks! They were Japanese soldiers hiding in the jungle. They had removed US Army uniforms from dead soldiers and came to chow! The boys said nothing, just nodded to each other, and kept quiet. They knew that these young Japanese boys were hungry, in fact, starving. They also knew that these young boys were like them, shipped off to a foreign land to fight a war that they wanted no part of. So they kept quiet and let this quiet enemy eat. No conversation, no apparent recognition.

"But there was another problem! Every day at 5:00 p.m., a Japanese Zero fighter plane flew over and strafed the chow line! Everyone had to run for cover until he passed over. After a wreck of this, the 'powers to be' called in for assistance, and an American P-40 fighter waited, hiding in the clouds. When the Zero swooped down to make his run, the P-40 dropped out of the clouds and engaged. The Zero went down, smoking into the sea. Problem solved." The captain paused. "No tears in this one, James, I had to tell! Your other stories I keep in my heart, old mate! I did not want to go against your will! You said you would write about Japan in a good way, no war or stress, ties on the better side! And this is good, and we are here to see the new Japan—also, the old beautiful Japan in its beginnings, its history, and its culture, and to see my old friend Ying, who has volunteered to be a storyteller on this trip. So James, got your pen warmed up?"

"Yes, Captain, I do, and you know what, the stories of mine you told were not in a bad way! There was no *bad stuff*, so to speak. As I guess that maybe someday more can be told. There are vets out there from your country and mine that would like to share. When I visited the war museum in Canberra, your capital, there were a lot of stories told about your side. It was something to see and put into your mind."

"Storytime is over, boys," the captain said to his crew. "We are passing the small islands. In a short time, we will be going up a beautiful inland bay of the Satsuma Peninsula to berth at Kagoshima, a Japanese city at the bottom of Japan, bordered by the Sea of China on one side and the Pacific on the other. There, we will pick up Dr. Ying, one of my best friends. He will be our tour guide and narrator for the balance of this cruise, and I implore you to follow his instructions as you would mine. He will quickly earn your respect because his mannerisms and knowledge are of the top. He most likely will give you respect in turn. We were coming abreast of two larger islands and moving into the beautiful bay leading up to our destination."

When we arrived at the port off the city of Kagoshima, Japanese dockhands proficiently handled lines and set up the gangway before our crew could blink an eye, actually took on their job and got it done!

Cookie approached the captain. "I have a surprise lunch if our guest arrives soon!"

The captain said, "Fine, Cookie, I can always depend on you being one step ahead of me! I imagine the guest will be here soon! Knowing him, he is waiting in the wings for our arrival!"

Directly, a brand-new minibus pulled up and parked. Darrel Ying waved and smiled as he began his ascent. We were all anticipating how this arrival would proceed. Friend to friend, Darrel stepped off the gangway onto the deck, stopped, and stared at Captain Mobley. The captain stared back. Then he yelled, "Ying Yang!"

Darrel yelled back, "Mobley Dick!"

They stood staring at each other. Our faces dropped! Was there going to be an altercation here? Then the two grabbed each other's shoulders, flashed big grins, and with hands on shoulders, started yelling and laughing, dancing around the deck! Like two old trappers meeting up at a rendezvous who hadn't seen each other for years, they then grinned and hugged, and the captain said, "Hello, old friend!" And Darrel did the same. We all let out a sigh of relief.

Then the captain said, "Come, let me introduce you to my band of friends!" So introductions were made all around, and then Cookie stepped out of the galley to bang his pan. Always a great greeting. We all headed to the tables.

As we go in, dear reader, I will give a little explanation about Darrel Ying. I had explained all this in a prior book, *North to the Aleutians*. On that cruise, we stopped at Darrel Ying's fine home in Japan and were treated royally! Sometimes I call Darrel Ying, Dr. Ying because at a very young age, he earned his doctorate degree from a prestigious college in Japan. Also traveling abroad in his pursuit of knowledge, including in other countries as well as the United States. Darrel Ying's parents were a Chinese father and a Japanese mother. He has aspired to be a powerful businessman in Japan and worldwide. One of his famous products, sold worldwide, was his teriyaki sauce. This is why Captain Mobley came up with the name Ying Yang for the sauce—a joke, really, about his mother and father—but

Darrel Ying did not adopt the name. Still, Captain Mobley likes to tease him with it. So the encounter on the ship! A trip to Darrel's home was a surprise on our Aleutian journey. And what a surprise it was!

After an excellent lunch, we rolled back for conversation. Later, Darrel said to Captain Mobley, "I would like to talk about this trip to Japan. May I have the floor while everyone is present?"

Captain Mobley replied, "Sure, Ying, you can have the table, but you can't have the floor! That's my deck!"

He chuckled. Ying smiled and said, "Yes, I forgot my nautical terms. May I have the deck, sir?"

"Permission granted," said the captain with a chuckle.

I glanced at Lei and said, "This is going to be a fun trip with these two!" Dr. Ying took the "deck" and addressed us with a courteous bow, very humble.

"Ladies and gentlemen, and I must say a very beautiful lady," he nodded at Lei and me. "We are ready to embark on a journey through Japan. I have been honored to be both narrator and educator on this tour. Captain Mobley has graciously turned the project over to me. I am very honored! You know, as we go along in life following the schedules and protocol, we will not succeed! We will just be followers. Sometimes, a man must mark his own path, even if some become confused! There is always explanation and clarification for those who seek the truth! Some have referred to me as a man of vision. I am not a *man of vision*. I strive to do my best and be an achiever and believer. Therefore, my agile little brain does not operate in a convoluted order to make myself clear and not to confuse. To see and know Japan, you must absorb their history, their customs, their beliefs, and their future. Then you will have within your grasp the real Japan! We can go from city to city, and what do you see? Beautiful cities, some quaint, some modern. But have you come away with the heart of Japan in your memory? No! I will show you the real Japan by showing you the lifestyle, customs, beliefs, and aspirations. I will show you city by city, but forgive me if I don't give you a repertoire of cities. My friends, you can see, but the heart of

Japan you cannot see unless you go into the history, the people, the culture, their rituals, and their goals.

"Soon this journey will take us from looking at the cities to listening to the memories that I retain about them, not always correlated to cities but to a life of the past. Thank you for your indulgence. Now for lesser but firm instruction, I have made arrangements for all aspects of this tour: payment, food service, lodging if needed, and a mini bus at each port of call. This whole venture is on me! No pay, no tip, no sweat. This is my deal, and I am grateful that my friend Captain Mobley has allowed me to do so. For me, it is a great honor. So allow me to pursue this. There is still time left today. The minibus is waiting. Let's go tour this beautiful little city before we leave. Tonight, Mr. Cookie, there will be no 'Cookie'! You will dine with me, as well as the rest of the folks, on the finest Japanese cuisine in Japan! Then we will all return to the *Sheila II*, and I will get to sleep in the beautiful stateroom that Captain Mobley has prepared for me. Eat your hearts out, boys. I'm not sleeping with the crew!" Everyone laughed.

"Tomorrow, the journey begins. We will not stop at my home to go out. I have saved that option for last. I have a special treat! Meanwhile, we will travel up the Pacific side and down the China Sea on the opposite side. At Kobe-Osaka, we have a spacious channel to bring us inland again. Follow the bag up to my residence. And for you, Captain Mobley, thank you for the use of your deck, and no, my home is not 'Ying Yang's.' There is a more sophisticated Japanese name that I will reveal to you there!"

Everyone roared with laughter; I think Captain Mobley was the loudest.

After a wonderful evening tour of the town, a gourmet meal, and a good night's sleep, we were ready to get underway in the morning—the journey was about to begin! When we all returned to the ship, the crew was ready to do their own thing: hit the sack, play cards, or whatever else piqued their interest at the time. As for Dr. Ying, Captain Lei, and I, we were too excited about tomorrow's journey, so we decided to stay on deck, sit, and chat for a while. The night was moonlit, and calm, with just a light, balmy breeze blowing in off the bay. We just sat together for a long time, saying nothing, just enjoying the time and company.

Dr. Ying raised his eyes and silently stared at Lei and me. A span of time elapsed as he determined how to proceed politely into this conversation. He stared at Lei, then me, then back to Lei. Finally, he quietly spoke, "Lei, you say you are from Samoa?" No answer. "You are a very beautiful woman! You may have been born in Samoa, but I think your ancestry goes beyond that. Your beauty tells me you are more than Samoan, maybe Tahitian, Tongan, or from other Pacific islands, you know, they traveled around, located in different places. You have the unusual beauty of other Pacific islanders. I know you were born in Samoa and think you are Samoan, rightly so, but still, your heritage shows through in your beauty." He became very silent, and then Lei, a little embarrassed, thanked him for his comments.

In a loving moment, he went on, "Lei, you will meet my wife at the end of this journey. Her name is Lotus Flower. I call her Lotus, her preference! Like you, she is very beautiful! And like you, somewhere in the past, she, or her beautiful ancestors, came down from a different race, which mixed with the Japanese islanders!"

Lei asked, "You don't think I am part Japanese, do you?"

Dr. Ying smiled, then laughed. "No, Lei, I don't, but somewhere back when." Lei smiled. He then switched topics. "James, how did you ever meet and capture a beautiful island girl?"

That took me off guard, and I said, "Dr. Ying, I don't quite know how to answer that. I almost lost her! Let me explain. Lei was a flight attendant for Qantas Air. On the first flight back to the States from Sydney, I met her! I was very interested but hid the fact. On the second trip back, she was on duty, and we became closer. She slept on my shoulder during her break. I was overwhelmed by that but resisted. I really knew I was falling in love, but no such luck for an old man! So flights back seemed to become manipulated." I glanced over at Captain Mobley, and he looked down sheepishly. "So you know, I myself did not know when or if my last flight would be, and this beautiful island girl would be lost." Lei gave me a sheepish look.

"So on what I thought would be my last flight, when we arrived in Los Angeles, the day broke! I did not know my friend Captain

Mobley had arranged for a round-trip ticket for me! Lei tearfully confessed how much she loved me, had loved me! I was smitten with love for her! We diverted to Samoa, she left the service, we built our life, and retrieved my dog Cocoa, and here we are!"

Dr. Ying smiled. "James, that sounds like a good fairy tale love story!" I chuckled. He went on, "Not to pry, but how would you explain your relationship?"

I said, "You are not prying, Dr. Ying, I would gladly express myself on this subject. You see, it has always been on my mind. You know, to me, marriage is not just all about sex. Marriage is about two people who meet. They fall in love! There are sexual encounters, yes, but that is not the whole story. It is about two people coming together, loving, and caring, and sharing with each other."

Lei was staring at me. "It is about feelings, love, touch, and smell. Let me explain. It is a man and woman together. When Lei and I go to bed, it is not all about sex. I want her closeness. I want to cuddle up to her back, feel the softness of her body, caress her shoulders and hips, put my arm around her waist, listen to her breathing, and take in her beautiful smell, which is heavenly to me. I like to bury my face in her beautiful hair. I like to take my hand and caress her forehead, back down through her hair, and then she breathes deeply and goes into a deep slumber. I cuddle closer and so I go into slumber. That's when my woman and I are one." Lei was looking down, eyes misty. Captain was looking down. Dr. Ying was staring at me.

"James, that is the most beautiful thing I have ever heard! I always wanted to express my feelings for my wife like that but never had the words. Now you have given me the words. Thank you so much!" The conversation turned to general chitchat as we enjoyed being together. Later, when we were tired, we all turned to our places.

As we turned into our bunks, Lei turned to me. "That was so beautiful what you said about us, honey!"

She kissed me softly on the lips, and I returned her love. "I love you, Lei," I said as I cuddled into her back.

She said, "And I will always love you. You are my man!"

In the morning, after a famous "Cookie" breakfast, we made preparations to get underway. The Japanese dock team did all the honors of removing the gangway, and untying the lines, so our crew did not have to lift a hand. Leaving this first beautiful city and bay, the *Sheila II* headed south to exit. Clearing the bay, we set course between two smaller islands and headed for the Pacific. Lei, I, Dr. Ying, and Captain Mobley were all on deck! Helm had taken control of the wheel. The crew was finishing their duties and eager to gather around to have *story time*, something that transpired over the journeys, and allowable grant by Captain Mobley, and a joy for all. This will be the plan of the day, henceforth on this journey between ports of call. Dr. Ying is the sole commander at this time and will bring to us his story of Japan: the culture, the history, customs, and goals.

The crew gathered around with Helm at the wheel, like children at the library ready for story time. Dr. Ying began without needing introductions since we had all lived together for a day. He started by telling us that our next port of call would be up a small bay to the City of Nagoya, located at the extreme end of the bay inlet. From there, a minibus would take us on a tour of the surrounding cities and countryside. This area, somewhat inland contrary to most of the cities that are coastal on both sides of Japan, was chosen because, as James had mentioned, the steep volcanic mountains left no decent flat areas in which to build. Additionally, although dormant, there was always the threat of eruption. Dr. Ying mentioned that this area was in his backyard, but we would not visit it just yet. He was saving that for last when we came down the west side of Japan for a little surprise—a tour of his home. If he had failed to mention, lodging, meals, and minivan transport were provided whenever we went inland or toured cities. Cookie, visibly delighted, grinned ear to ear when Dr. Ying added, "Thank you, Dr. Ying, I will still do breakfast for you and the crew!" All agreed.

The morning trip into Nagoya was the best of the route, and in proximity, it showcased more of the country-like features than the coastal cities. Dr. Ying reiterated what was said about coastal dwelling. It was necessary to occupy coastlines because of the proximity of mountains, where terrain and steepness prevented builders from practicing their craft. This portion inland was more conducive to settlement, thus several cities were born. The climate here was favorable, due to the southern coastal flow of the ocean. Two ocean currents influenced this weather: the southern current brought warmth, while the northern trend could bring colder weather in the north, thus the snows in winter.

As we journeyed north, it would be mild, with no snow—an important note to keep in mind. Dr. Ying added that Japan was not inhabited by primitive people making c. Instead, it was a mix of people who found and settled on this land. Predominantly, Koreans and Chinese moved onto the islands and had an influence on early growth. Christianity came and added its influence to the Buddhist and other religious practices here. Russia had a significant influence in the north, as did the English and Dutch in the south. The Dutch set up trade centers here, similar to what they did from Jakarta to Cape Town in Africa, resulting in a mixed population. Later in history, under various governments from ancient Japan to the present, Japan also built a navy and had a very successful merchant marine system.

Also in the early years, as the islands were inhabited and growth began, there were large stands of forest here, various pines, and cedars. Lumber was needed for the construction of homes, buildings, furniture, and heating. So the forests dwindled and some species became extinct. Forestation was not planned for, so as the population grew, the forests were depleted. Later, forest reclamation was established, but it was too late to supply the need, so Japan had to import wood, as well as many more commodities.

On a lesser note, as we travel inland, you will see preserved home sites of the early people. They are rough, round buildings with rough wood sidewalls and thatched roofs. They resemble the thatched verandas of the early Pacific islands but are fully enclosed for protection. You can see here, as the population grew, the demand for wood from the forests grew.

The first port of call and our first inland run was a good trip for the day. We all got a perspective of the coastal and inland areas of this region of Japan. The primitive building adventure was exactly like Dr. Ying's narrative. A return to the ship after a good meal in the city, and we were ready to move on to the next adventure.

The next day, after a good breakfast prepared by Cookie, gathering around the table in a full group, Dr. Ying began to speak again. As I looked around, all eyes were on this quiet Asian man. The crew looked at him with respect and friendship. They had not been with him long, but they could sense his intelligence, peacefulness, and pride—not a pride of boasting but a pride in his communication with others. His ability to take quiet and firm command of the situation had already earned him acceptance as a leader, albeit with respect to his present position. He was the master of the group, as their captain had instructed them to be. They were attentive to everything Dr. Ying spoke of in his gentle but firm way, conveying to his group the love and respect he had for his homeland, much like they had for theirs.

Ying smiled, then remarked, "Gentlemen, we have embarked on the first leg of our journey to circle the islands of Japan, and I will strive to show you my country as I see it. James has brought part of Japan's history to you in excellent form, and at the risk of repeating, I may add a little more. Before we continue our journey, I would like to ask if anyone has questions about a place they would like to know about. Please raise your hand."

There was silence in the room, then finally, one of the crew raised his hand. Ying nodded. "Sir, I realize that we are well north of Okinawa, the largest island in the small island chain, and also that this island is not on our agenda, but I am curious to know about this island since in the past relatives were lost there."

"Very good response, mate!" Dr. Ying quoted. "You worded that request with dignity and respect! I'm glad you did not ask with the overtones of the prior Great War there." The crewman blushed. "It is no wonder the crew looks at this man with respect! His nature and dignity define a man of vision." Dr. Ying chuckled, and then said, "Yes, son, I will tell you about Okinawa. I am glad you brought up the question. You see, to tell about this small island and the magnitude of its growth and advancement will actually reflect on the same, for every city in Japan! So let us say it is a preview of many cities, we will pass or stop and see on this journey. If you were to approach this island from the sea, as we are doing, you would see at a distance a beautiful tropical island with lush vegetation and beaches that look as white as snow. The mountains would be majestic, and the breezes would be balmy as the winds from the south caress the island! But that might be the old Okinawa. Through the centuries, this island governed itself, then as time went on, through conflict, Japan took over as government, then back to self-governance until after World War II, when it became governed by the United States, then in 1972, it returned to Japan. In the early years, the Dutch East India Company had a big interest there because of the silk trade. Their influence was great since they had enterprises from Jakarta to Cape Town, Africa. Today, their income is generated from the sale of fish, sugar, tobacco, and other grown goods, for you see, they have no frost and the growing season lasts yearlong. Their biggest incomes are from the silk industry, tobacco, yams, and sugar.

"As for the population, I cannot begin to tell you the number, because inhabitants there number in the thousands, and all of Japan would number in figures that would boggle your mind.

"This island has modernized to the extent of not only building bridges over to other islands but also constructing tunnels under the sea and modern modes of travel to other parts of Japan. Also, not to forget air travel. This may be a good time to interject."

"Where did the Japanese come from? Who was the first to inhabit these islands?"

"This research has been ongoing for centuries, and all the 'powers to be' cannot, through various means of tracing back, come up with a positive answer, only speculation. Of course, one theory is that they crossed the land bridge between Korea and the large island of Japan. Speculation only, because no proof! Maybe they migrated from China or other Pacific islands, but again, no positive knowledge of the movement. So I guess, I accept we are here!" grinned Dr. Ying. "As we travel and tour the cities, we will also see museums, shrines, and displays of ancient crafts, all lending to the life and habits of the people of old, and still, no link to the beginning!" As Dr. Ying ended his story, the crew was spellbound, and with chuckles, Captain Mobley called them back to reality.

We were now underway, heading north. Our travel pattern now would be up to Dr. Ying, as per Captain Mobley. Any city worth the stop, by Ying's judgment, we would have a tour and a meal, Japanese style, as promised by our exalted tour guide! Cities he wanted to talk about or points to be made, he told us on the way. It seemed like story time anytime, not scheduled for night talk! He asked Captain Mobley to make port at Yokohama, entering a small protective bay. This was in close proximity to Tokyo, the capital. He had vans waiting at each location to show us the city and other points of interest. He catered to the crew to stop at shops and street vendors hawking their wares. The crew was polite not to linger. Then an evening treat to a gourmet Japanese dinner, then maybe a show if it had the quality Dr. Ying preferred. The boys liked the one with geisha girls and song and dance enacting the past. Then back at the ship for overnight. Everyone was tired but happy.

The next day was Tokyo, the bustling capital of Japan. Dr. Ying wanted to give us a glimpse of the capital of Japan. Again, dinner and a show were spectacular!

As we pulled out midday and headed north again, we were allowed to sail close to shore so we could view the landscape and towns as we moved up the coast.

The next stop was Sendai, right on the edge of the sea. From this point, there were several island cities that Dr. Ying wanted to show us. We were out for a few days, van driving, quaint lodging, and experiencing a more primitive lifestyle—no big city hustle and bustle. It was kind of like stepping back into the past as the farmers worked the rice paddies and crops proudly. They used primitive carts and oxen, which none of the crew had experienced before. Lodging and meals were like stepping back in time, but the food, even if you did not know what it was, proved to be a delicious adventure!

Back in Sendai, Captain called for a day of rest, and Cookie once again took over as cook. Dr. Ying praised Cookie for his gourmet meals, saying they were much better than Japanese cuisine! Cookie swelled with pride.

Lei and I were on deck looking over at the activity on the shore. I asked, "Honey, are you worn out yet?"

She said, "No, why?"

"We are just about halfway up the coast. We have to make it to the north, then all the way down the other side!" I chuckled. "Most of the activity and population are along the coast on this side, what I call the busy part. The opposite side is mostly coastal towns back down."

Lei asked, "Do you think Dr. Ying will have any inland tours set up for us?"

"No," I replied. "I noticed he was pretty smart! He got all those tours in while on this coastal side!" Lei smiled.

As the *Sheila II* moved on north, Dr. Ying would come out with more stories. He had talked about the old ways—the culture and art that depicted the ancient way of life. Now he switched to a northern city. I presumed he would continue on this pattern since it was our objective to reach and see them. He started with Hokkaido, which is Japan's northern frontier comprised of several cities. It was Japan's northernmost frontier, dominated by a mountain range. Forests rise unto steep cliffs and rolling pastures, the Sea of Okhotsk to the north, the Sea of Japan just to the south, and to the west, the Pacific. The coast is washed by cool waters which keep the climate cool and the growing season short. This area was inhabited by the Ainu-Caucasoid people who lived by hunting deer and fishing for salmon. They were rapidly assimilated into the Japanese culture but retained their customs, religion, festivals, and crafts. They grew potatoes and rice, which became a food staple. The agricultural development of potatoes, fish, and rice became a major factor in the production and income of the area.

If one were to look over this area, one would agree that it resembles New England.

As Dr. Ying came to a pause in his narration, I asked if the Ainu people were considered indigenous like the American Indians. He paused in thought, then said, "It was unknown where they came from or originated, but society assimilated the people into the Japanese. I can't say outwardly they were indigenous." Dr. Ying was pouring a lot of information into his story, almost too much to absorb unless written down. So as the *Sheila II* tacked north, I couldn't help but remember from the beginning to now! We started out at a quaint seaport in the south of Japan. As we traveled north, Dr. Ying took us inland in the southern region which was mainly a farming district and folks were somewhat laid back. We saw primitive homes, rice paddies, and terraced gardens. Some homes were wealthy, some common. The people were friendly and cordial.

As we moved northward, things became busier but beautiful. The cities were populated with thousands of inhabitants, maybe in the millions! We viewed all types of industry from farming to industrial manufacturing, state-of-the-art electronics, manufacture of vehicles, all types, and pharmaceuticals, all mixed with custom, cultures, history, and politics!

We have been to shrines, cultural centers, fine restaurants, and busy cities, and Dr. Ying had spoken about all, and it was hard to imagine that one man can keep that much knowledge at ready recall! Yes, this quiet man was a walking information center. You could tell he loved his country. He also told you the most important and the most interesting things. We would make a stop at Shikoku soon since we were moving into the far north. Just a little place! Only four and a half million! But this place was jam-packed with a variation of farming and industrial skills! Everything was beautiful. Terrace gardens, rice paddies, and the huge rice crop are shipped to lower cities: Tokyo, Yokohama, Nagasaki, and many others.

"This city contains tech colleges, industrial complexes of various kinds, colleges, a huge shipping port, and also, most famous, quiet for now, Mount Fuji, the most famous landmark in Japan. The volcano still puffs smoke and steam but has not erupted for centuries. What a shame if it did! Such a complex area. Looking up at it, Fuji is snowcapped to the area spouting smoke; in fact, the whole mountain is snowcapped, and in this locality, it becomes heavily laden with snowfall and winter sports!" Dr. Ying said we should find a safe dock in the huge port! And prepare for a two-day stay here. There was so much to do and see! And of course, he would take us all on a tour to the top of Mt. Fuji, maybe close enough to look down into the crater.

Dr. Ying paused to catch his breath. "Any questions? So far, I have given you the real Japan. The beauty of these islands, a little history, a little culture, we have seen mountains and streams, fishermen on the water. People at work in the fields and gardens. We have not toured giant manufacturing complexes because I felt it might clash with the beauty of this trip. We have passed and viewed those complexes, and you all know the names of the famous products being produced. We still have to loop the top! And to the south down the other side, I hope I can make it interesting also. It is about the same as this side of the island, but cities are less major. The beauty's the same. Over the top, we will have some islands to view and test Captain Mobley's sailing skills!"

Then he looked at Captain and chuckled. No one said a word. I think they were all spellbound by this quiet man. "One other comment before we adjourn," said Ying. "You will notice a change in the air? A little cooler? We are now in the Pacific winds from the north that won't keep this island tropical. Also note that while the growing season in the south is longer, maybe yearlong, the growing season here is short, although these folks are big producers for the market it presses them to get their crops out in a short season. Okay, gang, thank you for your attention. I think we have grown to be part of each other!"

Where we were docked was somewhat away from the main hub of activity, but the muffled sound of all the activity resonated through the cabin walls. This hyper-busy docking port was busy twenty-four hours a day, doing business with many ships from all over the world, coming and going. But it was not overbearing; you could still sleep. I had been on ships before where systems ran with noise twenty-four hours a day. As I lay and listened to the sounds, I thought about the trip so far. On this side of Japan was where all the activity was: the major towns, major industries, major agriculture, and major government. The place where, through the ages, customs were formed, dynasties flourished and became extinct, major events in history occurred. When we started down the other side of this island, it was less major and almost like a follower, but the island's beauty was still there.

So Lei looked at me and asked, "What are you so deep in thought about?" I shared this with her; she then started thinking—

you know, women! They think differently than men. Then I started to chuckle.

"Now what?" Lei asked.

"Oh, just a thought," I said.

She poked me playfully and said, "What?"

"You know, Lei, Dr. Ying is providing all this to show us his country. He won't let us pay a penny! I was laying here thinking, when we leave, the van driver is done, so he puts his money in his pocket with a smile and goes home. Then the waitress puts her money in the tip cup and goes on with a smile! Then the restaurant owner tries to *bow* lower than Dr. Ying with a smile on his face, at the good fortune this kind, quiet man has brought him!" I chuckled again.

Lei turned to my side, hugged me, and said, "Close your mind, dear, big day tomorrow!"

"Good night, sweet."

"Yes, close your mind," Lei said. I tried while watching her drift off into a peaceful sleep. But my mind began to whirl with all the beautiful sights of this journey so far: beautiful, clear, rushing rivers, wooded lands, rice paddies that were laid out in perfection, terraced gardens winding around hillsides in a perfect pattern, cities, and towns clean and neat but loaded with many people, thousands of people coming and going, watching the habits and culture of the people. I saw the mystic shrines with fat Buddhas sitting squat and looking down at the people passing by. I watched citizens in their daily ventures, some in modern dress, some in garments of history. Technology prevailed everywhere in the cities as Japan moved to the forefront of this advancing world. I guess what amazed me was the millions of people that inhabited these Japanese islands. And all the while, listening to Dr. Ying narrate all this sight and knowledge, his talk was interesting about the tunnels and bridges being built to connect the islands together, a tunnel constructed under the sea to connect Iwo Jima to the mainland whereby the four million-plus citizens there could travel to and fro and likewise for the millions of people on the mainland to do the same. My mind was a blur as I tried to settle down to sleep. I guess my lasting thought was our trip up Mount Fuji to watch the famous volcano boil the earth within and belch smoke. When would the next eruption occur? All this and I hadn't even had time to ask Dr. Ying about the historic Samurai! But we would get to that, I thought as I drifted off to sleep.

We were berthed in the harbor at the city of Tomakomai, on the southern side of this great northern island of Japan. After Cookie's fine breakfast and talk over leisurely cups of coffee, the *Sheila II* was ready to get underway. Leaving the protection of the safe harbor, we entered back into the Pacific Ocean, preparing to move north. The currents were strong coming out of the north. We could feel the temperature starting to change from the southern current flow which allowed the warm air to cover most of Japan. To hear Dr. Ying explain this was one thing, but to experience it was another! Also, the ship pushing against the wind was another concern for navigation strategy.

Dr. Ying advised Captain Mobley to open the foul weather locker for the crew and guests to don warm knit sweaters and knit caps. Also, foul-weather jackets, hats, and trousers were available for severe weather. Lei looked good in her knit sweater and *tuque*. She frowned at me and asked, "What is a *tuque*?"

I chuckled. "That is the Canadian word for a sock hat."

Captain Mobley asked Dr. Ying, "How much transit time to round the top?"

Dr. Ying said, "Today's journey will get us north to the islands above Japan, and by nightfall, we will be headed down the west side to a small town near Sapporo—a safe inland harbor. Also, we will once again enter a warm air zone." Captain nodded in agreement. As Dr. Ying spoke to us, as usual with his stories, he advised us to take particular note of the islands above Japan. These islands were once Japanese territory. Then Russia invaded and took over the islands, and through international action, an agreement was instituted, therefore, half of the islands were returned to Japanese authority, and half were left to Russia. There are still squabbles over fishing rights between the two countries; also, there has been intermarriage between the peoples of the two countries.

The journey around the north tip of Japan was an exciting adventure in itself. As per Dr. Ying's prediction, when we rounded the top and headed south, it was time to restow the sweaters and caps; the weather was starting to warm. By dusk, we were approaching our next stop as predicted by Dr. Ying—a safe harbor near Sapporo. We secured the ship, and then Dr. Ying said, "I have arranged for a fresh seafood dinner at this little town at the harbor. Eat heartily, and sleep tonight on board. Cookie, you are on for breakfast. Then I have a van procured for a tour of Sapporo since it is the largest major city in the north." We all clapped and headed into town for supper.

The next morning, the van ride across to Sapporo was a different terrain to see, and the city was a new experience with the shops and somewhat change of customs.

The next morning, we prepared to move south and noted that the cities were quite close together on this side of Japan as well. We sailed close in to observe the cities and sights. As we were slipping past the southern tip of the north island, we opened a passage between the north island and the main island that would allow passage back to the Pacific. Back to the side, we saw all! Dr. Ying addressed Captain Mobley, "My friend, if you want to sail overnight, we can see most of this side, which is more or less a repeat. The cities are mostly coastal, as in the east, again due to the mountains. Also, not as major, since all the major activities of Japan occur on the east side!" Captain agreed to that. "Also," Ying continued, "I might suggest the next stop will be Itoigawa, which will provide a safe harbor."

The journey was putting us south down from the north island to about the midpoint of the major island. The topography was about the same as in the east, still beautiful with all the familiar sites as the east, but more peaceful with less industry.

Everyone on board was probably getting a little tired by now. I know I was and thought maybe it was time for a story. It was time for a story from Dr. Ying on the subject I was anxious to learn about this whole trip! So I asked, "Dr. Ying, where does our journey lead us next?"

He smiled. "Well, James, plans are to make nightfall bring us to Shimonoseki."

"Right," I said, not admitting I was totally confused and could not even pronounce the name. "And from there, sir?"

"Well, James, it is right by the entrance of the Inland Sea. From there, it will be a short journey up to Osaka, my home, where I plan to entertain all of you folks before you make your departure."

"Okay, sir, I have been wanting to ask you. Can you tell me any history of the Samurai warriors?"

A big smile came across his face. "James, I will be glad to! That is one of my favorite pieces of history!"

"So, James, I will give you a short history and description of the Samurai warrior. To go into a depth description would lead us into a political harangue, which gets very deep! Let us say that the Samurai were the ruling force from the twelfth to the nineteenth century. Of course, you know in the history of Japan the country went through many dynasties of ruling classes. So looking at the Samurai during their time frame of rule, we recognize that they were stern warriors who lived by what was more likely ruled by martial arts that were trained and somewhat developed by the warrior himself. These new martial arts were developed and incorporated into their system. Little children were trained with stout sticks to battle and overcome their adversary. The goal was to be a top gun, so to speak.

"Going into combat as an older boy, the best were incorporated into the ruling factor of the village or district from where they came. The top Samurai was the chieftain who then answered to the ruling leader. Everyone strove to be as good as the leader! In time, they also developed suits of armor, which they stooped to enter, or had an assistant to aid them. In time, as they became more powerful, the horse was incorporated, and they were commonly called the Shogun. I guess, James, this is why I say they were men who lived by the sword. Later, I will comment on this again to you in another facet that I want you to know about!"

I said, "Thank you, Dr. Ying. That was good and gave me the curiosity to learn more!"

He replied, "James, I also thank you! And since you are my friend as well as this whole crew, I would like to drop the formalities of *doctor*. I am your friend, and Ying or Darrel is sufficient, but not what Captain Mobley calls me sometimes!" and laughed. Captain Mobley gave a sheepish grin.

Well, as Ying said, we made port just about the time the story was finished. Cookie was up and ready to provide us all with a delicious supper. Afterward, Lei and I, along with Ying and Captain Mobley, went on deck to chat and also to enjoy the Pacific breeze blowing a balmy wind up across this southern main island of Japan.

Early to bed and early to rise, we moved into the far inland sea and headed for Osaka, Darrel Ying's home, or should I say domain? Because his holdings were vast, he was a polite, common man.

As planned, when we pulled into his dock, there was a driver waiting; also, his wife was there anticipating his return, and with her was a young boy about five or six years old. Captain looked astonished. "Darrel," he said. Darrel smiled. "I have been busy, Captain! That is Kato, my new son. I retrieved him from a bad situation, as an orphan. Now he is my son! I will raise him and train him to be like me, his father. He will be smart and polite, with good values like me. I will train him in my business which, in time, someday he will take over." Darrel smiled a soft, proud smile.

Captain Mobley had tears in his eyes as he grabbed Darrel up into a big bear hug. "Darrel! I am so proud of you!"

Greetings were all around, and then the crew and all were transported to Darrel's home for an evening of fun and feast. He had a big grill fest for us. There was a skilled Japanese man at the grill waiting to serve. He was slick with all the tricks and movements an expert grillman has and was dressed in Samurai clothes. Darrel took me by the arm and eased me over to him. In his quiet tone, he said, "James, this is Tom Nakanishi, a former engineer and now an officer in our Samurai organization, which we are trying to promote much like the organizations you are familiar with. The ancient Samurai lived by the sword of war! We Samurai live by the sword of peace! Our goal is to bring comfort and assistance to all the poor widows and orphans out there!" Then he smiled that soft smile of his. "I want to introduce you as one brother to another. His lodge name is Yang, as a compliment to my friend Dick Mobley, Captain that is!" Then he laughed, and I expressed my thanks to him for doing so.

I looked for Lei, and she was tied up with Darrel's wife, a beautiful Japanese lady named Lotus—really Lotus Flowers, but she likes to go by Lotus.

The celebration went into the night, and soon we departed back to the ship, with short goodbyes in the morning, ready to head for home. When we were taken back down from this palatial estate, Darrel, his wife, and son got out. Captain Mobley looked at him, puzzled.

Darrel announced, "Kato said he wanted to sleep on a real ship! So Lotus and I, with Kato, will sleep in the guest stateroom and bid you farewell in the morning!" The captain roared with laughter, as did we all. Cookie stepped forward and took Kato by the hand. "Come on, son. I will give you a tour of the ship, and then I bet we can find some treats in the galley for you!"

After a good night's sleep, a tearful farewell, and the Yings finally waved from the dock as the *Sheila II*, with full-blown sails, headed down the Inland Sea and out into the Pacific for home.

After a long voyage, going home seems to bring peace and satisfaction to your heart. Coming home is like an ending to a story. But since you are the one coming home, you can make it end your way. I looked at Lei, and she looked back at me. We didn't have to miss each other because we were together. In my heart, always will be. Off the horizon, we saw a tiny tropical island appear. That's Samoa! We put our arms around each other, and that was the real home. But the beauty of Samoa was included also because, you see, that was the place we ended up together, in love and ready to face the challenges life brings. It's our little space in this whole wide world until we get the call to ascend to another place that will be more beautiful than "the spoken word can tell!" And you know what? We would have our little place there also and love all around us. And you know what else? An unknown author wrote a poem about a rainbow bridge. Fantasy, you say? Well, yes, but you know what? Cocoa and I are going to cross that rainbow bridge, together, when we go up!

Thank you, and God bless!
James

Delaware

Odyssey Down Under
Part XI

*Drums Along
the Delaware*

By
James Gardner

I wish to dedicate this book and the series to Cocoa, my Lab. He came to Anita and me as a young dog during a downtrodden time in our lives. He was with me through Anita's passing and was my companion for twelve years. Cocoa passed away in January 2023. He has been featured in all my books, including this one.

James

About This Book

We are off on another adventure with Captain Mobley and his good ship, the *Sheila II*. He wants to return again to the Great Lakes and challenge the course up the Saint Lawrence, as Captain Cook once accomplished on his first journey, where I met him and our journey began! Come aboard and see how this story unfolds. Let your imagination guide you!

We will visit my boyhood haunts and talk about the Miami and Delaware Indian Tribes. I'll mix my imagination with real life to spin another story. I also want to confess: Mixed into this story, I have interjected situations from prior books in the sequence to unlock the mystery. Past books are a good read!

Author's Comments

In the Bible, the Great Teacher says, "There is a season for everything under the sun!" Always a beginning and an end. Sometimes I wonder when my season will end. My seasons are parallel to yours, dear reader—some good, some bad. We strive to stay in the good. I try to be spiritually correct. I have a date with Anita in paradise that I want to keep. I will refer to the religion of the Samoan Pacific islanders in this book, as well as the American Indians.

Samoans believe they descended from the Garden of Eden. Indians believe that the Great Creator brought them from the earth. In my book *In Quest of Quanna*, I like the answer Quanna gave the fleet commander when he questioned why Quanna was building a church for his people when there was one available in the fort. "Because," said Quanna, "White man reads about God, but the Indian talks to God!" Interesting! I leave this with you. Enjoy the read!

James

Odyssey Down Under

Drums along the Delaware

Once again, it was Sunday afternoon, and Leilani and I were relaxing in our hammock, with Cocoa beneath us, having dog dreams and jerking once in a while. I looked at Lei and asked, "Sweetie, I wonder where Cocoa's dream is taking him? Wouldn't it be neat if we could go?"

Lei replied, "Let him go on his own! We get enough travel from Captain Mobley!"

I chuckled to myself. "That's my Lei!"

Women always tend to outthink men. That's why they are smarter than men! Just to think, it all started with an apple! Eve knew that by eating that apple she would not die! We, of course, did not—until she started a whole generation of us people!

That pulled my thoughts into the now. The Samoan people believe that they always were. That is to say, if you asked a Samoan where they were from, they would look at you in question and say, "Here!" You see, they believe that Samoa was once part of the Garden of Eden. Maybe east of Eden? I chuckled. Lei poked me and asked, "What is on your agile little mind now, James?"

"Church," I replied.

"Oh," she said. "And so?"

"So it was pure to the word and no fantasy mixed in," I said.

"So, James, did you like going with me?"

I said, "I went with you, didn't I?"

She growled. "Awww!"

"I'm kidding, Lei. Yes, I went to worship, and that was important to me!"

She smiled. "That's good, James. I want to keep you on the right track!"

I asked, "What do you mean by that?"

She looked at me very seriously and said, "Because I want to keep you on the right track!"

"What do you mean by that?" I asked.

"Well, James, there is always an ending, and when it is all final, I want to be with you in paradise!"

We were silent for a moment, and Cocoa raised his head and looked at us. I looked at Lei and said, "We will be there together. Now give me a big hug."

Lei turned and embraced me. We held together for a long time, and Cocoa laid his head down. We must have dozed off because the cellphone jarred us awake. Lei picked up; there was chuckling on the line. She didn't answer. She handed the phone to me and said, "It's for you."

I said, "Hello!" and the reply was, "Hello, mate. How's it going?"

"Well, Captain Mobley, there would not be enough words to explain," he roared with laughter.

I asked, "What's on your mind?"

"Well, James, we are planning another cruise! I need you again as a first mate!" I knew he didn't want me as first mate, he had Jason Helm, but he just wanted me aboard for our friendship. He continued on without my asking, "James, I want to make a return to the Great Lakes, maneuver back up to Saint Joseph Island where we met! Kurt and Hawk plan to keep in touch by radio! They can take Cocoa with them! At the prescribed time, they will fly into Saint Joseph. From there, we intend to fly up to Mountain Ash Lake and meet with Eagle Feather one more time. Their ladies will be with them, and Lei will be with you!"

He stopped, and I sat stunned. After a quiet moment, with Lei staring at me, I replied, "Captain, you poured all that out without me even saying I would go!"

He asked, "Will you?"

I looked at Lei; she nodded yes. "Yes, Captain, we will go! What about customs?"

Captain chuckled again. "Here is the icing on the cake! There was a change in the Canadian government. The powers that be looked into what was done to Hawk in the past, they did not like it! They gave Hawk an honorary citizenship with the right to travel in and out of the country with guests!" Then he laughed. "So, James, I will get back to you shortly. We will pick up ports of call during the journey. I would like a stop at Tahiti to see my old friend. Anyone who desires can shop, and take in the shows and such. From there, we move to the Canal, which I detest, but it's a necessary route. Once in the Atlantic Ocean, we can plan stops. First, maybe Corpus Christi to top off fuel and supplies. The base there allows Cookie to shop in the commissary at a big discount! I'll keep you posted!" Captain hung up.

At that, of course, it boggled my mind as usual to be extended the invitation on such a journey. I had clicked the phone on a conference call, so Lei heard it all. Her comment was, "Wow! One captain, six guests, and eight crew members, one first mate, one cook! I hope Eagle Feather can catch a lot of fish!" I laughed at her arithmetic.

The day of departure arrived quickly; we were excited about the upcoming big trip but sad that we had to leave Cocoa behind. He knew this as he sat in the jeep with Hawk. Hawk had come to drive us to the dock to meet the ship. We could see the *Sheila II* on the horizon heading in. Hawk looked as forlorn as Cocoa. "Folks, say your goodbyes to Cocoa now. I don't want him to see the departure."

Lei and I hugged Cocoa and told him all was well, and to mind Hawk until we met up! For you see, Cocoa didn't realize that we would meet up later in the trip and fly to Mountain Ash Lake again where he had shared an encounter with the white wolf! Hawk pulled away as the ship was maneuvering dockside, a quick tie-off to secure our boarding and immediate cast-off! In and out! No delay! The captain was at the wheel and the crew was attending to their duties. Cookie became the greeter this time, and he was thrilled to do so. Other folks held back, out of the way.

As we moved out into the bay, the crew and ladies could come and make their greetings, hugs all around, and excited laughter. The captain gave it time, and then motioned for Helm to come take the wheel. It was his turn for the greeting. With misty eyes, he gave Lei and me a big bear hug. "Gosh, mate, I sure have missed you two!"

"We have missed you too, Captain. It has been a long spell since we traveled to Japan!"

"Well, James, I told you how this was going to come down! It may be the biggest one yet, except for our trip to England to pursue Captain Cook's roots!"

"I know, Captain. That is fresh in my mind, but so are all the others, even back to our first meeting!"

"James, are you prepared to write a log on this one?"

"Yes, Captain, I am!" Lei, standing by holding my hand, looked back and forth at the two of us in agreement.

"Do I get a preview?" he asked.

"No!" I said.

He paused a moment and then remarked, "No!"

"Yes, Captain, no, because this time I am telling Indian stories, mostly history really, and I'm not totally prepared yet!"

"Well, Hawk tells Indian stories on his charter flights!" he remarked.

"Yes, Captain, those are about Ojibwe Indians, Captain, and I will be talking about Miami and Delaware tribes."

He looked at me and said, "What forever for?"

"Because both of these tribes had a place in my history. I can't tell you why now because it would reveal the connection."

He chuckled and said, "I don't know about you, James! But I know it will be good!"

"Thank you, Captain."

He chuckled again and said, "Do I get a preview?"

"No!" I said.

"In fact, story time will not commence until we are in the Atlantic Ocean."

"What's that got to do with it, James?"

"Teller's choice!"

The captain roared with laughter. He put his arms around both our shoulders and said, "Let's go see what Cookie is conjuring up for lunch!"

So we were out to sea again, and Tahiti would be our first port of call. Now sea duties commenced, and every hand had a job. I worked into the watch list by choice; watches could occur at any time of the day or night. They were four hours in duration. Then you are free!

In the navy, I had to stand four hours on and four hours off, then back for another four! I was stuck in a hot engine room, not on a beautiful deck with air and sea breeze. Usually, when the captain had the watch, Lei and I stayed with him to chat, and vice versa. It gave time for us to chat. According to tradition, the cook always brought the midnight watch a cup of nutritious soup to sip before taking your watch. The soup was so good! Hot broth with some noodles, more broth than anything, so you see, Cookie was carrying on this tradition and always stayed up until midnight to carry soup to the watch. When the captain or I had the watch, he carried three, because he knew three would be there.

After a few days, Tahiti was in sight, shining like a gem in the ocean. It was so beautiful! As we docked, the girls came running down the dock, screaming and with leis in their hands. Each one placed a flower over our heads and gave a kiss on the cheek. The boys loved it, even though their girlfriends and wives were present! Captain turned the crew loose on liberty. Off to the shops and shows they went. Orders were to get underway the next morning. Lei and I wanted to go with Captain Mobley back to see his friends and family up on the mountain. I don't remember his name, but that's okay. Captain made travel arrangements to take us to the path leading up the mountain. It was a long climb, both up and down; as we went either way, the view was spectacular! When we reached the clearing, all the kids ran to greet us. The man was homeschooling them, and they just *broke out*! The little girl who chose to come to live with her uncle's family was growing up—a pretty girl! We all greeted each other, and Captain Mobley told his friend that this would not be an overnight visit this time because time was pressing.

He told the story about what his journey would be like this time, and they all sat around wide-eyed and took it in. He said he wanted to share time with them while in the area. His friend chuckled and said, "That's good, so we have time to share fresh pastry my dear wife has made, along with Kona coffee that came from Hawaii," he boasted. His wife lowered her eyes and smiled. So after a good talk and good snacks, we were bound to go. All the children gathered around us with hugs and goodbyes. Down the mountain path again, happy for the visit, and Captain Mobley had a taxi waiting for our return to the ship.

On the way, Lei remarked what a pleasant visit this was and far more interesting than seeing the shops. She asked Captain Mobley, "How long have you known this family, sir?"

His reply was, "Gosh, I don't know! I met my friend during the war when we patrolled this island. Then when he married, I came over for the wedding, then the kiddies came, and the family grew, and I kept coming whenever I was in the region." He paused then added, "You know, it is interesting about the young girl. Her mother brought her to her brother for a visit when she was having a hard time. When she got herself straightened around, she came back for her. By then, that little sweetie had bonded with her uncle's family and wanted to stay! It was a tearful time, but her mom agreed and let her stay on. The girl loves her 'Mom' but loves this family also. Like us, her mom comes for regular visits, and times are good."

Lei said, "Oh, Captain, that is such a lovely story, and thank you so much for sharing with me!" When we were back aboard the *Sheila II*, we were in for another surprise! The crew and women were back! The ladies got their heads together; they said they had enough sea voyages and were not too sure about going to the end of this long journey. So they made a decision: they would let us go on. Then after a few more days of Tahiti shops, they would use Qantas Air or Pacific Air for their return trip to Sydney. The captain was surprised and looked forlorn. He finally said, "Okay, ladies, I guess that will be alright."

Cookie was looking over to Lei with a smile on his face and winked his eye. Lei quietly returned the wink and smiled. I looked at both for a moment, trying to figure this out, and then it hit me: Cookie was glad to let them go. His wife wasn't on board. He was glad that things got back to normal! As far as he was concerned, Lei was just one of the crew, like me. So Cookie went all out to have a fine breakfast for all the next morning. Then leaving was like a show-boat drama. We untied and were ready to get underway.

The welcoming Tahitian girls came running down the dock and joined with the girls staying in the goal. All were jumping up and down, waving and calling to us. The boys looked forlorn, only one smiling: Cookie! As we broke harbor, the captain had a forlorn look on his face and just shook his head. Time for James to snap him out of it. I sidled over to him. "What's the course, sir?"

"Due south," he said. "Isthmus of Panama! And those blasted canal locks!" That was my clue.

"Well, Captain, if you are short on women, maybe we should bypass the locks. Maybe we should go on down to the Galapagos—see if the Duchess of Vienna has returned!"

He reared around at me and said, "James! Maybe you would like a swing in the Pacific!" I laughed, then he laughed and broke out in a roar of laughter. "Thanks, mate!" he said.

"Captain, not to pry, but what is distasteful to you about the locks?" I asked.

"Well, mate, it makes me uneasy, I guess. You see, I always felt helpless in the locks with someone else in control. What if I was confined and a bad factor tried to board? I would have to take them down, you see, kill a bunch of radicals?"

"Well, Captain, they would have to get past the United States Army deployed there to guard the canal. Also, remember there is a small base on the north island of the Galapagos to keep a watchful eye!" I replied.

"You're right, mate, just a little of the jitters, I guess. We'll make it a good go!" he said.

I stepped back for a moment. Lei was looking concerned. "Who is the Duchess of Vienna, James?"

I laughed. "Now, honey, that is a story in itself. I'll tell you that one when we are all relaxed in the hammock!" Then we giggled, and she was in turn with me.

Captain Mobley was intent at the wheel. I could see he was not going to delegate a watch until we cleared the locks. "Captain, do you want me to relieve you?"

"No, mate, stand by. Your company and Lei's would be nice. Maybe a good time for a story, James? Maybe when we get into the locks I'll start story time? I'll probably last up the east coast of the Atlantic!"

He raised his eyebrows. "James, I was just kidding about Hawk telling Indian stories in flight! Are you joking or serious?"

"Serious, Sid. I have a history of two tribes that were in my life. In Indiana, it was the Miami Tribe, and in Delaware, where I grew up, it was the Delaware Tribe. There is a small surprise that I wish to reveal but only at story time. The crew has read my log on Quanah, leader of a Comanche band, so a little more Indian history may be entertaining."

"Okay, James, I'm excited. The locks are a good start. Also, it's going to be a long run up to the Great Lakes."

"This is going to be an exciting journey! What prompted it?" I asked.

"Don't really know, James. I just got it in my craw to go one more time and challenge the Saint Lawrence as Captain Cook once did during the Seven Years' War between England and France. He surveyed the Lawrence, you know, and found that a particular sand-bar had shifted sides. He gave the all-clear, and the ships went up and captured Quebec! Of course, when we go, we will sound the bottom to be sure. Also, getting together with Eagle Feather one more time before us old duffers fade away!" He chuckled. "Maybe Indian stories are in order! I was getting prepared to brush up on my history. This story will contain some history of two tribes interacting together at one point."

The Isthmus of Panama was on the horizon when the radio crackled. Helm picked up on the call. It was from Hawk! He and Curt were airborne on a passenger tour but were also keeping a check on our position. Helm turned up the volume.

"Hey, James. Hawk here! Just wanted to check on your position and let you know that Cocoa is fine! Hey, James, did you say Cocoa was a Labrador or an Airedale?" Then he roared with laughter. "He is doing just fine and has become a good entertainer for our guests! Also, James, I hear you are going to tell a few Indian stories! You are cutting into my territory!" Then he chuckled. "I am just kidding, James. I don't want to miss out on those stories! Are you keeping a log?"

"Yes, Hawk, I am, and you won't miss out on the Indian stories. I'll see you get copies! Also, my friend, it will be a real live Indian story when we get to Canada—Eagle Feather's stories!" I replied.

He chuckled. "Okay, James. I'll check it off. We are getting close to our destination. I have to get off and help Cocoa entertain!" Then he chuckled again. "I'll be tracking you folks through the canal and up the east coast of the Atlantic! See you next when we get together at Saint Joe!"

"That was a refreshing call," I said to Captain Mobley. He smiled and set the course for the Panama Canal.

When we moved into the first lock, no one on board had to be notified. Helm quickly took over the wheel, and the crew, along with Lei, the captain, and I, gathered around the wheel area so all could listen. I looked around at the anxious faces.

"Gentlemen, my stories this trip will be a lot of history, maybe not as exciting as Captain Cook and Captain Bligh!"

One of the crew spoke up, "That's okay, James. We are anxious to hear more Indian stories. We've heard all that Hawk had to give."

"Well, men and lady, you remember when I gave you the log on Quanah, the Comanche leader? Well, there is a little excitement in this history also."

The crew responded, "Yes, and we want to hear about where you grew up and the things you did!"

"Well, that may not be too exciting a story, but we will see. Living in Indiana for half my life after a tour in the service, I found an interesting connection or incident between the Delaware and the Miami tribe. Most of the Hoosiers, Indiana folks, think that the Miami tribe was concentrated around the Mississinewa River near the town of Peru, Indiana. But you see, this was a vast nation, like the Comanche, with connected bands stretching from New Orleans up and all around most of Ohio, running north into Michigan, maybe very close to the Ojibwe and Chippewa in Minnesota. So you see, it was a vast, strong nation. They liked to settle along rivers, lakes, and streams where fishing and hunting were good, and food sources were plentiful. Their sacred bird was the blue heron. The most famous chief was Little Turtle, whom I will touch on later. Although the folks in the colonies thought that Indians were heathens, they had a religion of Indian Christianity that they practiced.

"After living peacefully in their own habitats for many moons, the United States government felt that the lands were territories to be expanded into. They did not consider that this land belonged to the people, the tribes. Legislation opened the borders, and the settlers rushed in with the attitude that this was free land for the taking. This sparked the Indian wars, and Little Turtle was the greatest leader in the Miami nation. The Indian wars were battle after battle, and Little Turtle became a foe to be reckoned with. Many forts and many historical generals came and went during this time period. Exhausting battle after battle with many losses occurred before the Indian nation was contained. Most of the Miami bands were sent by the government to reservations in western Arkansas and Oklahoma. One small band in Indiana put up intense resistance until the government decided to recognize them as the Miami Tribe of Indiana, still current and still living around the county that is called Miami County. They have a charter and are continued to be recognized by the government. There has been a monument erected on a trail near the river, a historic monument erected by the government. All the names of all the famous chiefs are on this monument, many chiefs! And one name stands out on the listing of all the honorable chiefs of the Miami tribe. Francis Slocum is listed as an adopted honorary chief in line with the rest of the famous.

"So you see, going back in history and tracing all the lifetimes and accomplishments of these leaders will bring to light all the American generals, all the forts that were established, and all points of conflict that are still with us today. And what about adopted honorary Chief Francis Slocum? We will make that connection when we look into the history of the Delaware Tribe."

We were coming out of the first locks into the lake between the locks. The captain stepped to the wheel, relieved Helm, and the crew resumed their duties. It was sailing time now across the lake and to the remaining locks emptying into the Atlantic Ocean pathway.

At the wheel, Captain Mobley's face looked peaceful and not strained as it did in the locks. I said, "You look much better, Captain, since you are free of the obstacles of the first locks."

He looked at me and said, "James, did you have obstacles in your life?"

"Yes, Captain, I did!"

"Then, James, how did you overcome them?"

"By force!" I said.

Captain chuckled and said to the wind, "Won't question that!"

We were quiet for a moment, and then I said, "Captain, I have a Bible story about an obstacle. Want to hear it?"

"Yes, James, I do. There is no restriction on my ship about any reference to the Bible. That's God's Word, and all good captains of the sea respect that!"

"Well, you see, Captain, there was this prophet named Balaam who had a great influence on his people, the Israelites. He was summoned by a rich ruler of another land.

"'Balaam, your people are camped on my border, and I am nervous. So come and talk to them, move them out! They will respect your word!'

"Balaam told the ruler, 'No problem, they are peaceful.' So he did not go. Again, the ruler contacted him. 'You must come and talk to your people.'

"Balaam said, 'I will talk to my Lord and see what he will allow me to do.' He then said, 'My Lord tells me not to disturb His people, so I will not come!'

"A third time, the ruler called and said, 'Balaam, I really need you to come and talk to these people! I will give you land, silver, and gold!'

"Balaam thought about this, and the reward was tempting! So he contacted the ruler and said, 'I will straight away come!' He gathered his supplies, saddled up his ass (Bible reference), and started his journey. Upon the road he was to travel, the Lord stationed an angel with a two-edged sword. As Balaam approached, he did not see the angel, but the ass did! He stopped short. Balaam whipped him and urged him on. He wouldn't go! Balaam cried out, 'Move on, beast!' But the ass refused, and then he talked to Balaam!

"'Master, there is an angel of the Lord with a two-edged sword and has sworn to kill us!' Balaam saw nothing, so he urged the beast on. Approaching the angel, the ass turned sharply and headed into the wilderness. Balaam jumped off, put the bells down, and started to severely beat him, cursing him. Balaam's eyes then opened, and he saw the angel of the Lord!

"The angel then said, 'Prophet, why do you beat this poor animal? Did you not think it odd that your ass talked to you, disobeyed you, and tried to keep you from coming into harm's way? For if you did, I would have killed you!'

"So you see, Balaam had a great obstacle in his life, but his mind was so ramped up by the thought of all the land, silver, and gold he would acquire, that he threw caution to the wind! The Lord had spoken! 'Leave my people alone!' So you see, that ended the journey for Balaam!

"Sometimes you need a clear mind to keep yourself out of harm's way!"

Captain looked at me and said, "James, is that how the Bible words it?"

"No, sir, not exactly. I just told it in my own words!" He roared with laughter.

Cookie then came toward us, his apron tied to his head and flowing down over his shoulders like a robe. What's he up to now? He came between us and remarked, "If you guys need an extra prophet, I'm here to volunteer." We all had a hearty laugh! He had been eavesdropping in the galley over the radio to our conversation! Then he pulled some fresh goodies from under his apron and gave us a treat.

How quickly we had sailed that lake! As we approached the last of the locks, Captain called Helm to the wheel. The crew was all grinning; in the locks, story time would resume! Through the remainder of the locks and with Helm at the wheel and the crew gathered around, I was ready to begin. Captain sat down by my side, and Lei was close, touching my other side. Boy, talk about support. I was off and running.

"Gentlemen, on this part of the trip, we will talk about drums along the Delaware. About the Delaware Indians, also known as the Lenape people. Let me assure you that volumes of history, customs, treaties, and changes in location over centuries have occurred. Reference and history books are full of it. So much it would boggle your mind!"

I looked around at the perplexed looks. "But, mates, I am here to tell you a story, so from my vivid imagination, a story it will be!" Looks changed from perplexed to smiles.

"As their nation grew, the Delaware, so to speak, finally took in the span from Oklahoma and Wisconsin up to Ontario, Canada. The time frame I will talk about was holding from northwest, upper northern Hudson River area, upper New York, Pennsylvania, New Jersey, and Delaware. I'm going to pull it down to the Delaware River, Delaware Bay, New Jersey. At the time I am referring to, the Delaware, Lenape people were living along the Susquehanna River in Pennsylvania and the Delaware River Valley in New Jersey. Now, friends, we are pulling it down to my boyhood playground!"

Lei squeezed me. "A little background on the Delaware people: they farmed, fished, and hunted alongside rivers and streams, much like the Miami Tribe. Their Christianity was the same, customs similar, and language very similar. That accounted for the communication they could have with each other. Also, what amazed me was their looks. The men were handsome and the women beautiful! One Indian chief's daughter in a photo was absolutely beautiful!

"So you see, this brings things down to my beginnings! The river I grew up on, the river that was my playground, the cliffs I dug in as a boy searching for arrowheads or pieces of pottery. These were my Indians, so to speak, just as the Miami were my Indians when I lived in Indiana near the Mississinewa River Valley basin and walked by the monument dedicated to the famous Miami chiefs. But what about Francis Slocum, the name engraved on this monument with all the famous chiefs? It says 'adopted Miami chief,' so that's pretty honorable!

"Well, here is the story that both the citizens of New Jersey, Pennsylvania, and Indiana believe. Back in time when the Delaware were migrating or being pushed out—it seems to me more like pushed out because of settlers pushing in on the lands—as they were traveling west from Pennsylvania, they looted and killed along the way. They came to one family, the Slocums. Two small Slocum boys hid. Francis, a young girl of ten, watched her parents get slaughtered! The Delawares scooped up Francis and took her with them. Later, she was bartered off to a Miami chief along the Mississinewa. She was assimilated into the tribe and became one of them. Growing up, she married a Miami chief and bore her own children. She was happy and well-loved by the tribe.

"Several years later, when her brothers were grown men, they conducted a serious search for her. They finally found her, and a glorious reunion occurred. The brothers tried to persuade Francis to return to Pennsylvania with them. She refused. You see, she was happy in her life, marriage, and children of her own. So the monument depicts a woman of the tribe who was loved, respected, and reached a high status!

"You know, mates, this came to mind when I wrote the *Quanah Log*. When the Comanche attacked Fort Parker in Texas, Cynthia Ann Parker, who was ten years old, was carried off and lived with the Comanche band. She, too, married a chief and bore three children—one daughter and two sons. The son named Quanah grew up to be the leader of this band, never to be defeated in war. When he volunteered to surrender in captivity, he built churches and schools for his people and taught them White man's occupations to survive in the world. After he was pardoned, he became a very well-respected and wealthy person. The United States named him Chief of all Indian nations in the United States."

We were pulling out of the last of the docks and heading toward the Caribbean Sea. Cookie asked, "What's the next story, James?"

I looked at him with tired eyes. "Cookie, let me catch my breath. There's a long journey ahead, and the stories will come!"

He nodded, and Captain Mobley in the background just chuckled. Lei rolled her eyes. Moving up the coast of South America, Captain said, "James, if it wasn't so far back to Madeira, I would pick up some fine wine like Captain Cook used to do!" I just let that comment pass by. Instead, to change the subject, I asked what the next few stops would be.

Captain said, "I'd like a stop at Corpus Christi. I'd like to see that base commander again and take on a little fuel to push off. Then maybe a quick stop at Charleston to take on a few extra supplies, then on up to Delaware Bay and let you be the tour guide on your boyhood haunts!" Then he chuckled. I said nothing.

We no sooner docked at Corpus Christi, and the base commander was running up the gangway with an extended hand to Captain Mobley. "Hello, my friend!" he shouted. "What brings you back here again so soon?"

"Well!" the captain said. "Hello to you, mate! I wanted to see if you were still in command here! No telling when we will pass by again, although maybe on the return trip!" They were still shaking hands vigorously. After a pause, the commander asked Captain Mobley where this cruise would take us. After the captain told him our complete itinerary, the commander just shook his head. The dockhands were already hooking up the fuel lines.

Captain said, "Good friend, I intend to pay for this! No freebies!"

In turn, the commander said, "I'll give you a little Aussie! As long as I am the commander of this base, mate, you will have a free go here!" Captain Mobley roared with laughter. When they finished slapping each other on the back, they shook hands like old friends.

We got underway and had a good sail across the Gulf. Then turning north, we were Carolina-bound. It was a smooth and swift trip to Charleston. Cookie and the crew went ashore for the supplies, and the captain, Lei, and I stayed aboard. A break for the crew and some quiet time for us three.

"Northbound and down," we were heading for Delaware Bay. When we approached the point where the Delaware River entered into the bay, I called the crew together.

"I am not in charge here, mates! Captain Mobley is! But while keeping a watchful eye on your duties, I want you to remember what I told you about the Delaware Indians. You see, they lived along this river before they were driven west. Also, James—that's me!" Laughter. "Wrote a log about another James who, in the 1800s from this very spot, bought a horse from a Delaware Indian and headed west in search of an Indian named Quanah, a big leader of a band of Comanche. Also, I told you about the similar event of two different children in two different places being abducted and carried off— both girls ten years old. Also, mates, this is my turf in my boyhood, and a few stories will come from that."

As we moved inward, Captain Mobley asked, "James, any worry about sand or mud bars here?"

"No, Captain. This river is a mile wide with a large shipping channel kept open. Ships of all sizes—merchant ships—ply these waters from mobile docks to shipping ports in Philadelphia! So no problem with navigation! Our last port of call will be Red Bank. If there are no docking facilities, we will all go ashore in the longboats!"

All the crew was listening with rapt attention, so I just continued on with my narration. "Mates, this part of the Delaware basin was thick with Delaware Indians. After history evolved to my time in life, it became a playground for boaters, skiers, hunters, and fishermen."

A little farther up, we were approaching the mobile docks. "Mates, from these docks on, I will be talking endlessly until our journey upstream is complete! Please hold questions until we head on up north, and then we will have time for discussion. Now when you look at these docks and inland, you will be seeing the third largest oil refinery in the world. Ships come in from all over the world to take on refined oil! I have seen many flags from many countries come in here. It would not be unusual to see sailors from all countries walking into the town of Paulsboro to shop, tip a few beers, or ogle the girls!" There was laughter.

"Then you could watch freighters and tankers from all countries going upriver to Philadelphia, past mobile docks. If you look inland closely, you will see a large foundation. In my boyhood, there was a Coast Guard lighthouse on that site. Up the steep hill was the Lighthouse Keeper's Home, and boys, it was a large colonial residence. My friend and I played on that foundation under the lighthouse structure. In our minds, with the tides lapping and receding the foundation, it could be anything! A pirate ship, a United States Navy Destroyer, or a boat heading up an African river. You see, imagination can make anything!

"One day, the lighthouse keeper came down the hill. He asked why we were always there, so we told him about our play games. He chuckled and said, 'Come with me, boys, up into the lighthouse cabin. It is time for me to change the graphite rods.' He went to great lengths to describe the operation as he changed the graphite rods and then struck an arc to relight the beam from the reflectors! This I will never forget.

"A little farther upstream is another foundation. At one time, it was Fort Billings. The town nearby was called Billingsport. During the Revolutionary War, a large chain anchored to the foundation was stretched across the river. It was spaced with grappling hooks that were to rip out the wooden hulls of the British warships! Across the mile-wide stretch of river were two islands, one called Hog Island and the other called Tinicum. I always dreamed of going over to them but could not. One boy in the neighborhood, Norman Swindell, built a small boat in his basement. He sailed to Hog Island once but never told anyone about it. From then on, we called him Hoggie. So you see, I know only legends about the two islands. It was said that a pack of hogs was turned loose on Hog Island and the population grew—good for hunters! On Tinicum, the only thing I heard was that Dupont stored munitions and gunpowder on that island during World War II!

"Now, mates, we are heading for the gem of the Delaware, Fort Red Bank in Red Bank, New Jersey. This was my most favorite place in my boyhood. With all the water and history around me, no wonder I could not wait to grow up and join the United States Navy!"

The crew roared with laughter.

As we approached Fort Red Bank by riverside, I suggested to Captain Mobley that he might sound his way in to gain as much depth as he could, then close in to anchor. He nodded in agreement and then started to laugh. "What?" I responded.

"James, they won't think the British have returned and fire upon us, will they?"

While he laughed, I said, "Oh, brother," and just rolled my eyes. Lei in the background was giggling.

When we beached with the long boats, I suggested a firm tie-off in case of a tide change. Fort Red Bank astonished its guests with the colonial buildings and cannonballs embedded in the stone! It looked like they were placed in the mortar when the stone went up, but no, they were fired into it with great force from the British cannons aboard ships in the Delaware. We toured around and saw the massive defense cannons on the ground and crates of grapeshot beside them for loading. How would you like a passel of grapeshot the size of golf balls or even tennis balls fired at you out of a rustic cannon?

Then there was the colonial house built with old timber and massive stone, a beauty in itself, the inside must have been the command center with all the beauty of the hardwood structure. Yes, it was a beautiful place to behold, and all present became silent with pride—not that they were American but were Aussies taking pride in what their American brothers went through. I stayed silent for a long time, so much so that Lei pressed against my side and slipped her hand into mine. Captain Mobley was quietly staring at me. He finally asked, "Anything wrong, James?"

A pause, and then I said, "Nothing wrong, mate, just thinking back across life itself." Red Bank was the climax of this short run, and the crew was so impressed with my neck of the woods. Going back down the Delaware was like a newsreel in reverse—short and sweet!

When we broke out of the Delaware Bay into the Atlantic, we were underway for the north and the Saint Lawrence River. Watches were again in order. Also, Cookie's fine meals and midnight soup! My watches were good, always with Lei and Captain Mobley. We had talks to share.

Leaving Charleston and moving up the eastern shore, I told Lei about the Outer Banks and the horses there that never leave. I told her that was another place I always wanted to go but never did. Lei asked where the horses came from. I explained to her how they came from the Old World. They belonged to the conquistadors when they came to discover the New World and were just left behind. They survived, bred more, and the herd never left the outer islands. They are protected now. But it must be a sight when you can see the herd run! Lei got quiet for a while. I knew that the horses were running in her head—another exciting event that she had never seen in her lifetime. To watch her was worth a thousand words!

On up the coast, it was beauty by day and spectacular lights from the harbors and the shoreline by night. What came to me was that old beautiful song "The Harbor Lights." Lei said, "James, you are such a romantic, but I love you for it!"

Before we knew it, we were passing New England and pressing the shores of Canada. My thoughts for a few moments went to an old friend who lived in Nova Scotia, Canada. She was a good author, even though her stories were a little on the strange side! Soon we reached the entrance to the Saint Lawrence River. Wow, we were having a good time. Old Captain Mobley was catching each puff of wind! He called to me, "James, would you recommend sounding?"

"Yes, Captain, I would, but at the point in the bend where Captain Cook measured the shifting sandbar. Past that, we are home free." When we approached the area mapped also by James Cook, we found by sounding that the passage was best on the left bank in front of us. This also must be done on the return trip!

Soon we were passing Quebec, the French fortress that the British slipped in and captured during the French-British Seven Years' War. Again, thanks to Captain James Cook for turning the tables in favor of England! Our passage through resulted in moving into Lake Erie, then north into Lake Superior. I asked Captain Mobley to sail past Mackinac Island and up around Colborne Island on the north side. He agreed.

"Do you have a story, James?" he asked.

"Yes, I do. During the Revolutionary War, Mackinac Island was a fort, American, while on Saint Joseph Island, the British had a fort. Many battles occurred between the two islands with ships, no winners! Also, we will pass around Colborne Island, which was a stomping ground for Hector Nelson. His deer camp and all? Many stories can be told about this island that I have encountered, but we go on. Maybe story time another day!"

Captain chuckled. "Okay, James, you're on!" Lei just stared at this man with a mind she never knew.

Saint Joseph Island was a beautiful sight from the Great Lakes, with the causeway running from the mainland out to the island. We approached from the backside to make harbor and dockside. Just as we slipped into the dock, the dock attendant ran to greet us. He had known us from the very beginning of our journeys!

Next, an old fifty-four GMC came rolling in. "Hey," I exclaimed. My old truck and Hector Nelson driving." It was a grand reunion all over again, and Hector met Lei and was all smiles! I asked why he did not drive the old GMC to Colborne Island over the ice. He said he got to like the old girl so much he just kept her.

When evening started to fall, Hector said he could put us all up in his camp cabins for free. Captain Mobley spoke for us all, which was a relief to me. "Thank you, Hector," said the captain, "but we will all be okay here. Friends are coming in the morning."

Hector said, "Okay, Captain Mobley, the dock superintendent, and I will keep a good eye on things." The dock area, sea, and woods were enough to tour. I took Lei around to see the sights and told her the story about the Pudding Stone. She was impressed!

We all settled in for a good night's rest and sat on deck to watch the glorious sunset. After a good breakfast the next morning, as we sat down, we heard the drone of plane engines! Hawk and Curt, in their seaplane, hit the water like a big graceful bird! Things were moving fast! As they tied up, Cookie yelled, "Just in time for breakfast, mates!" Cocoa came bounding out of the plane straight for Lei and me! He was ecstatic! We all sat down for breakfast and gave thanks for what we had and were also thankful that Hawk, Curt, and, yes, Cocoa made it safely from that long journey from Samoa.

After a leisurely breakfast, Captain Mobley cautiously mentioned to Hawk and Curt, "How long did you want to stay here and when should we leave?"

Hawk jumped up and said, "Why not now? We just fueled up at Saint Ignace, Michigan!" So everything exploded like a Chinese fire drill, everybody grabbing up what they brought for the north country!

Curt yelled, "Get all you need! We have room to spare!" Cocoa was barking, all excited; he was going to get back on the plane—not on a ship! Hawk chimed in, "We will make it by late evening!" We loaded up and swooped out of the harbor like a big bird! We banked around and headed north into the north country. Mountain Ash, here we come!

Mountain Ash Lake from Little Rapids is about a four-hour drive, so from St. Joseph Island, it was a quick trip! I asked Hawk how we were supposed to contact Eagle Feather that we were coming. Hawk grinned. "Eagle Feather will meet us on the dock!"

Lei frowned at me in question. I said, "How do you know that? How did you reach him?"

Hawk just laughed. "By Indian way, no problem, no worry!" I didn't pry anymore. I knew Indians had their ways and were also deeply involved in the spirit world.

As we approached the Mountain Ash area, the big lake came into view. Hawk circled the lake and started the approach to land. Sure enough, there was Eagle Feather standing on the dock to receive us. Hawk burst out with laughter, while we all sat dumbfounded! We landed and started to disembark. Eagle Feather grabbed Lei and hugged her first, then Hawk, his adopted son, Curt, Captain Mobley next, and me last with a long and tight hug. The old Indian had tears in his eyes, and I had tears in mine. "Old friend" was all I could get out. Eagle Feather just shook his head. We had a bond.

Eagle Feather had a fire, fish smoked, and fresh vegetables from his woods garden. The crew was all excited to be turned loose in the north country they had never seen. I laughed to myself. "Wait until they are down in their *swags* (sleeping bags) and the wolves howl and start to circle the fire!"

Hawk asked Eagle Feather if the government was still harassing him for wandering the north woods. He started to chuckle, "No, Hawk, all gone. They made me the Honorary Chief of Mountain Ash area. They even put a plaque on the logging road entrance. It says, 'You are now entering Mountain Ash Preserve. Chief Eagle Feather is Land Manager.'" Then Eagle Feather laughed.

He then turned to Hawk, his adopted son, and embraced him. In turn, each of us received a hug and handshake. He kept Leilani for last, and she got not only a hug but a kiss on the cheek. Then he turned to me. "My friend, it is so good to see you! As many moons went by, I was hoping for your presence! I love your woman Lei as well. Glen would have been proud of you if he still lived, but as a spirit, I think he knows." We held tight for longer than the others, for we were special friends. We were the first to meet!

I said, "It is good to be with you again, even for a short while. I have thought about you often, Eagle Feather. You will always stay in my heart." We stood silent, looking at each other. Cocoa came and nuzzled his side, and the old Indian reached down and caressed Cocoa. He smiled and said, "I remember when we met on your first visit back! Sometimes you called him *Buck*!"

"Yes," I said, "and what about your wolf dog?"

"He is nearby. I call him wolf dog sometimes, but I named him Lobo."

I said, "Lobo is a fine name!"

He nodded, then went on. "I have trained him to stay under cover when people come. I need to know if they are friend or foe. I do not want to put him in harm's way!" He turned and gave a call. Lobo came out of the bush! He was big, with steel gray eyes that could look through you. His coat was gray-white-tipped in black. He came to me first, with Cocoa by my side, and it was as if they had met before. I could not resist stroking his massive head and reaching down to caress his neck. He leaned in for more attention. Lei moved to my side, smiled at me, and took her turn loving the big wolf dog.

Eagle Feather smiled and said, "Does he bring back memories, James?"

"Yes!" I said, "Memories of my wolf pup, my now big white wolf who is a spirit wolf!"

"Yes, my friend, he will always be yours! And yes, he still roams."

The others looked on in wonderment, astonished at this *thing* between Eagle Feather and me. The crew turned to unload gear and supplies from the plane. We had food to share, along with Eagle Feather's fresh smoked salmon hanging over the fire. We were off and running—five days of fun, pleasure, exploring, and sharing time with Eagle Feather. Once again, many stories around the fireside at night opened the crew's eyes in amazement. There were the old stories of past visits as well as new stories of the present.

Around the fireside one evening, Lei moved closer to me, took my hand, and asked, "Honey, will you try to contact your wolf pup this trip?"

I thought for a moment. "Yes, Lei, I did have that in my mind, but you see, we have already been together. We have all bonded together, so that is a good thing, you see! I don't want to have such a meeting with all the people around and too many questions. The white wolf, spirit wolf, and I have a pact between us, and of course, Cocoa. We have a promise that when our time on earth is done, we will walk with the white wolf in another realm!"

Lei smiled. "And me?"

"Yes," I said. "And you!"

The others, talking, did not catch any of the conversation, but Eagle Feather did. He looked me in the eye and said, "Well said, my son!"

As we sat around the campfire each night with stories being told, Lobo lay by Eagle Feather, and Cocoa lay by Lei and me. The two dogs would flick their ears, move their eyes around, and almost give the indication that, yes, they did understand these stories and were taking everything in! On the last night in camp, the fifth day, we were all slumbering by the fireside. The night air was balmy, and the wolves were more active in the distant forest.

I heard some rustling in the bush nearby camp. I knew that sound; I had heard it before. I said very quietly, "Yes, I know you are here, my wolf pup." Cocoa raised his head, his ears tense. "I want you to know I will always love you, my white wolf. Cocoa and I! Remember that someday we will walk with you as spirits in another place." Lei raised up then. She looked at me, kissed me on the lips, and lay back down, moving in closer.

The morning was bittersweet because it was time for departure. We had brought some jowl bacon along with us. Eagle Feather had stoked up the campfire and was cooking biscuits made from wild grain. He had also found some duck eggs! Coffee was perking. Cookie looked over breakfast and said, "Wow! I've been outdone!" Everyone laughed. Then it was load-up time! The crew turned and started loading the plane. I chuckled because, in a few hours, they would have to unload!

We all gathered on the dock for our goodbyes. There were handshakes and hugs all around, even a big kiss for Eagle Feather from Lei. It came down to Eagle Feather and me. I was misty-eyed, and so was he. I felt a tear escape and run down my cheek that I could not hold back. You see, I knew this was it. We would never see each other again. His tears escaped as well. I grabbed him in a big hug. "Goodbye, old friend. You know and I know we may never see each other again. But I promise you this! There will come a time when our spirits will meet and stroll around that great place called Paradise, where roses bloom!"

He nodded. We all boarded. Curt took the copilot seat. Hawk gave Eagle Feather one last hug and cast off. The engine cranked, we taxied out, then hit the throttle. The big engine roared, and we were flying down the lake and up! Hawk circled the dock twice where Eagle Feather stood with his wolf dog Lobo, waving at us from below. Hawk wobbled his wings in response.

In a few hours, the big De Havilland skipped down on the waters of St. Joseph Island and taxied to the dock. We disembarked, and Captain Mobley asked Hawk and Curt, "What's the plan?"

They said they would sleep in the plane that night, come for Cookie's breakfast in the morning, and be off!

Sounded like a plan to Captain Mobley! Lei and I sat on deck that evening, enjoying the island before we were to get underway. Cocoa came and sat with us; I dreaded the separation again.

We all gathered in the galley for a fine "Cookie" breakfast. He went all out! After breakfast, Hawk looked at Lei and me. "Curt and I think that you two should fly home with us!" You could have heard a pin drop. Cookie was looking at us, shaking his head yes. Captain Mobley took up the conversation. "You know I hate to give you folks up, but going home is a return trip back the same route. I think you have a good offer here! I think you need to return with Hawk and Curt. I can't stand to see a separation between you and Cocoa again!"

We were elated! "We will accept the offer!!" A cheer went up. After another big goodbye, we climbed aboard with Curt and Hawk. Cocoa was elated! We went skipping across the water again, saying goodbye to St. Joseph Island. Airborne, Hawk said, "The flight plan is to fly across Canada to Victoria Island, then the Pacific, passing over Hawaii and down to Samoa. Anyone want a Hawaii stop?"

"No!" was the unanimous shout. We were homeward bound.

Captain and I stood on the grounds of Red Bank, looking at the cannonballs embedded into the walls of the old building, standing still after all these years of history. It was a beautiful old building of native stone and beautiful to the eye inside and out. I stood there amid the cannons and racks of cannonballs, and life came flooding back into my memory. I stood silent for a long time. Finally, Captain Mobley asked, "Are you alright, James?"

"Yes," I said. "Just thinking about my life, where I have been, and where I am going." Captain looked at me in question. I looked back at this close friend of mine, and yes, he was part of my thoughts.

James started singing, "We are southbound and down! Hawk put the pedal down!" We all laughed; it was great!

We were tired, yes, but when the Island of Samoa was on the horizon, we were happy to be home. Things went fast: descent, dock, and unload. The two guys kept their jeep at the dock, so Lei, Cocoa, and I were taken home. Curt said they would not stop for a visit because we needed to settle in.

We unloaded and said our goodbyes and thank-yous. Cocoa rolled in the grass and ran around in circles, the most life I had seen in the old dog for a long time. We were tired! We threw our gear on the porch and headed for the hammock between the two coconut palm trees. Cocoa took his position below the hammock, in easy reach of a petting hand and also close enough to take in the conversation and movement.

Lei and I settled into the hammock, and she pressed against me as close as she could. All I could say about that was, it was as good as it could get! This was quiet time, and I was trying to be quiet, but how could I when a good-looking woman kept scooting closer? She moved in as close as she could get, and the fragrance of her sweet body was about to overwhelm me! Cocoa was already snoring in his dreamland. She wiggled closer, and I played possum so I could get all I could get.

She said, "James!"

I stayed quiet.

She turned over and kissed me smack on the lips. "James, do you hear me?"

"What?" I said.

"Do you hear me?"

"Now I do!"

She replied, "James, after each trip, you always have words of wisdom. Where are the words now?"

I said, "Us," trying to appease her a little.

She repeated, "*Us*," with a little emphasis. She pushed closer and kissed me hard on the lips. I was about to go out of my mind!

"James, tell me about *us*!"

"Okay, do you remember the first flight I took back to the States?"

"Yes."

"And you were the flight attendant?"

"I remember," Lei said.

"Well, when you had your break time at night, you came to me, sat down, covered us both with the blanket and fell asleep on my shoulder."

"Uh-huh."

"Well, Lei, I fell in love with you. I wanted this woman on my shoulder in the worst way. You booked on my every flight back, and the love grew and grew. At my age, I couldn't believe that it was possible to have you! But it did happen, and Lei, I am so happy here in this swing with you. Your fragrance overwhelms me. Your love and kisses I adore. You are a part of me, and I love you intensely. And so, my dear woman, the words of wisdom are not about a trip or an event but about *us*. So you see, you are a part of me, in my mind, and you will always be a part of me no matter what."

Lei was quiet for a long time, then she rolled over and looked deep into my eyes. "My love, I never knew your love was so intense, but I love you for it! I want you to know that I love you, and I will never leave you!"

"I believe that," I said. "You are part of my very fiber, so we will always walk together, even where the roses grow."

Odyssey Down Under

Pacific
Journey Six

Another leisurely Sunday afternoon in American Samoa with my love, Leilani. Yesterday had been a big day for us. The island was celebrating a religious holiday, giving thanks for being regenerated from the Garden of Eden. Most Samoans believed that where they came from was Eden and that they had always been there. Interesting thought, but not too bizarre. Didn't we all get our start from there back when things began?

Leilani had a big part in the pageant and was dressed in native costume. She danced and sang, and when she did, she captured the hearts of the people—mostly mine! She was so beautiful, and it amazed me how I could be so fortunate, late in life, to have such a beautiful and loving partner.

Today was a rest day—a do-nothing day—as we relaxed and watched the puffy white clouds pass into the horizon where the sky met the sea. Yes, Samoa was truly a South Sea island paradise. I could want for no more. As I watched Cocoa, my dog, snoozing softly at Leilani's feet, I said to myself, "I even got my best friend here with me."

When I came to Samoa, Cocoa was left at the farm in the States under the care and watchful eye of my best friend, Jim Chastain. Missing him badly, Curt and Hawk arranged a clandestine fly into and out of the States to retrieve him. Now that was a class story in itself! But now, the three of us were close-knit together in a paradise world.

The silence and meditation were broken by the jangle of the cellphone. Lei picked it up as Cocoa and I watched her reaction. She looked at us and said, "There is someone on the line chuckling!"

"Okay, tell him I'll pick up in a moment!" Cocoa was up now, ears alert! Lei had a pouty frown on her face. Captain Mobley was on the phone.

Lei said, "I guess I'm going to lose you again for a while!"

I said, "Well, Lei, I don't have to go! I will stay here with you and Cocoa this time. Just say the word."

She replied, "No, James. No matter how sad for me, you must go! It is what you and Captain Mobley do, and he would be lost without you on the trip. As he says, his *first mate*!"

"Okay, baby. I'm reluctant to go, leaving you and Cocoa behind, but it will be another journey of a lifetime, and we will have stories to share when I return. You know it's almost like receiving orders again to go!"

"Yes, James, and Captain Mobley is patiently waiting on the line! Give him your reply."

So taking the phone, I said, "Hello, Captain Mobley."

And the chuckle turned into roaring laughter! "Well, James, g'day to you, mate. I was waiting 'til you and Missy decided if you could pull away from each other long enough to talk!" More laughter.

"Yes, Captain. We had a quick talk, but remember, you had a big hand in this romance blossoming."

He chuckled again and said, "Yeah, mate. I began to wonder if you were going to get the drift! Happy, aren't you?"

"Yes, Captain. Very happy. Thank you for stirring your little stick!" Another chuckle. "So I presume it's another journey cropping up, right, Captain?"

"Yes, the crew and I have sat long enough, and it's time to get the hull of the *Sheila II* wet with sea again!"

"I hope you are not going to take Captain Bligh's water clear to England?"

"No," he chuckled. "Plan to stay in the Pacific islands. Haven't mapped it all out yet. Was hoping you'd give a hand in that. When you get here, we will finalize the journey. Want to see more islands you have not seen to write a log about, and also want to see old Ying Yang up in Japan!" Ying Yang was the name Captain Mobley gave to one of his best friends in Japan. A rich man, Darrel Ying, of Chinese descent—mother Chinese, father Japanese. Captain Mobley had his fun this way, and his friends really were not offended—they loved the attention!

"So when can you come, mate?"

"After I kiss Leilani one hundred times and contact Curt and Hawk for a fly into Sydney!"

He laughed. "Sounds good. At the journey's end, I will get you back on Samoan soil!"

Now Curt and Hawk, as noted in past logs, were good friends of Captain Mobley, and now mine as well! They ran a flying service in the islands and were based in Samoa. They had two refurbished De Havilland planes, seaplanes with turboprop engines and classic interiors, and each could carry twelve passengers. Hawk had been transplanted to Samoa from Canada, a story told in a past log, and he was of the Ojibwe tribe. Curt was the one responsible for making this union happen! With two planes, they could fly separately when the tourists numbered more than twelve.

They liked to fly in one aircraft so they could be together—best buddies! Both knew the islands well and could tell good stories. Hawk liked to tell Indian stories once in a while, and his passengers loved it! I was proud to say, through Captain Mobley, that they were now my best friends also. Just a request, and one or the other was ready to transport me wherever I wanted to go.

So I'd request a flight to Sydney, and it would be on! We might fly alone or maybe with passengers. If passengers didn't have Australia on their flight plan, they got a free ride anyhow and a treat to a short free stay in Sydney!

When flight day arrived, I notified Captain Mobley, and Leilani and Cocoa saw me off on the flight. It always was a sad, tearful experience, and even Cocoa would lay his ears down and put on a sad face! But duty called! And the return was a joyful and glorious event!

So flight day arrived, the captain was notified, and we were off! When that De Havilland scooted across the water and lifted off, with the turboprops humming, it was an exhilarating experience. Also, coming in, the engine slowed down, the pontoons kissed the wake, and the plane taxied to the dock. It never ceased to excite me! Hawk and Curt were both with me on this flight, in between passenger schedules, giving us time for a catch-up and a brief visit with Captain Mobley before the return flight.

The flight seemed short, and as we taxied into the dock, Captain Mobley was standing there ready to give us a welcome. "Hello, mates!" he said as we climbed onto the dock. Then we all took a walk down to the *Sheila II* for a short visit with the crew and all!

After settling in and with Cookie preparing a bonanza supper, Captain Mobley got down to business and hit the charts! The call to supper came, and it was fabulous! There was a little French accent to it since Cookie and Miss Duprey were together now!

Captain Mobley asked how the flight was, so I recapped the flight over. "The flight was good as usual, Captain. Hawk was the pilot and Curt was the copilot. There were no passengers and no apparent problems. The sky was blue with beautiful white puffy clouds that I remarked about to Curt and Hawk. They said yes, it was beautiful but ominous too. They are thunderheads and maybe a preview of what is to come. Other than that, it was a smooth ride!"

After the meal, Curt and Hawk made their goodbyes and were off again for the flight back to Samoa. I thanked them again for their generosity, and they said, "No problem, anytime. Have a safe journey and contact us on your return run."

When things settled down, Captain Mobley had a conference with the crew. "Men, I want to be up and get underway by eight thirty or nine in the morning. Right now, we will be leaving Sydney Harbor out into the Pacific and heading north to the Solomon Islands. The journey from there is yet uncharted, so James and I have a big task to plan the rest of the cruise! His input is important. We will review the charts tonight and complete the island journey we intend to take. Hopefully, James will keep a written log of the journey as he usually does." Then he looked at me with a big grin on his face!

In the morning, it was a busy time, getting the *Sheila II* ready to get underway. Ropes were slipped and stowed, the gangway was retrieved and stowed, and all hands were at their stations, ready to perform whatever their captain ordered. Captain Mobley started the diesel engine to move the *Sheila II* away from the dock and out into the bay. As soon as we were clear, the crew readied to unfurl the sails and put us into wind power. Captain Mobley motioned for Helm and me to stay with him on the bridge and enjoy our exit from Sydney Bay. It was a glorious day, and all seemed peaceful and well.

As we exited the bay into the Pacific Ocean, we saw a gray area ahead of us. As we moved on into what we thought would be a little squall, things started to change. The rain started to come a little heavier, so rain slickers were in order for all of us. All hands stayed at their stations because things could get unpredictable. The wind picked up at our aft, and the sea began to roll some swells. Then the wind came fierce at our back, and the waves grew larger and larger, producing whitecaps. Visibility was nil!

The captain moved on ahead, his face stern and his big hands grasping the wheel. He reached down and turned on the communication system that was piped to each station on the ship. The crew stayed alert but gave anxious looks to the captain. The helmsman at my side was watching the captain intently to see if he needed to jump in and support. Captain Mobley's face was stern and focused straight into the storm ahead. The crew kept an eye on the sails and their eyes on the captain. I remained still with Helm.

As I looked at the captain, I thought about the *Old Man and the Sea*, where the old man had his battle with the sea. Then I thought about our journey south of New Zealand, keeping toward the southernmost island that sometimes spurned sea storms. The one we got into included sleet and hail! The captain pulled us through. Now looking at this situation, I had been in storms like this on the Atlantic, but in a steel ship, not out in the open! We went on!

Helm kept his eye on Captain Mobley, and the captain was grimly staring straight ahead into the storm. The crew was getting anxious, and Cookie locked himself in the galley! The captain knew that with this wind and the sea up, he could not turn about—make a return! To do so would put the ship's side in full contact with the wind and sea! This would cause a capsize! This would put his crew in harm's way! So we went on!

It was a look of determination to beat this beast of the sea, as he had during various times in his career in the Aussie navy. We went on! Helm and I stayed quiet and glued to the bench on the bridge, the crew worried and anxious at their stations. The captain's grim look and strong hands carried us through.

Finally, the sea started to calm, the wind and rain died down, and we moved out of the storm into bright sunshine! I immediately thought about Curt's remark about the thunderheads. A cheer went up from the crew! Helm smiled. I sighed in relief. Captain Mobley grinned and said, "Beat it!"

Cookie opened the galley door. "Is it over? I peed my pants, and the cake in the oven fell!" Everyone had a good laugh.

The captain announced, "Okay, boys, north to the Solomons!" Then he reached down and turned off the PA system, and with a grin, said, "Enough of that!"

Helm said, "Okay, Captain, you've had enough dealing with the storm. Let me take the wheel for a long watch and free you and James up!"

So the captain turned the wheel over to Helm. Helm was the only one the captain would trust to take this ship in and out of the port on a dark night's watch. In the maritime service, Helm, as a helmsman, took many a ship in and out of ports, weathered storms, and big ships at that. Sometimes the captain would say, "Take us home, Helm," and Helm would be in his element! So we were on a north course to the Solomons now.

In a little while, Cookie came out of the galley and announced, "Lunch will be served according to shifts. Today's lunch menu will be storm sandwiches served with mustard!" Everyone just looked at him, and Captain Mobley shook his head and chuckled!

Today looked like the storm was over, and now we made it a succession of nice days—sunshine, good wind, and decent seas! Sometimes, you know, something tweaks your mind and your thoughts drift back to times past. Being on board sometimes put my mind back to the ships and journeys of my naval career. Sometimes it went back to my boyhood as I watched the tides come up on the riverbank. It also fascinated me to be there long enough to see low tide and what it exposed, only then to shift back to high tide with the water rising and coming in, covering what was exposed!

I also enjoyed watching various ships plying the Delaware River. Ships of all sizes, makes, and from many different countries. Up and down the river, doing their trades. It's no wonder that some folks are drawn to the sea! Soon, my thoughts and I said, "Well, Captain, you ready to go down and try one of those storm sandwiches?" He just chuckled, and we went down.

Munching my sandwich, I thought, we haven't even made a plan yet for what, where, and how we are going to set the course for this trip. We need to get busy. All I know is the Solomons first and thereafter see the islands not touched before, setting a circular course to bring us back to Samoa. Some of the islands I will call war islands. These were touched by battles in World War II. Some even have sunken relics of warfare machinery, ships, tanks, etc.

The Solomons consist of thirty-five islands and atolls. They are located north of Vanuatu and Fiji, off the island of New Guinea, across from Papua, which was notorious as a prisoner colony. It is governed by a monarchy. Located in the Solomon Sea, it was a place of interest in World War II. Some familiar names you may have heard about are San Isabel, Santa Cruz, Honiara, and Guadalcanal. There may have been a Japanese-prisoner-of-war camp there, and the battles of Guadalcanal are etched into everyone's memories. Captain Mobley intended to make our first stop there with shore leave for the crew to see a piece of history. A favorite place of the crew was the War Museum of World War II in Canberra, Australia.

As we approached these small islands, they looked much like the other South Pacific islands in nature—so beautiful from the sea. Almost a paradise again with the threat and desolation of the war healed over. A short visit to Guadalcanal, and we were ready to move on.

That night, Cookie fixed us a good supper, one he said would put meat on our ribs for the journey! Throughout supper, Captain Mobley was very quiet and did not join in on the conversations. I looked at him with a wary eye but said nothing. As all the quiet came into play, I quietly said, "Something on your mind, sir?" You could hear a pin drop in the galley. All eyes were on Captain Mobley and James.

After a moment, Captain Mobley began to speak. "Gentlemen, James and I have planned this journey to continue on from the Solomon Islands clear north to the Northern Mariana Islands, then east to the Wake Islands, then south to take in the Marshalls, and then on down to the Kiribati Islands. Then a southeasterly direction down to Tokelau, which places us above the Samoa Islands and home to James.

I feel that the farther north we go, we are traveling to what I call the *war islands*, all the islands subjected to the most fierce battles of World War II. There is beauty there, yes, but also memories that are ugly. Men, we could come see these islands and many more stops we choose in the future. Something here is eating at my soul!

When Hawk took us to Fiji and his uncle Magnus took us on a tour of the fifty islands surrounding Fiji, James had a long story about Captain Bligh, the mutiny on the *Bounty*, and Captain William Bligh's purpose for the journey there. That got into my blood. Last trip I insisted we travel the Bligh waters clear around the Cape of Good Hope and up to the Caribbean Islands. We did that. For me, it was a tribute to the greatness of one of our heroes.

Now, gentlemen, I feel a very strong pull to travel the waters that another hero has plied—the waters Captain Cook traveled coming into the unknown waters of the Pacific Ocean. Waters that only the Polynesians and Melanesians had traveled on their way in here. Seas and islands that had never been discovered by the white man and uncharted seas of islands never seen by the English before!"

The captain paused for a moment. A little misty-eyed, he continued. "Men, I want to make this cruise a tribute to the famous hero of our time, Captain James Cook! Much the same as I did for Bligh! I want to travel a piece of the three journeys on the actual compass bearings that Captain James Cook took on his discovery and charting of these islands!"

Again, Captain Mobley was silent. There was dead silence in the galley. I sat dumbfounded, no words coming forth. Then softly, one of the crew members spoke. "Captain, I and this crew would sail to Hell and back with you. You know that, sir? Change course, and we are ready to go!"

A big cheer went up! Everyone roared in laughter! Then Cookie, who always had to get in a bit of humor, said, "Captain, do you think I ought to call Simone, my wife, and say, 'See you in two years, baby, we are going to England'?" That brought in another round of laughter.

Captain Mobley said, "Okay, men, the course has changed. Tomorrow it is southeast toward the Cook Islands and on to Tahiti!" Another cheer. Then Captain said, "James, we will be passing south under the island of American Samoa. You can wave as we pass by!" There was more laughter!

Then Captain Mobley informed us, "We will be picking up pieces of Captain Cook's journey waters. No, we are not going to England, nor the Bering Sea, and also not around the Cape of Good Hope. We already made the journey traveling Bligh waters to the Caribbean. Also, we traveled the same distance when we went to Newfoundland, the US Great Lakes, and where we picked up James! So, mate, are you sorry now you climbed aboard the *Sheila* and got yourself all into this fine mess?"

"No, Captain, there was never ever a doubt in my mind! I trust you with my life, and in my eyes, you are another Captain James Cook! The sea called you as a young lad, and you pursued it through the ranks up to the commander of your own ship!"

Captain looked a little embarrassed at the praise. He didn't know what to say next, so he asked me, "James, do you have any prior knowledge of Captain Cook?"

"Yes, sir, I do, and also a log. We can tell this story during the evenings when everyone can attend. Judy Watchmen can pick up in between the log entries. Incidentally, when you mentioned picking me up at Saint Joseph Island, Captain Cook had a big hand in charting the Saint Lawrence River, and I will bring that out."

"Okay, crew," Captain Mobley said. "It is sailing by day and stories by James at night. I guarantee you will be enthralled as was our small crew on the Fiji Island adventure!"

The next morning, it was time to get underway, and it was done in short order. Pulling out of Guadalcanal and heading southeast, Captain Mobley was at the wheel, looking over at me with the biggest grin on his face. This would be a long journey, nonstop, with changes at the helm, everyday living, and stories at night.

As we opened this log, it was about Captain James Cook, a continuing story. So let's realize that the everyday travel and duties were in place. Let's proceed with the reading of the log and learn all we can about the man, Captain James Cook. With thoughts generated in my mind and pausing to feel the ship rise and fall in the gentle sea, it captured my mind. Then the flutter of the sails seemed to flutter a message to me of a distant time, long ago, when Captain James Cook may have taken this very course!

My daydream was broken by the voice of Captain Mobley. "You still here with us, James?" he said with a chuckle.

"Yes, Captain, I am, and I was daydreaming about being with Captain Cook on this very spot! Trying to get down and put myself in that place long ago."

"Sorry I broke the solitude, James, but I was about to make a request."

"Go ahead, Captain."

"James, you know we have all traced the history of the noble Captain Cook, but do we really know him? Do we really know what made him tick?"

"Yes, Captain. He was a very exceptional man and a man of vision, so to speak. A completely unusual man for those times, he was always thinking far beyond anyone else and had this profound ability to succeed in anything and everything he set out to do! To add to this, I've been thinking of all the accomplishments he made! Also, what a loss it was to the world when he was killed in Hawaii on his second journey. How much more he could have contributed to the world in knowledge? He was at the pinnacle of his life and career."

"How true, mate, and even now I feel some remorse about this. I guess this is why I was compelled to take this journey. Not to travel his complete path, but at least some of it. Kinda like a tribute, you know?"

"You should put all of those thoughts in the minds of your men. Let them share the concept of this journey."

"I will do just that, mate, and as you unroll your log, we all will get a new concept of Captain James Cook!"

"To learn the most, Captain, I will start back when Cook was a boy and growing up into the man he became! James Cook was born on the North Coast of England to a Scottish farmer and his wife. Over the course of time, he was one of seven brothers and sisters. Tragically, all passed away at some point, leaving only James.

"As a young boy, much like most boys, he had chores on the farm. Being on the North Coast and in close proximity to the sea, most of James's attention was drawn to the sea. He was an obedient boy and showed promise of stronger capabilities even at a young age. He would visit the coast to watch passing ships, tides going and coming, all animal and plant life, the rocks, and the beaches. I guess that was where the sea captured his heart. He took everything in and retained it.

"It was said at an early age that he showed signs of leadership, deep thinking ability, and decision-making. Even at play with his friends, he was a leader. His decisions were his decisions and not subject to change! He held to his plan no matter what.

"At seventeen years old, he left home as many young children did, to take up an apprenticeship with an individual. The first lady he worked for saw promise in James and taught him trigonometry, so this skill was planted securely in his mind.

"In his second apprenticeship, his employer took an interest in James and his ability. His employer, being friendly with those in power in the maritime service, recommended James to a person of influence. James was enlisted as an apprentice seaman. Soon, James was a seaman, and achievement was in his blood. In a short time, he became master and was in command of his own ship.

"To spend a career in the maritime service and retire would make for a very comfortable life. But aghast as his friends might feel, James had different plans. He left this unique service, perhaps due to patriotic feelings, to join the Admiralty! He enlisted as a lowly seaman, which at the time was a motley lot—drinkers, brawlers, etc. But James had a plan. He had a new vision, so to speak: to study, perform, and move up!

"He quickly moved up in rank to a master's position and was assigned to the HMS *Eagle*, a sixty-gun flagship. Being in the Royal Navy was an honor to James. The captain of the *Eagle* became close with James. Seeing his potential, he recommended James to be captain of his own ship.

In the meantime, the *Eagle* encountered a French 50-gun warship and engaged in battle. The French ship was sunk, and this pushed relations to the limit since France and England were already rattling sabers of war!

"Somewhere in the course of time, with all this movement and advancement of James, he had time to engage in marriage. Cook had two sons and one daughter. This all happened about the time that he was mapping coastlines and Canada, which we will address.

"The war was heating up, and Captain Cook was reassigned to Canada. His assignment was in Halifax, Nova Scotia. One day, while exploring the perimeters of the beach, which he did regularly to become completely accustomed to the area, he saw a man with an instrument shooting perimeters of the shorelines. The man turned out to be a man by the name of Holland, and he was a hydrographic expert. Cook asked him to let him try that. He and Holland struck up a friendship, and Holland taught him the skill. Soon, Cook was mapping everything in sight, even the Saint Lawrence River.

"Discovery became a great joy for him. Also, another skill, and a precise one. All of his charting he sent back to England for the Admiralty to see. He was soon outperforming the best cartographers the Admiralty had. Soon his work was noticed, and he was called back to England and presented with an award for his excellent work! Explorer/Navigator, Fellow of the Royal Society, Honor Historic King George IV, Post Chaplain in the Royal Navy.

"James was returned to his post in Canada. He continued mapping and charting, happy in what he was doing, but the Royal Navy had future plans for him!

"War was heating up, and Britain was wanting expansion in Canada. Two major cities were in mind—Montreal and Quebec! The French, in turn, knew that England would make a move on the cities to further their expansion. Both cities were heavily fortified. Both cities were wealthy and had goods acquired from the land. Both would be hard, serious battles for takeover, but if successful, would be the open gates to move into Canada and claim it for England!

"While battle plans were being made, Cook decided to take one more look at the Saint Lawrence River, which was access to the two major cities. The plan was to take two ships up the Saint Lawrence as far as possible, then load up longboats with men and arms to slip in and have a surprise attack on the cities. Quebec was the first major city and protector of the Saint Lawrence and the coast. Montreal would be an easier quest!

"Cook alarmingly discovered that the tides had switched the sandbar to the opposite side of the river. He quickly charted the safe route and passed the information to the British forces. The raid was successful, and Quebec was secured!

"After a settling time, James was happy with his assignment and thought he would be continually mapping and charting his surrounding area. He was also an expert in astronomy. It was once said that he was the best captain and navigator, that he could take a ship anywhere, never discovered, and leave assessed and be a success!

"But James's happy life of mapping, charting, and mailing back to the Royal Navy was about to end. They had bigger plans for Captain James Cook. In one of his forecasts, he had charted where, at one point in the South Pacific, yet uncharted, there would be an eclipse! So we found ourselves about to go on the first journey. He was dispatched from England and was put in charge of the HMS *Resolution*, with all sorts of astrologers, gentlemen, explorers, botanists, and the likes to make the journey with him and the crew. They were to study and record what they might find. Cook was to make records of any land masses, set coordinates, and make discoveries if possible."

Everyone on board, most especially Captain Mobley, was moved so far by the story! A break was needed to get back to reality and do what was needed to check the course, prepare chow, and wait a day and watch to resume our journey. We got so wrapped up that the ship ran itself! Only Helm had his skillful hands on the wheel.

When we resumed, we had to remember that when Cook rounded the Cape of Good Hope, he entered a world not yet entered by ships into the South Pacific, except by ships and canoes by the Islander people who came there first. Nothing was charted, discovered by white men, or had any dangerous locations noted!

Captain Mobley wanted to travel on part of Captain Cook's routes into the Pacific. Just part, not all, and also now charted and safe, thanks to Captain Cook.

We had stopped the story at this point to attend to the business at hand. As afternoon slipped into evening, everyone was doing their own thing. I turned in early; the day seemed tiring, although all was well. I lay in my bunk, and Captain Cook just wouldn't leave my mind. I wished I had the watch so I could occupy my mind on guiding the ship.

Finally, I decided to just get up and go topside. As I climbed the few steps to the upper deck, I saw Helm at the wheel. I realized the captain was off watch now and Helm was on for his turn.

"Anyone want relief?" I asked.

"No," was the answer by the shake of their heads. The air was balmy, and the small rustle of the sails in the perfect wind. The ship was moving underfoot in a gentle up-and-down motion. Captain Mobley was sitting by the rail, meditating or just keeping company with Helm.

"Can't sleep either, eh, mate?"

"No, just restless, I guess, Captain. No problems. It was a good day."

The captain chuckled. "And a good story, I might add, mate!"

I answered, "Yes, and I am glad you allowed all the crew to sit through our story!"

"Yes, James, no problem. All was well and no need for the boys to hang at their stations. As long as the sea cooperates, I'll keep it the plan of the day. The crew can't wait for the next episode!" He laughed. "Although it is not an episode but some history on their favorite sea captain!"

"Well, thanks, Captain. I'll give it a good go, best I can, and as close to the real thing as I can. I might receive some dispute from the experts, but so be it. It is what I have studied and presented in my own words, maybe with a little loose imagination slipping in." And I laughed.

"No problem there, James. I like how you covered Captain Cook's younger days and his rise to excellence. I had never heard that part."

"Another thing I did not mention because it was not written down, an unseen thing! Captain, can you imagine the parting with his family when he was dispatched for the first cruise? Leaving England for a long journey into an unknown world, maybe two years or more in the night, maybe tragedy at sea and no return?"

"Yeah, mate, that would be a real worry and a fright for a good woman and kids. But you know, that's just how it was back in those days. It was accepted as duty calls!"

"Well, Captain, if all goes well, we will get into the first journey soon."

In the morning, everyone was all a-chatter about Captain James Cook. The story—no, the reality of it—was taking root. Cookie had, as usual, prepared an excellent breakfast. Finally, Captain spoke up. "Okay, boys, the plan of the day is to stay the course as usual. James and I are going to go over the maps and charts, and if the plan changes, we will inform you."

*****

NOTE: The plan of the day during my navy days was announced to the whole ship from the quarterdeck by the officer on duty. He also announced revelry, the uniform of the day, along with the plan, and informed all hands to report to their duty station. The quarterdeck was the precise area where you entered or left the ship. Upon going and coming, you saluted the flag, then turned and saluted the duty officer, asking permission to leave or enter the ship.

*****

Captain Mobley and I went over maps and charts, trying to determine the exact course Cook took for different islands. With these in mind, Captain Mobley could accomplish his goal of tracking Cook's waters.

We went up on deck, and Mr. Helm was at the wheel, in control of the ship. Captain Mobley called to the crew to report aft to the upper deck for a slight change in plan. The crew arrived and mustered around, all ears.

Captain Mobley announced to his crew, "There is only a slight change in course for the present time until exact tracking can be found. Resume your duties as planned. Any change will be notified by Mr. Helm."

I motioned for attention, and Captain Mobley nodded permission. "Captain, if time allows, I would like to go back to yesterday's story and add a little something that came to mind, followed by a little personal story?"

Captain Mobley started chuckling. "James, I was wondering how long it was going to take you to come up with a story. You have been silent too long! And I miss your stories!"

"Well," I said, "this story is for all! When I thought back to yesterday's report, I felt something personal that I wanted to introduce. As Captain Cook entered manhood and was serving his country, he wasn't just someone history remembers for traveling the Pacific, discovering, and documenting exotic places. In the early days, he was entrenched in military affairs and wars.

"Think back now, gentlemen. You are on the HMS *Eagle*, one of Britain's finest. Captain James Cook is the master of this fine ship, a warship sporting sixty cannons. It meets up with the enemy, a French warship toting fifty cannons! You realize that you are on the *Eagle* when the battle begins! Cook is in charge! The cannonballs are coming over like hail! You know, a big iron about the size of a bas-ketball! They are tearing down rigging masts, making large holes in the deck and hull below. Also, these huge balls are hot! Blown from the muzzle of the cannon, full of packing and gunpowder. Many of your mates are wounded or wiped out! You yourself are wondering if you are going to survive this! Put yourself there! I did! It's not a comfortable feeling, is it?

"So the bottom line is, talented man, discoverer, map and chart man, also the best of the Royal Navy! He could also do battle in defense of his country! I'll leave you with that thought in your mind when we continue the story tonight. In respect to that, I have a story of my own." Captain Mobley grinned.

"When I was a young boy, I had been born and raised in the east. I once had the opportunity to visit Fort Red Bank in Red Bank, New Jersey. It is not far from a little place called Newman Springs. I was impressed by what I saw and went back many times—one time with my wife to show her a fine piece of history.

"Fort Red Bank is on the banks of the Delaware River. It was a real hot spot during the Revolutionary War. The British were coming up the river, no doubt to siege or seize Philadelphia. The battle was hot! The giant limestone buildings had been preserved. A beautiful building, but on its northwest side, cannonballs and grape shots are embedded in the stone, left in place. Thank goodness the impact must have been tremendous, and the building stood.

"To make an impression, a tornado drives a timber through a wall without splintering around it! The cannonball was there, not added, not mortared in. Many cannonballs were by each cannon placement on the grounds. There was a box of grapeshot handy to stuff in the cannon to fire. Grapeshot is like buckshot, but larger, more like golf balls or musket balls. Can you just imagine something like this coming at you in a thick spread?"

I looked around, and everyone was staring right at me. I had a captured audience. I had made a point about what Captain James Cook and his crew endured.

Captain Mobley smiled. "Love that story, James! You never brought up that one!"

"True, Captain. May I make one more point, or should I say a missed point?"

He nodded. "Go on!"

"Well," I said. "Going back to the first cruise you introduced me to, we left Saint Joseph Island, sailed through the Great Lakes, down the Saint Lawrence River to the Atlantic. As we traveled the eastern seaboard, seeing many places, why did I not remember Red Bank? We could have turned into Delaware Bay, up the Delaware River, and anchored off the fort!"

Captain Mobley laughed. "That would have caused quite a stir, mate. Folks would think the redcoats had come back." I laughed with him. Then he said, "Maybe we can put that on our agenda when we set up a cruise for dear old England." He laughed, and I just stared back at him!

Things settled down then. Helm was taking the watch at the wheel. So everyone gathered around on deck so all could share and hear the ongoing story of Captain James Cook. We thought we were free of interruption now until Helm's radiophone came on. He answered. He had a short conversation, then he spoke over to Captain Mobley. "Captain, it's Hawk. He picked up on us. Asked what we were doing? He said his last vector in on us was in Guadalcanal! Now we are in the South Pacific heading southeast?"

Captain chuckled. "Tell Hawk, yes. We changed our mind from proceeding north to the islands. We changed course back down to the Tahiti area in pursuit of something more interesting!" Captain then said, "We may put the north on hold for another time!"

Helm relayed the message back to Hawk. Silence for a moment as Helm relayed the message. Then he said, "Roger and out." Helm looked back at Captain and said, "I just love that Indian boy!"

So we directed our attention to the continuing story of Captain Cook. So I started off. "At the risk of repeating myself, mate, let's have another look at our esteemed Captain Cook. Sometimes I marvel at his life and himself. All the steps this young man took to better himself in his life. We now see him as someone who desired only more knowledge and perfection in his life, from a maritime sailor, successfully switching to the Royal Navy, to advancing upward to more knowledge, studying plant life, and ocean-to-shore characteristics.

"He became a highly professional hydrographic surveyor, chart writer, and many more skills. His work became recognized by the Royal Navy, and he was called back from Canada to receive some of the highest honors in England. Yes, the Royal Navy had plans for him, and as we journey on, we will cover the assignments he had to undertake.

"Cook was a big-framed man, pleasant, and one would say handsome. He dealt with a pleasant attitude and supported his crewmen and others, but he could also be stern in situations that needed immediate authority with his crew, islanders, and others. When he had a plan, this plan was it! No influence of change.

"He also was married and had a lovely wife and children. Their relationship was always loving and very close, even though his deployment meant many long months away from his wife and children. The couple always remained loving and loyal, as we will see when we get into historical facts later in the story. Deployments can be for a great length of time, a real strain on relationships and family. But this you have to endure. When you belong to the navy, you do what the navy demands!

"As we will see later, Captain Cook had many important people of science, botany science researchers, and the like on his journeys with him. I can imagine Cook's intelligence would be equal to theirs, even though he was not a trained professional. Cook was a natural, a man who learned from exposure, life, and living. He was, in myth, a kind of man of vision. Even his intelligence reflected on his crew, who were also intelligent and understanding individuals who would sail into harm's way with him, knowing he was their captain and would take any precaution for their protection."

All eyes and ears were upon me now as I moved into the story. We were gathered on deck again with Helm at the wheel. Captain Mobley spoke softly to Helm. "Mate, can you continue the course for a while? I want to hear this!"

"Aye, Captain. No problem. I feel comfortable here, and yes, I can hear."

So I continued where the story would pull Captain James Cook back in at some point. "With the war between France and Britain coming down to an end, and Britain being in control, James was still in the service. He was busy charting and hydrosurveying most of the coastline of Nova Scotia. He was buried in the work he loved. He signed and dated all his work and sent it back to England.

"His supervisor, Colville, was completely surprised. Not only surprised but pleased with Cook's work. So precise, so accurate, that he ordered almost eight months' wages to be added to James Cook's pay and honored him with the title of Piloting Master of the Saint Lawrence River.

"After a brief service in Newfoundland, Cook returned to England. Cook now not only had his work published, but he also submitted all signed work to the Admiralty. His Rear Admiral, Colville, posted a letter stating that James Cook should be considered for greater undertakings.

"Soon, greater undertakings transpired for Cook. He was deployed to survey the rocky and stormy shores of eastern Canada. James went two weeks late to his duties but was forgiven, for James had fallen in love! We don't know much about the courtship due to the loss of records, but on December 21, 1762, James Cook, thirty-four years old, courted Elizabeth Batts, age twenty-one. James took Elizabeth to the Parish Church of Saint Margaret, in the village of Barking, to be married.

"Then come March, James was preparing to leave again for the New World. Now I can't tell you much about this marriage other than the knot was tied! But it was a secure marriage of love and loyalty! You know many separations have occurred due to deployments, but not this one.

"So James was deployed back to Canada, not to survey the area he loved, but to survey the islands off the west of Newfoundland. Since the war, France and England had entered into a treaty for France to have possession of these islands because of their North Atlantic fishing trade. Before their release, England wanted a secure survey of the islands in question. Cook, now back in Newfoundland, had been granted his ship, HMS *Grenville*, and was then sent to Labrador to survey its coastline.

"He returned home in November to find Elizabeth had given birth to a son. She named him James. Cook found and purchased a house on the outskirts of London and settled in.

"Working happily on his passion, Cook refined his charts and surveys, being careful to sign them and submit them to the Admiralty. His work was well received.

"Cook remarked that his work on the islands placed him in the company of fishermen. He said he learned something about nature by being around them. One Newfie had this to say about James Cook and his Newfie brag:

'We have always respected Captain Cook here. He was a bloody good seaman. His charts and surveys have saved a lot of lives over the years. Captain Cook was a superb hydrographer and master of the craft!'

"By November, he had assignments and covered most of the North Atlantic in the *Grenville*, his first voyage as sea commander! In December, Elizabeth Cook delivered James's second child and named him Nathaniel.

"In 1776, the first of Cook's work on Newfoundland was published. Then next, Elizabeth gave James a third child, a daughter whom she named Elizabeth.

"Also in 1776, a heavy fog blanketed Newfoundland. At this time, a lunar eclipse of the sun was forecasted. James went to work calculating positions using latitude with longitude and his passion. He vectored in the exact place at the center point where the eclipse would occur. He then submitted his findings to James Berins, who was deep into astrology and also a prominent member of the Royal Society. Berins submitted this to the society with the comment that Cook was a good mathematician and an expert at his work!

"The Lords of the Admiralty picked up on this. James Cook was recognized by both societies, which increased his visibility. He found himself placed in high places!

"In 1776, James was planning another trip to Newfoundland, his present assignment. He was eager to return to his mapping, surveying, and hydro survey practice. However, other people in the Admiralty had different plans for him! The people in the hydrographic department were planning another trip for him. They were about to dispatch Captain James Cook on a trip to paradise!

"On the good ship, the HMS *Resolution*, the flagship, and Cook as commander! So, mates, we are about to embark on Captain James Cook's first journey into the South Pacific!"

Captain Mobley looked at me. "Gosh, James, I never knew all of that!"

"Well, Captain, neither did I until I started reading up on his life. Then I thought I should bring forward what most people never heard."

"Good, mate. Glad you did!"

"Should I start the first journey, Captain, or close down for a while?"

"No, James, start the first journey. We will be in Cook waters soon, so let's go on for a while!"

"Aye, aye, Captain!"

Then Captain turned to Helm, who was manning the wheel. "Mr. Helm," he said, "when you are full into Captain Cook's waters, change your course to due south and head for the Society Islands. I want to circumvent those islands as Captain Cook did when he went south out of Tahiti!"

"Aye, sir," was the response.

We sat silent for a moment, and Captain Mobley looked at me in question. I responded, "Captain, sir, just out of curiosity, do you intend to follow all the courses that Captain Cook made in his three journeys?"

Captain burst into laughter as the crew looked on, questioning. "No, James, good point! I had said that I wanted to change this trip to Guadalcanal to follow Captain Cook's waters. Rightly so. I just wanted to take the same course that Cook took on his journeys. But James, not all of them! This one will suffice for my passions!

"Remember back to our journeys, James. From last to list. Recently, when we took the Bligh water journey, we actually sailed around the Cape of South America. Then again, so did Captain

Cook. These times, when we went to New Zealand, we actually circumvented New Zealand, running into a sea storm in the South! Then in the north, we went inland to the place he described as a land of plenty.

"Around the north of New Zealand to Tasmania. Plus, we embarked from Sydney, Australia several times, and visited several islands where he charted and explored. The trip to the Aleutians—we went up the Asian side of the Pacific, whereas Cook went up the American side. So in essence, we have traveled most of the courses that Cook took! The last two societies for us cover about all of it, so I'm satisfied." Then he roared with laughter! The crew and I just looked at the captain in amazement.

Then I asked, "Captain, did you plan all those trips around Captain Cook's journeys?"

"No, James. If I said I didn't, I would be a liar! I did not have Captain Cook in mind when I planned those trips. Funny how it turned out that we were running his courses! It wasn't until the Aleutian journey that I became aware that Cook had been dispatched to the Bering Sea to assist and possibly discover a northwest passage.

"Also, we did track his course from Alaska down to Hawaii, but not intentionally. So to make a long story short, when we took the Bligh water trip, the realization came to me that this one piece of the journey would complete the course of Cook! So that was the reason for my persistence." Then he chuckled that low rumbling chuckle.

We all looked in awe, but so be it. Once again, things settled down, and I prepared to start the story. I said to the crew, "Bear with me because this will be a very long story! Much longer than Mutiny on the *Bounty*! A few facts before we begin. Captain James Cook, in my eyes, was a man of vision, a hero of his time! He became a hero to Britain for most of his accomplishments. As a boy, he took charge and endeavored all his life to learn and improve!

"Showing promise from a very young age, he had the ability to rise above the best! If you were in his crew, you would be considered the best! Captain Cook chose only the best! And I must say that as the crew of the *Sheila II*, you are the best because your Captain Mobley picks the best also!"

The crew all blushed! Captain Mobley grinned. Yes, he had the best.

I went on. "Gentlemen, we have all been on some long journeys together. Even down and around the Cape. So in the days of Cook and Bligh, remember, to leave England and reach the Pacific, you had a long journey down the Atlantic, around the Cape, into an uncharted Pacific. These journeys were not short! If storms prevented your passage around the Cape, you were required to cross back the Atlantic, round the Cape of Africa, into the Indian Ocean, and find passage to the Pacific!

"Also, girlfriends, wives, and children were left for very long times, hoping their loved ones would overcome all the perils of the deep and come home to them again. So keep that in mind as we go through the journeys with Captain Cook.

"To set a little background, going back to the eighteenth century, an explorer sea captain by the name of Alexander Dalrymple had passed through the South Pacific, chasing the legend of Marco Polo and other Dutch explorers who spoke of a large continent in the Pacific, unexplored and unclaimed.

"England, since the Seven Years' War with France, was anxious to explore the uncharted waters of the South Pacific. They wanted confirmation of existing lands and also such lands claimed for England for possession and expansion. Good old King George was in favor and could finance the cost of such an adventure.

"Since Alexander had already been in the area and had done some mapping, he approached the Royal Society as the man for the job. The Royal Society thought he was best for the position, but the Royal Admiralty declined. They were in favor of a young sea captain who had proved he was qualified for the job. This Cook did not know, for he was planning to return to Canada in Newfoundland and continue his mapping and charting that he loved so well, but the Admiralty had other plans for this young man.

"James Cook was contacted by the Admiralty, promoted to lieutenant, and commissioned to the HMS *Endeavor* as captain and head of the expedition. Not only was the intent to seek and find new land, but he must also hydrograph, chart the land, explore all fauna, any man or beast, and claim all for the British crown. Also, the country was excited about the alignment of planets and an eclipse of the sun by the planet Venus which was soon to be.

"The ship was ordered to be stocked, staffed, and refitted to accommodate the journey. Aboard with James Cook would be astrologers, botanists, artists, and explorers. All were of the highest caliber for not only the planet alignment but also for studying and categorizing all plants, animals, terrain, and inhabitants.

"The ship's carpenters were engaged to build a series of small cabins, very small, on deck to house the guests. The destination for this venture would be Tahiti. Cook's coordinates had pinpointed the actual point of contact to view, and the astrologers were in agreement.

"During all this preparation time, Cook had the opportunity to visit his wife, who was in her fourth pregnancy, soon to deliver James his fourth child. James Cook had secured a relative to stay with his wife and children while he was on this trip. Then it was off to Plymouth to take on a large cargo of supplies for the journey.

"On a cloudy day in August 1776, the *Endeavor* pulled out from her moorings at Plymouth. Cook then retired to his quarters to open and review his orders. As he opened the sealed oilskin envelope, as a young captain just promoted and assigned to the HMS *Endeavor* and embarking on a prestigious journey for the crown, he had to feel some excitement.

"His first port of call was the island of Madeira, then to proceed on around the Cape into the Pacific to King George's Island, so named, which was Tahiti. This had been agreed upon as a good base for viewing the planets. Cook was to go south then and search for other lands or islands if not already claimed by another power. He was to develop good relations with the inhabitants. The scope of Cook's tasks did not disturb his purpose.

"When they made Madeira, Cook had delivered several foods: many eggs, goats for milking, 300 gallons plus extra wine, 270 pounds of beef, and live bulls to slaughter at sea. They also took on gallons of water. Then the *Endeavor* started her long journey across the Atlantic into the northeast trade winds, finally approaching the islands.

"Here in the great Pacific, this little wooden ship was making a voyage of unimaginable magnitude to endure many possible pitfalls to complete their mission. There must have been twenty times over of doubt, worry, and fear, with Captain Cook worrying for his men. But Captain Cook never showed any emotion, standing as a strong pillar before his men.

"At a speed of eight knots, less than eight miles per hour, the *Endeavor* finally made its destination. April found Captain Cook approaching his first Pacific island, Vanuatu, positive that the edge of this island was part of the archipelago group. Sailing through this group of islands must have been a welcome sight for sea-weary sailors. It had been eight months since the *Endeavor* left Plymouth!

"Cook wrote, 'This was truly a paradise for his weary men.' Tahiti, coming next in all its splendor, was a place where the men were tall, muscular, and handsome. The women were, all we can say, beautiful and very seductive!

"To cultivate good relations between islanders and crew, Cook set up rules of trade that only designated materials could be traded—nothing of iron or any material that could be made into weapons. Not even a nail! The women especially would trade anything for a nail! Many a ship had gone back to sea only to find they were short on supplies for repairs.

"Immediately, Cook set his men to build Fort Venus, as it was named, to be not only a fortification but also secure housing for men and instruments. The pending view of the Venus eclipse was soon to come. Cook selected the best location for viewing and set his men to work. The extra cabins built on the ship to accommodate guests were dismantled and reconstructed on land as an observation post. This he named Fort Venus.

"Posted by guard one night, several Tahitians got by security and stole everything they could get their hands on—equipment for the sizing of Venus! It was time to get tough and take action. The crew and English had identified the perpetrators: a group living by Fort Venus. They and their chieftain, Tupala, who was a distinguished priest in Tahiti and advisor, were seized and kept in safekeeping.

"Things escalated, and Tupala, angry, denied having anything to do with it. A Tahitian court exonerated Tupala, but he stayed angry with Cook. After many apologies and gifts, Cook mellowed Tupala from his anger, which could have jeopardized the Venus project. All equipment was returned safe and sound, and Venus was back online.

"Finally, on the day of viewing, when Venus was to start its journey across the face of the sun, Cook had made preparations from England to have on hand watchmaker tools—tools to set in precision several clocks placed around a hollow log, which would provide stability. With the instruments now ready, the waiting began.

"Finally, a black spot started to edge across the sun. The air was perfectly clear, and the only disturbance came from heat blasting in the atmosphere around the planet into the surrounding space. Its disturbance affected the views some. The alignment of the planets was right on target. The sun's rim moved slowly across. Viewers had a dark cloth which they could quickly use to take a view. When Venus made its journey across the sun, it became dark, and dusty in appearance, not a blackout as some would expect.

"Cook was somewhat displeased with the results, but the fact was his calculations and predictions of the point of happening were right on target. His precision instruments had proved accurate. Captain James Cook's mission was complete. Now for the continuing orders within the oilskin orders packet! It was time for the adventurous work spelled out in that pack!

"The first order of business before opening the orders pack was to prepare the ship. This meant refurbishing the ship from top to bottom, making all necessary repairs to sails and masts, cleaning and revarnishing the deck with marine spar, addressing recaulking where needed, and even going as far as re-tarring the hull. When complete, the *Endeavor* would be shipshape and have a new custom look.

"Then Fort Venus had to be dismantled and all precision instruments had to be safely stowed away. Fort Venus was carefully dismantled, and the ship's carpenters returned all materials back to the ship and rebuilt the small cabins on deck to accommodate the various guests. During all this activity, the Tahitians prepared a barbecue for Cook and his men. It was dog meat from Tahitian dogs. Cook wrote that 'they had never eaten sweeter meat. Therefore, we will secure some for the future.' He also added he never despised dog flesh.

"On the morning of June 6, Cook set sail in the *Endeavor* to circumvent the island. After the Venus sighting, he was ordered to investigate the island, people, and fauna, and to complete information on the coastline with his mate, Banks. This he did, plus the two spent two days on foot within the island to observe, study, and record.

"In the meantime, the high priest whom Cook had accused of robbing Fort Venus's equipment had mellowed. Probably because Cook had showered him with gifts and apologized. He came on as a guide for Cook and Banks, and a thorough tour of the islands was completed.

"He also expressed a desire to sail with Cook, acting as his guide and interpreter in the island-searching venture. His main goal was to sail a return trip to Britain, where he had hopes of meeting the king.

"When the *Endeavor* weighed anchor and sailed out of Tahiti, they had spent three months with the land and the people, and leaving there would be something of endearment in each man's heart. There was a story told that two men went into the island paradise with two Tahitian women. When confronted, they said they would not return to the ship but wanted to stay there and marry the women! When Cook went to talk to them, they must have realized that it would be in their best interest to come back aboard.

"The blustering blue sea beckoned to James Cook and the *Endeavor*. The course was southward, but before chasing unknown continents, he changed course to the north of Tahiti to search for any land or islands above Tahiti. Tupala was now on board by choice, and as he said, he wanted to see Britain (history did not say if he returned to Tahiti, but I imagine he stayed on in Britain as well as others who had been taken there).

"Tupala was a good navigator, trained in the ancient ways, and also a good interpreter, for most islanders could understand the Tahitian tongue. He served as a go-between with the natives and strange White people. He proved his worth as he guided Cook through passages in the reef around some islands. He also had the ability to predict favorable winds.

"Bearing again south into uncharted waters, Cook came upon a group of islands. He called them the Society Islands (maybe naming them for the British society in England?). He named each of the islands: Huahine, Raiatea, Taha'a, Bora Bora, and Maupiti.

"For three weeks, he crossed among these islands, noting places, making friends, reviewing supplies, and claiming territory for the Crown. Soon though, the *Endeavor* and crew were ready to venture into uncharted water in search of that land that was talked about.

"With Tupala navigating, the first clue that he knew of was running due south. A solitary island would arise on the horizon. Rutu was a chain of islands near Australia. On their first stop, the Islanders were mainly Tahitian originals, so he spoke and lived in the old ways.

"After checking TuTu, Cook headed on south to Moore islands, but there was no sight of any continent. For two more weeks, the *Endeavor* traveled south to the 40-degree point, now 1,500 miles from Tahiti. Still no sign of a larger landmass.

"Cook's orders directed him to go westward to the land mass. Discovered by Dutch explorers near Tasmania in 1642 and 1643, which were on a sketchy map showing the western shore of New Zealand, showed parts of Australia, parts of Tonga, and parts of Fiji. The Tasmanian map showed only shoreline geography, but in six months, Cook mapped and explored twenty miles of north shoreline.

"He endured all kinds of hardships during his mapping—storms, winds, uncharted waters, ice at the southern tip of New Zealand, exploring no man's land, tussles with nature, and much more. Striving to keep his crew safe and healthy and remember distinguished guests on board.

"As Admiral Haslan once said, 'Cook's survey of New Zealand is one of the most awesome accomplishments in the history of cartography and hydrography, especially whenever you consider the difficulties he faced and the rudimentary equipment he had to work with. It's truly astonishing!'

"Cook then went westerly to New Zealand. His gentleman aboard sharing his cabin continues to update journals, category specimens, and paintings, all in an eight-foot-by-twenty-four-foot cabin! Not only cramped and clustered, it was a stable atmosphere, and many highly technical conversations must have taken place! Now Cook was among the best of the best intelligent beings, and his mind was taking on the energy and knowledge that would be discussed.

"Land was cited as they continued their journey. Though it was another continent, it was not New Zealand. Cook decided to land and trade for food, such as with the Tahitians. But these were Māori Indians and warlike! The landing party engaged in a struggle! A musket was fired and a Māori was dead. Not knowing the reason, the Māori made a few more thrusts. Then picked up their dead companion and left.

"After the skirmish with the Māori, Cook moved up the coast, finding more landing places with Māori of a friendly nature. Cloth was traded for yams and sweet potatoes. There were plentiful edible greens, clear streams for fresh water, and also fish. From the shoreline, oysters could be harvested, washed, and eaten.

"When they left this coastal area and sailed up and around the top, Cook ran into dangerous winds and serious currents. When he reached the north tip, he made a record of this. He definitely knew he was leaving New Zealand and, by the charts, Cook knew he was on course for the coast of Tasmania.

"He found a safe harbor, stayed for three weeks, and made any necessary repairs. The coast offered abundant wood, more fresh water, and again fish from the streams. These things appealed to Cook, and he marked the charts for later return voyages.

"Cook charted his landings and went inland to inspect the terrain and inhabitants. Botanists examined and recorded all types of plant life, building information on all they found, including sketches to put into their logs. Records were kept on inhabitants, who were sometimes friendly, sometimes hostile.

"As they left and moved up the coast, they entered the waters of Whitsunday. The water was deep, and the sailing was smooth. One of the hands had the detail for sounding depth. So far, so good: smooth sailing. Then a reading of twenty and twenty-one fathoms! A close margin for a ship drawing fourteen feet!

"Before the mate could throw the lead weight again, the *Endeavor* hit the Great Barrier Reef and was lodged. No efforts could get her loose. There was damage to the hull, and it was taking on water. Emergency repairs had to be made. Captain Cook thought that the change of tide would lift her off, but as the tide came up, so did the water in the hole. More pumping, more repairs. Finally, she lifted off the reef and started to float.

"The *Endeavor* was listing to starboard. Initially, pumping got the ship upright, and repairs provided a temporary fix. With leaks still coming, Cook ordered all unnecessary cargo to be deep-sixed (thrown overboard). Most of the cargo went over, including several cannons. With the cargo gone, the ship floated, but because of a broken mast and tattered sails, it could not function properly.

"Then a calm came up, and it made matters worse. It looked like the Great Barrier Reef had swallowed another ship. Cook was determined to go on, not back up. He ordered the crew and longboats over the side, with a man in front, bow sounding, and the crew laboriously rowing. They slowly pulled the *Endeavor* through the channels of the reef, sometimes with the hull scraping the sides of the reef.

"After all the labor and two calms, the leaking *Endeavor* was pulled free of the reef and limped over to the north shore of Australia. Cook named the reef the Labyrinth.

"On August 21, Cook took possession of the whole eastern coast, naming it New South Wales and claiming it for England. Confident now of his mission completed, he had reached the continent in question and named it for the Crown. His next determination was to get repairs for his ship and plan his return to England.

"He found help to get on to Jakarta, the Dutch port. There, Cook bought supplies and reoutfitted the *Endeavor* for the voyage home. In Jakarta, many of his crew came down with sickness, and twenty-nine died. On the voyage home, more sickness plagued the rest of the crew, along with tattered sails, weak equipment, and daily maintenance issues.

"When the *Endeavor* pulled into England, she was overdue for repairs and refitting. Charts, surveys, and findings were turned over to the admiral. Cook expressed hope that they were sufficient and accurate to the best of his ability, with humility. The admiral received them, overwhelmed with pride!"

I looked around. There were tears in everyone's eyes. I expressed my gratitude. "Gentlemen, I was proud to bring this story of your hero—in my humbleness."

For the crew, this concluded the story and the first voyage of Captain James Cook. Now there were two more voyages to tell about before the log was closed.

Cookie said, "I was so taken up I forgot about lunch! I'll get everyone a big gourmet sandwich and cookies. Drink of your choice." He hustled off, and I looked at Captain Mobley, who stood with a large grin.

I asked, "Captain, Cookie was enthralled with the story, also true, but he is several generations down from Captain James Cook, his name being Jack Cook! Why do you think he chose to be a gourmet cook instead of a sea captain?"

"I don't know, James. I guess I'll have to answer that with one of your quotes! Whatever turned his crank!" Then he roared with laughter!

When we were on the Society Islands, it was a good break from the sea. The captain did more of a steady go across the Pacific to Tahiti from Guadalcanal. It was a long voyage. Then from Tahiti, almost back up to the equator where the Society Islands are just down under. Still, Captain Mobley wanted to circumvent these to be in Cook's waters, a part he never attempted before.

But as we tacked around the islands, he picked out Bora Bora for a rest stop, to take on needed supplies, enjoy a little entertainment, and have a good meal. Back underway again, we were on course for Tahiti.

As things settled and became commonplace, Captain said, "James! Don't you think it's time for the second voyage of our hero, Captain Cook?"

"Gather the crew around, and we will get started."

As everyone found their spot to sit, and Helm took the wheel to favor Captain Mobley, Cookie came hustling out with treats to feed us as we ventured on! Good old Cookie!

"Well, when we last left Captain Cook, he had somehow amazingly beat the Great Barrier Reef and got into Jakarta for temporary repairs to get seaworthy. There were many losses by the time he limped into England with the *Endeavor* badly damaged.

"So picking up from there, I take you back into England and pick up on his life from there. His events in life leading up to the second journey!

"The *Endeavor's* homecoming caused a rift of excitement in London. The newspapers flooded the story of Banks and Solander's voyage. The two were the toast of high society. Overnight, they became the pinnacle of fashion in London society. Banks even visited King George in his country home! Banks was running full force in this delusion of grandeur! His accomplishments escalated out of proportion!

"James Cook quietly retired to his home in Mile End Old Town. While society clamored for Banks and Solander, John Montague took Cook and presented him to His Majesty. Cook told of his voyage and explained his charts and graphs. He commented on all the possessions claimed for the crown. He was proud when he left the place with the promise to be promoted to commander!

"But happiness was also stained with sorrow. His four-year-old Elizabeth had perished just three months before his return. His infant son had died immediately after birth. His reunion with Elizabeth, his wife, eight-year-old James, and six-year-old Nathaniel was joyous, but to the boys, he was an important stranger.

"Another voyage was being considered by the Admiralty, and it was approved after a conference with the king. It was to be two ships commissioned to the Pacific for exploration, seeking new lands, charting, and surveying. Cook was sure he would be considered for the journey.

"Just ten weeks after the *Endeavor's* return, all this took place. Another expedition for the exploration of the Pacific, lands, and continents, surveying and charting! There had previously been voyagers through, but no definite location or description had been mapped or written down. After the ten weeks, the Admiralty had the proposal in place and was ready to approve the mission. Cook, now commander, was to head it up.

"Cook's choice of ship would have been the *Endeavor* and another ship to accompany it for safety, especially after the Great Barrier Reef disaster. But the *Endeavor* had been repaired and was already dispatched on another assignment. Cook then inspected two ships built at Whitby, and the navy purchased both. The *Resolution*, at 462 tons, was fractionally larger than the Endeavor, and the second ship, *Adventure*, was slightly smaller.

"In the spring of 1772, Joseph Banks was contacted to again make the voyage with Cook. Unfortunately, Banks had a swelled head from all the acclaim of the first voyage. He purchased all kinds of equipment and had an entourage of scientists, botanists, artists, draftsmen, and two horn players. His demand for his convenience was to add another full deck on top of the deck of the *Resolution*. Even in rippled water, this ship would capsize! Also, in retrofit, all masts, rigging, and sails would have to be relocated on the new top deck.

"Of course, there was no way the shipyard would retrofit this ship, nor was the Admiralty going to approve or pay the bill for a fool's folly. After three fits and a bad spell, Banks ordered all his equipment off the ship and left. Joseph Banks would not be returning to the South Pacific.

"Cook returned to Yorkshire for the Christmas season with friends and family. By summer, both ships were ready. Tobias Furneaux, a stalwart but imaginative officer, assumed command of the Adventure. He had sailed to Tahiti with Wallis.

"On June 21, Commander James Cook took leave of his family, less than a year after he had returned to them, and took the *Resolution* to Plymouth, where the Adventure was waiting. At 6 a.m. on July 13, with a fresh breeze from the northwest, the two ships left Plymouth Sound, and soon the two ships were out of view.

"It would be three years before Cook would sight these shores again. He would meet many challenges, from icebound seas to the beauty of warm tropical islands. He would travel the most monumental journey in the Pacific, discovering, exploring, mapping, and surveying every possible landmass he could find. He would chart all islands that had been previously passed by, reported but not charted, and prove or disprove mythical landmasses or islands.

"Leaving port at Plymouth, Cook stopped at Madeira for fresh water and food. Also, most important, a large quantity of wine. In the order were a thousand bunches of onions, an important ingredient for his special diet to ward off the danger of scurvy on the long voyage.

"While there, he heard tales about a botanist named Burnett, in his thirties, who was waiting to board with Banks's party. After hearing that Banks would no longer be on board, the young man disappeared. Cook wrote, 'Every part of Burnett's demeanor and actions were to prove his demeanor of a woman.' Banks, in his grandiose plans, had even arranged for a female companion for himself as he was womanless.

"The two ships arrived at Cape Town on October 30. A clerk noted that all of the crew were in perfect health. He believed it was the result of Cook's diet and demand for cleanliness.

"Cook's first objective was to stay in the South Atlantic and move on down to the extreme South Arctic. The French explorer Bouvet had passed through the Arctic in 1739 and, through a dense fog, thought he saw a landmass, rocky and hard-cut by glacier ice. He decided it belonged to a greater landmass, and he named it Cape Circoncision. It appeared on at least two maps along with sightings of ice.

"The cold became oppressive as the two ships left Cape Town heading south. Soon, Cook ordered heavy trousers and thick wool jackets. Later, he included heavy red baize caps. The two ships moved through miles of ice, often mistaken for land. They encountered icebergs, two hundred feet high and twenty miles in circumference. Penguins and albatrosses were sighted.

"The Lieutenant on the *Resolution* recorded that they were now crossing the area of Bouvet's sightings of the Cape, but no landmass could be seen. Conditions became very dangerous. Rigging froze like steel, ships' sails became like sheets of metal, and equipment froze and broke. The crew could hardly endure it. Frostbitten hands cracked and bled, fingernails turned black and came loose. Still, they pushed on.

"The ships were soon stopped by a field of ice that seemed end-less. Hour by hour, they watched for three weeks with no sight of land. Then four inches of ice and sleet fell on the decks, with the temperature dropping to five below zero. Sails froze stiff like metal. To touch them meant serious injury. The freeze began to attack moisture in the eyes and nostrils. Eyebrows and beards froze stiff.

"In January 1733, Cook concluded after a thorough search of the area that the French explorer had not found land, only mountains of frozen ice. What Bouvet had taken for land was a speck five miles away in a vast ocean. The mapping was marked incorrectly, and in a thousand miles of ocean, Cook was some four hundred miles from the southeast direction of the Frenchman's Island.

"Cook heard of another doubtful track and set sail in search of it. A French navigator by the last name of Trénarce (I won't quote the full name—too long to list!) found that if you thawed ice there, it was about the freshest water you could find!

"Cook plunged on the south and crossed the Arctic Circle—the only one ever to do so! Then packed ice stopped him, and he veered to the northeast in search of another piece of land reported by another French explorer. This too was unfounded. Cook resolved that there was no landfall there. His equipment was advanced for the time, and he was meticulous in his search.

"Again sailing in tandem, the two ships sailed out of Cook's Strait (so named) on June 7. They crossed hundreds of miles south of Cook's track of 1769, circling to the east. No land was found. As they moved along, the weather became warm and pleasant. On August 17, the first land was seen: Tuamotus, a small island group.

"Cook was anxious to get to Tahiti. The health of the crew on the *Adventure* had declined. Furneaux, their captain, was excellent in command but short on dietary management. Some of the men had died of scurvy. One was the cook, of all people! Tahiti would bring much-needed provisions. Also, the hearts of the men stirred with memories of good food, beautiful countryside, and exuberant flower-scented women—a time in paradise.

"All faced drowning before reaching shore. By some mistake, the night watch on both ships allowed them to come in too close to the reef surrounding the shoreline. The wind died, and both ships, in the surge, drifted into four feet of water. The *Adventure* was on a collision course with the reef when, at last, her anchor hit bottom and held her off. Finally, a little breeze pushed both ships away from danger.

"The spearman remarked that he wished there wasn't so much swearing from the others, and Captain Cook became so distressed when it was over that he went to his cabin, feeling sick to his stomach. He was stressed so badly that the spearman suggested a double brandy—'an old Swedish remedy,' he said—and Cook recovered soon enough.

"All the scurvy victims on the sister ship also resolved that the visit would be short. There was a shortage of pigs, and petty thievery was increasing among the islanders. Cook decided it was time to leave Tautira and move on to Matavai, where he was better known.

"Breadfruit was out of season, and pork was also scarce. His move had not prospered much. Also, the great Arii Tuteha was killed in a race war! His successor was timid and insensitive, a young man named Tu-in Fu, which meant 'great Tu who was next to God.' Cook managed to establish a genial relationship with him. On September 1, the ship departed Matavai Bay.

"Cook again went to Huahine and Raiatea. He was received there like royalty, with feasts and dancing. The great leader there embraced James Cook like a son until tears ran down his face. He truly earned the admiration and love of the islanders in Polynesia.

"When Cook left, he sailed west, hoping to confirm islands that Tasman had seen in 1643. Six days out, he passed two small islands engulfed with coral reefs and jewellike in color. He decided to name them for the Admiralty. The scattered islands within would eventually be named the Cook Islands!

"On October 2, Cook came upon a scattering of green mountain islands on the horizon. Coming closer, it was a scattering of 150 islands of the Tonga group. These islands were so similar to Tahiti that Cook came to cherish them just as much.

"As the ships drew close, the Tongan men and women came out to meet the ships. Friendly and excited, they clambered aboard, anxious to trade, eager for a bit of cloth or a nail. They were a happy group, and Cook ordered the bagpipes to be played to entertain the islanders. In return, the chief had three young girls offer a song in response. Cook gave each girl a necklace in return.

"The Tongans had with them a root that they chewed bits and pieces of, then placed in a green leaf, mixed with a little water, and made a brew. Cook was the only one who tried the brew. Everyone else was a little queasy about how it was made.

"For foodstuffs, Cook turned to Tongatapu. He edged along the south coast, diverting around the reef, and came to an area where the waves crashed over porous rock, showing tributaries that were passable.

"Although Cook only spent four days at Tongatapu, he and his men were enamored by the beautiful island and its friendly people. Every person along the way was cordial and helpful. Cook remarked that it was like the most fertile plain in Europe.

"He came upon some women making tapa cloth from the tapa tree, a laborious trade of stripping and soaking the bark into sheets seventy feet long and twelve feet wide, then pounding it into sheets and strips to make garments for special occasions.

"Leaving out at the east end of Cook Strait, a gale struck the *Resolution* and the *Adventure*. It became a storm with mountainous seas and drove the *Resolution* far to the south, and sight of the *Adventure* was lost.

"On November 3, Cook was able to slip into Ship Cove. For three weeks, Cook waited but saw no sight of the *Adventure*. He figured that Furneaux had decided to head for Cape Horn and make his way home.

"Before setting his own course for the Antarctic, Cook buried a message in a bottle by a tree and marked it 'Look underneath. On October 27, he sailed south.

"Only days later, the *Adventure*, badly damaged by the storm, limped into the cove. Furneaux found Cook's note and planned to catch up with him. With repairs almost complete, he sent a boat and men out to gather wild greens. They did not return. The next morning, Lieutenant Burney was sent out to find them. He found parts of the boat and the shoes of the men.

"Then he came upon a carnage that was shocking and unbelievable. The men had been slaughtered, apparently by the natives. Sickened, Burney returned to the *Adventure*. He and his captain had no stomach for revenge.

"With haste, Furneaux made ready to sail. He crossed the Pacific, searched for Cape Circoncision, and returned to England in July 1774.

"The *Resolution* at this time was heading south to the Arctic Circle. She found herself again in snow, ice, and fog. Mishandling by the ship's crew brought her precariously close to a giant iceberg that was missed by inches.

"Conditions were appalling, and Cook was forced to move north. Ropes were frozen like wire, sails were frozen in place like heavy metal plates, and the cold was so intense that men could hardly function. As 1774 began, Cook was steering the first u-shaped curve that took them 1,500 miles north and into the very heart of Dalrymple's continent and back into the Arctic Circle.

"His men were eating repulsive salt pork and spoiled bread. He plunged on south farther than anyone had traveled before. On January 30, snow-white clouds brought the sight of packed ice ahead with ice beyond, rising to ice mountains. Cook was overwhelmed. He wrote that this discovery confirmed that Cape Tribulation was indeed a reality and precluded any survival for any castaway. It would be a new constellation for seamen to steer by. With this achievement, he would go down in history.

"He was not ready to go home. He had refuted all theories that a large island could be present in the Pacific. He continued to stay in for another nine months, in spite of the hardships. He had refuted all theories that a large island could exist in the frozen wastes of the South Pole region, and he continued his exploration in the next nine months. He had discovered and rediscovered dozens of islands emerging from the ice. By December 1774, every important island group in the South Pacific had been located, identified, and charted.

"Then James Cook was struck down with bilious colic that put him bedfast with all the horrible effects of the sickness to endure. We will not go into all the symptoms and dangers that he had to endure being confined in bed and aboard a ship with primitive remedies. But enduring all, he was far from well when the *Resolution* approached its next objective, Easter Island.

"As they approached Easter Island, all we can say is it was a forlorn sixty-two-mile speck in the eastern Pacific. It was discovered in 1722 by a Dutch explorer, Jacob Roggeveen. It was surrounded by thousands of miles of Pacific Ocean, where powerful breakers pounded the volcanic rocky shores. It was a doomed existence for any seafarer shipwrecked upon its shores.

"The first Polynesians who came found a colder climate, an environment with little wood and water, and few necessary means. Isolated, they turned to religious expression. This was the land of the enormous statues that lined the shoreline, carved out eons ago and moved by the natives with ropes and manpower, step by step.

"It's said that around three hundred inhabitants settled on the island. When food supplies diminished, they turned to cannibalism. Cook and his men were awestruck by the natives and marveled at the statues and how they were moved. The islanders had a passion for hats, which they snatched off visitors' heads. Their foodstuff included bananas, but not in abundance. When trading, they often traded their neighbors' crops and demanded payment before exchange.

"After three days and some of the crew showing early signs of scurvy, Cook decided to move on. They faced a 2,300-mile journey to the Northern Marquesas. While the men still wondered if the race was of giants to make the huge statues, and why they hid their women, Cook was wondering how the Easter Islanders arrived there and how much they resembled people of the more western islands. Besides the physique, their language was the same as other Polynesians. He wondered if, over time, they had become a different nation with different customs.

"The Marquesas were discovered in 1595 by a Spanish noble-man with his Portuguese pilot. The volcanic isles rose majestically from the sea with lush green foliage. A beauty to behold. In times past, these islands drew famous writers and artists to their shores to further their craft. It was here that Cook wanted to stay for a while and renourish his crew, deprived of necessary foods for five months. A market was set up, and trading of goods took place. The trading went on as usual, with Cook offering nails, hatchets, and iron goods in exchange for foodstuffs. One man, eager to trade for a fine fat pig, finally offered red feathers from Tonga. Then the market disin-tegrated, and everyone wanted feathers in exchange. Cook became frustrated that his rules were broken and decided to move on before trouble erupted. He weighed anchor and set course again for Tahiti. Everyone who kept a journal wrote about how the heavily tattooed men were stout and muscular and kept their women at a prudent distance. The women were beautiful and remarkably fair.

"Cook, moving westward, bypassed the romantic island of Fatu Hiva on a pleasant southwest journey. For a third time, he tacked through the Tuamotus to anchor in Matavai Bay. As usual, the English were greeted with flourishes of friendship. Old loves were rekindled, and new ones ignited. Like his former visits, Cook found food in abundance. Many houses and new canoes were being built. In general, other signs showed that peace was restored."

I paused in my story and looked at the crew. All eyes were upon me in question. I then said, "Gentlemen, I want to pause here for a moment to reflect on what Captain Cook wrote. 'Arriving at Matavai Bay, as always, the English were greeted with flourishes of friendship. Old loves were rekindled, and new ones ignited.'

"Now my friends, I understand what all the excitement is about each time the *Sheila II* touches port at Tahiti! All the girls screaming down the dock, screaming with flowers in hand!"

The crew burst out in laughter. I went on, "I guess after this trip, I will have to check the level of the mail keg!" All roared with laughter, and Captain Mobley grinned and gave me two thumbs-up!

"Okay, guys, back to the story. As we continue with Captain Cook finding peace secure, Cook planned to stay two or three days to let Wallis check any error in Mr. Kendell's watch against latitude and longitude. The sojourning lasted for three weeks. The familiar joys, confusion, and problems ensued, and he was forced to inflict punishment on crew and natives alike. He held his hand as long as possible. Perhaps the spectacle of the Tahitian naval review of thirty-three double canoes, very well equipped and armed, remained in his mind as he reflected on his relationship with the islanders.

"He stated this relationship in this statement, 'Three things made them our fast friends. Their own good-natured benevolent disposition, gentle treatment on our part, and the dread and fear of our firearms. By ceasing to observe the first, we would have a worse effect, of course, and too frequent use of the latter would have excited a spirit of revenge and perhaps taught them that firearms were not such terrible things as they imagined. They are very sensible of their superiority. They have us in numbers, and no one knows what an enraged multitude might do.'

"Sailing southward, Cook reached a high jagged island that he decided to investigate. At first landing, the spearman was struck with a stone, and two men fired without orders. The Indians fled, and Cook decided to try to land again down the coast. He went ashore with two boatloads of men to leave gifts in some deserted canoes. His party was promptly attacked, with one native charging with the ferocity of a boar. Spears whistled, and musket fire scattered the attackers. Cook quickly returned to the *Resolution*. He thought no good was to come of these people or these islands. He named it Savage Island. Moving on to Nomuka, one of the Tonga islands, yams and coconuts were offered for trade."

I paused. "Here is one for you boys," I said to the crew. "While Cook was standing on the beach one morning, an old woman approached with a ravishing, beautiful young woman. The old woman said to Cook that he could have the girl in exchange for his shirt! Cook declined on the basis of poverty. Then the old woman insisted she would take care of the shirt. Cook refused."

When all failed, the old woman spit in his face, speaking with rage in words Cook could not understand. Cook retreated to the boat. In one quick moment, he was reduced from commander to a midshipman who could not handle the situation.

"Midshipman Elliot penned a statement about Cook's encounter. He wrote that they had never seen Cook swayed by an encounter with any of their fair friends but had also been called down as an 'old man and good for nothing.' Despite the encounter and a little petty theft, things were good, and the Tongan people always remained friendly. Even today, the Tongans are very proud of their heritage and go out of their way to be friendly, most especially the children. Underway again, the *Resolution* sailed under pleasant weather and gentle winds. Next was to properly map a group of islands that were incorrectly charted by a Portuguese explorer in 1605.

"Cook sighted land on July 17, 1774. For the next six weeks, he established the character of this volcanic group of islands that he named New Hebrides. He conducted a running survey of the chain of islands, chunks of land running 450 miles across the sea. Volcanic rock with some active volcanoes on some. The inhabitants were Melanesians, friendly like Tahitians. At sunset on July 21, the *Resolution* anchored in a bay of a large island, Malekula. The next morning, with a green branch to signify peace, Cook waded ashore, hoping to establish trade and get firewood. Confronting him were several hundred men armed with spears, clubs, and bows and arrows. Cook distributed medals and tried to speak to them in all the phrases he knew. In return, he received a small pig, half a dozen coconuts, and a little water. The natives were not interested in the medals. All they wanted was for their visitors to be gone. Cook obliged.

"Noticing the distinctive appearance of these people, Cook made a sketch. They were almost black or dark chocolate, slender, not tall, with monkey faces and woolly hair. The men wore only penis sheaths, and the women, a kind of skirt. For cosmetics, men used black paint, while women used yellow dye. All the Europeans found their language fascinating. Cook also observed that they could pronounce English words with ease. Another entry further down the beach bore more confirmation. Cook needed wood and water and moved on.

"He came upon an island with active volcanoes but encountered the same situation as before. Hundreds of natives on the shore were armed. He distributed trinkets and tried to negotiate. The natives wanted the men to come ashore and would not back up. Some ventured to the ship and offered two coconuts and a yam. That duly paid for trade. The old man made several more trips, landing with three boats, armed marines, and seamen. Cook faced two groups of men, a thousand or more. They refused to move back, even after musket fire over their heads.

"The throng dispersed, leaving one old man, an elder, who brought produce to the ship. Cook had his men stake out lines to a freshwater pond. They carefully stayed between them as they filled the ship's casks. Then he asked permission from the elder to cut firewood. Because of the elder's actions, the natives came drifting back. They did not attempt to steal or even touch any of the Europeans' possessions. They would not allow the strangers to go inland, but they did allow the cutting of firewood and gathering of stones on the beach for the ship's ballast. During the two August weeks spent here, an uneasy accommodation prevailed. The elder became a constant friend.

"After restoring his supplies of wood and water, Cook sailed from the harbor, which he named Fort Resolution. For eleven days, he looped through the islands of New Hebrides, placing them on his chart. In September, the *Resolution* was again plying through uncharted waters. Cook meant to reach New Zealand as quickly as possible, resupply, and take advantage of the southern hemisphere summer to explore the high latitudes before returning to England. However, he still had time to explore any lands he might encounter. That land appeared on the horizon just three days later: New Caledonia, a lush green mountain rising above the trees. The Pacific rolled over a great reef to shore. The reef surrounded the island, but finding a break in the reef, Cook made his landing on September 6.

"The Melanesian crowd that gathered around him proved to be shy but friendly—a pleasant change from the New Hebrides natives. Cook remarked they were good-natured people and left his mind at ease. Cook traced the entire coastline of the east, staying clear of the reef. He planned to go in to explore the south coast, so he moved on. A little further south, he ran into a tiny island, now known as Norfolk Island, famous for its elegant Norfolk pines.

"On October 19, the *Resolution* lay at rest at Ship's Cove. In three weeks of furious activity and with the men stuffed with greens, the ship was overhauled for the voyage home. She left Ship's Cove on November 10, and with a friendly wind, reached the west coast of Tierra del Fuego. In five weeks, Cook explored the storm-lashed coastline, which he reported as the most barren yet.

"Christmas was spent in this barren place. A carefully hoarded Madeira wine was served, along with roast goose, boiled eggs, and goose pie. Five days later, the *Resolution* gained the cape and entered the southern Atlantic Ocean. There they would search for signs of Dalrymple's most northbound continent.

"On July 30, 1775, three years and eighteen days after departing, Cook anchored again in English waters. But on December 28, poised on Cape Horn, he gazed back at the Pacific Ocean. Perhaps with a touch of wistfulness, he thought he was leaving it forever."

I looked around. You could have heard a pin drop. I quietly said, "Well, gentlemen, this concludes our hero, Captain Cook's, second journey. When the captain determines it's time, we will cover the third and final journey."

We were in Cook waters now, moving toward Tahiti. This was Captain Cook's favorite island, and also Tonga. On many stops by Captain Mobley and his crew, it became a favorite of theirs as well. The island of Tahiti was just ahead now with all its splendor.

As we reached dockside and the crew was securing the lines, a commotion rang out. The girls came down the dock, flowers in hand, calling greetings to the boys. The crew looked at Captain Mobley and me with a grin and turned to meet the girls. Captain Mobley and I just looked at each other. He was grinning and shaking his head.

A short stay in Tahiti, and it would be time for us to get underway. Destination Samoa.

After we were seabound and secure, Captain Mobley was anxious to hear the story about Captain Cook's third and final journey.

We all gathered around, and Helm took the wheel to keep us on course.

Third Journey

"When James Cook returned home to Britain, the news of his journey and accomplishments had already reached the country. The society lionized his achievements, voting him as an esteemed member. There was a great reception throughout the kingdom. King George anxiously listened to his report and then promoted James to post captain. At this point, James Cook was at the pinnacle of his career.

"The Admiralty also appointed him to the board of the Greenwich Hospital, a position of prestige that offered excellent pay plus abundant free time. This pleased Elizabeth Cook and their children, James and Nathaniel, who had been deprived of husband and father for six or seven long years. As soon as the *Resolution* said she lost another infant son, James accepted his new position but on one condition. 'I may quit if I receive a call from my country to renew active service.' Already rumors were starting that another Pacific journey was in the making. The *Resolution* was already in dry dock for repairs and refitting for another journey. Cook did not expect to command it. After battling the elements, poor food, and the responsibility of strain and hardships, he was forty-seven years old and had been constantly at sea for thirty years. Instead of relaxing, he busied himself with logs and journals and composing a chronicle of the *Endeavor*.

"His life changed course in 1776 when, at a dinner party with friends Sandwich, Palliser, and Stephens, the story was told that everyone wanted Cook for commander, but no one wanted to ask him to take the risks again. The Admiralty took this and deliberated long enough for Cook to say he would take the direction of the Enterprise. In less than six months' time, Cook had committed himself to a third voyage. He also took on a huge task—to search for or disprove the myth that a Northwest Passage existed between the Atlantic and Pacific in the barren frozen land of the north.

"A man by the name of Omai, who had come to England on the *Adventure*, would be on this journey with Cook. Once again, passengers other than crew—dignitaries, naturalists, and explorers—would be on board. Naming the crew members would be tedious, so let me say that young James King would be Cook's second lieutenant. A familiar name to you, William Bligh, who later became captain on the mutinous *Bounty*, became master of the *Resolution*.

"In the last week of June, Cook bade his family farewell and took the *Resolution* to Plymouth to join the *Discovery*, which he would command on this expedition. On the way, he observed ships that were on their way to America to quell the rebellion, an unhappy necessity. Later, we learned that Benjamin Franklin, high in government at that time, issued a decree that the ships of Captain James Cook should not be harassed or fired upon if encountered. Captain James Cook was on a mission that, if successful, would honor the whole world.

"When Cook arrived at Plymouth, he had happier news. The society had awarded him a medal, the Copley Medal, Britain's highest honor for intellectual achievement. Finally, on July 12, 1776, the *Resolution* slipped her moorings and headed southwest—but without the *Discovery*. A crewman was in a bit of trouble, cast into prison, and later came down with consumption. But the two ships joined up at Cape Town, with Cook picking up supplies in the Canary Islands. Due to shoddy workmanship, both ships experienced problems on the way. Weak masts, improper caulking on interior rigging, and sails all posed a threat of danger and created a wet environment for the crew. Cook ordered repairs at Cape Town.

"When the young native had an audience with the king, the king was so impressed that he ordered seeds, plants, and livestock to be purchased to take to the islanders as a token of gratitude. Omai gave up his cabin to livestock. Cook had taken on ample of all species. Carpenters in the shipyard had built stalls and the like on board to house the animals.

"Cook left the Cape in December, now in tandem with Clerke on the *Endeavor*. Cook was adamant about searching through the cold lands below the Cape in search of the mysterious continent that was never found. From Christmas Eve to December 30, he searched through the fog, ice, and severe cold. All they found was hardship. Glad to leave this cold, blustering, wet country, they moved on.

"On January 24, the southern coast of Tasmania came into view. Soon, the two ships were anchored comfortably in Adventure Bay. Fresh water was ample, and food was grass. In Ship's Cove, he kept marines on guard against attempted massacres he had experienced before. The men worked armed to repair the ships. Food, wood, and water were gathered. Omai would be the interpreter if they were confronted. Before he left, Cook released a boar and a sow, which are now the wild hogs of New Zealand.

"In March, Cook set his course for Tahiti off the schedule he intended. He wanted to be well on his way to North America in the summer to pursue the search for the passage. With ill wind, people out of sorts, and livestock short of fodder and water, he was not going to make his goal of reaching North America now. He would stay in the tropics, prepare for an early start, and make it northward.

"In 1778, he was too far off course to do anything else. The first land he spotted was Mangaia, the southernmost of the Cook Islands. Finding little to be offered there, he sailed on to Atiu. The reception was better, but the short supply of needed provisions forced him to move from island to island until he reached Palmerston Island. There, he found abundant water, and foraged for livestock, fish, sea fowl, and grass, which Omai skillfully cooked for the men.

"Cook, on the other hand, was starting to change from this journey. He was tired, his temperament short, and he lingered longer from place to place, knowing that a short distance away was a new venture to seek. As he left the Cook Islands and headed for Tonga, Cook took the same track by which he had gone in 1772 to the island of Nomuka, where he bought good supplies of food and water.

"A powerful young chief by the name of Finau encouraged Cook to travel to Lifuka, where goods were better and more plentiful. He sailed with Cook there. Cook bought and paid handsomely. The chiefs there saw wealth and plotted to kill Cook and his crew and take the ships and wealth.

"Thirty years later, an Englishman in Tonga learned the facts that Cook never knew. They planned an evening of feasting and dancing to entertain the Englishmen. At a given signal, they would fall upon them, kill them, and seize the wealth.

"On the afternoon of May 20, Cook and his crew were invited to dances by which they were greatly amused. They were totally off guard. The Lifuka chiefs had orchestrated the attack by night, where Finau, the Tongan grandee, had perpetrated that it be done. By day, he was mad that his order was disobeyed, so he canceled the attack and returned to the *Resolution* for his dinner.

"The night chosen for Cook's murder was the most spellbound of all his years in the South Pacific. Sensuous dances were performed by the women in the light of coconut torches, naked to the waist, their breasts glistening with scented oil, and their hair interwoven with flowers. They swirled and undulated to the beat of the long drum, and the English were entranced. The feast prepared for Cook and his men included a roasted suckling pig, Pulu made from coconut milk, taro leaves, fish, yams, and fruit, cooked in an earth oven.

"So Cook and his men left Lifuka pleasantly satisfied. They sailed for Tongatapu through dangerous coral reefs. Cook stayed among the friendly islands for eleven days. This journey lasted eleven weeks on his third voyage. He became very friendly with the Tui, equal to a king.

"In August, with great relief, Cook reached Tahiti and could release all the animals that the king desired to give to Chieftain Tu and other high-ruling officials. He felt relieved of the heavy burden of transporting these animals a great distance, with their troubles combined with him. He put the men to work caulking the ships and persuaded them to conserve their daily grog ration to be helpful in colder climates.

"On September 30, Cook departed Matavai Bay for the last time. Omai had decided to stay and settle down. Cook ordered his men to build a small house for Omai on a piece of land that Cook had acquired. They also planted vegetables that they had brought from Tonga. Omai was a shallow and silly young man, but he had captured the hearts of everyone on board. Thus, it became a long and tearful farewell.

"On December 8, 1777, another farewell occurred on the Society Islands. Some crewmen wished to stay in the tropics with their acquired women rather than face the frozen north. After a flogging by Cook and a stern talk on the pitfalls of desertion, they returned to the ship. Charles Clerke and William Anderson, both sick with consumption, begged to stay. Death was evident in the frozen north. But in the end, their plea unspoken, they sailed with the ship.

"On December 22, they crossed the equator. This was the first time that Cook entered the northern side of the vast Pacific. Now Cook and Clerke both expected a long journey north. Within weeks, they came upon an island paradise—the Hawaiian Islands. Cook moved toward the last of his great discoveries. As he approached the shore, canoe-loads of people met him. Much to his astonishment, they spoke a language similar to the Tahitians. They had the appearance of Polynesians. Cook was in awe as to how these thousands of people had migrated this far to these volcanic islands.

"Hawaii would become the most complex discovery he had made with its people, customs, beliefs, and rituals. Anchoring in Waimea Bay on the island of Kauai, and being greeted by people falling prostrate at his feet, he was impressed by the strands of taro, the village, and the shrines with three-tiered altars.

"On the beach, trade started with the greatest of order. During the shore party, an unfortunate accident occurred. Williamson, in charge, shot an islander trying to climb aboard, feeling threatened. This angered Cook. He then decided to reset the anchorage of the *Resolution*, but a burst of wind pushed him from the bay. He chose to move further north.

"Cook took the *Resolution* and *Discovery* northward. The people on the beach were saddened by his swift departure. He sailed away on February 2, 1778, with no plans to return. Nine months later, he would stage back to an anchorage he would never leave.

"On March 7, 1778, the long coast of New Albion came into view. There was nothing remarkable about it, concluded Cook. He recorded its hills, valleys, and forests. A northern extreme formed a point which he called Cape Foul Weather.

"Strong gales sent the *Discovery* and *Resolution* along the Oregon coastline for five days, moving north toward what is now the state of Washington. More storms and gales beset the ships. Short on water and still fighting storms, the ships found Nootka Sound almost immediately. The ships were surrounded by canoes, wary of Cook's friendliness until he handed out ship's biscuits that they mistook for wood. They yelled in welcome. Cook found them to be a mild people, eager to trade. They were ready to accept anything shiny or metal. Every piece of brass not needed from the ship went into trade.

"After docking there for a while and enjoying Indian songs, retail, and carvings, it was time to give the decks a good scrubbing. What began as a stop for water turned into weeks when one of the carpenters found rot in some of the decking. This was going to be more than a simple water stop. The stay evolved into four weeks. The masts had to be repaired, and rotten sections needed rebuilding. Trees from the woods—hemlock and cedar—had to be split, worked down, and planed into boards for the repairs.

"Cook, in the meantime, gathered greens, nettles, and wild garlic. Midshipmen rowed him around Nootka Sound, giving Cook an opportunity to explore the surrounding area. The crew remarked that it gave him a sense of peace, but upon returning to the ships, he was again remorseful. With the ships repaired once more, Cook sailed on April 26. The Indians were left with new hatchets and saws. Dressed in masks, they sang a farewell to the ships departing from the shore.

"Almost immediately, storms struck, rising to hurricane level and driving the ships far out to sea. Land was not sighted again until May 1, off the coast of southeastern Alaska. The storms vanished, and Cook named this area Cape Fairweather and Mount Fairweather. He followed the coast as quickly as the gentle breeze would allow. Orders from the Admiralty had stated that he should not lose any time exploring. Hastening on to latitude 65 degrees north, just below the Arctic Circle, he began his search for the Northwest Passage.

"In June, at the head of the Gulf of Alaska, he entered an inlet heading due north. Cook thought it might be a part of the long-hoped-for Northwest Passage. Sailing north, it became a cul-de-sac, and ten days later, they sailed out. Within days, they came upon a deep-water channel between tall peaks. Hope again arose. Cook insisted on exploring this waterway. He found no passage. For days, the ship plied the beautiful inlet to another dead end.

"Cook's orders gave him a year to succeed or fail, then he was to return to England by whatever route seemed best. He was expected home in 1779. Cook moved along the Alaskan coastline in fog and chilling mists. The peninsula was pushing the ships southward for 725 miles to about 54 degrees, reaching the Aleutian chain. Hearing breakers on the outboard bow, they were on a collision course. Cook yelled for anchors to be dropped! Later, as the fog cleared a little, it could be seen that they were in imminent danger. Cook then moved through the mist. North the ships moved into a nasty jumping sea, dodging ice as far north as the eye could see.

"On August 17, 1778, Cook saw a great light shining off the ice in the north. Moving on, with large ice thickening, Cook saw a channel in the icecap and zigzagged about the Chukchi Sea for ten days, seeking a route through the ice. Drizzling rain closed in on the northeastern coast of Siberia. Always, the ice defeated him.

"On August 29, Cook wrote that it was not possible to find a passage in this ice, at least not this year. To proceed would only endanger the ships and crews, possibly resulting in an ice-bound condition or wreck.

"On October 3, he anchored in Unalaska's Harbor, which he had found in July. Water was plentiful, as well as wild berries, halibut, and salmon. The carpenters could repair the leaking seams on the *Resolution*. Cook and his officers ran into some Russians who had been there for three decades, slowly expanding their fur trade. Throughout the Bering Sea, Alaska had become their headquarters. Pelts were traded from the Aleutian Indians and sold in China for a great price. Cook had not realized the value this land had to offer.

"There was a lot of friendly interaction between Cook and the Russians that later sparked interest from England and the United States, eventually leading to the United States negotiating a purchase. But for Cook, the founding of a northwest passage remained a myth.

It was never there. Tropical breezes from the south would replace the chilling gales of the north as the *Discovery* and the *Resolution* plied the waters to the south, destination Hawaii.

"At dawn on November 26, a small outline of land appeared on the southern horizon. Cook could see an elevated saddle hill that seemed to rise into the clouds. The mountainside was covered with lush green and ended in a deep rocky coastline, broken with dangerous surf. He had come into the Hawaiian Islands from the east. The first island he saw was Maui. As they moved toward the coast, people, cultivated fields, and houses were seen. But Cook made no attempt to anchor. For fifty days, he coasted the islands of Maui and Hawaii but made no attempt to land.

"The men were frustrated. For months, they had endured the hardships of the cold, dark north. Now with paradise in sight, they were confined. Cook had a new policy, and he stuck firm to it. Upon sighting land, there would be no private trade, no unauthorized firearms, and no trysts with island women aboard. To his dismay, venereal disease prevailed from his very first visit with the islanders he met off Maui, probably transmitted from Kauai since his visit earlier in the year. The islanders came in droves, climbing aboard, eager to trade with pigs, roots, fruit, and cartloads of food. They wanted to trade any iron goods they could. The women made offers to the men, promising favors if they would invite them in. Things got out of hand, and the women had to be ordered off the ship. They left with indignant stares. After a few days of this, Cook took advantage of the wind and moved south to the island of Hawaii. He continued to keep trade going during the day but shut it down at night. No one was yet to set foot on this island. They were still short on rations, and a crisis blew up over a drink.

"The provisions had included sugarcane, so Cook had it made into a wholesome beer. The officers tried to smooth things over by saying the crew liked the beer, but Cook received letters of anger and complaints about the beer and the fact of being confined onboard. He retorted by saying the letters were mutinous, and in the future, they should not expect the least indulgence from him.

"Cook was changing on this voyage. For two preceding voyages, he had been the father figure, and all his concern went to his crew. No one really knew Cook was keeping counsel to himself and not even discussing plans with his own trusted officers. After losing his temper in this episode, he almost lost his ship.

"A surprise storm almost blew him to shore. His quick thinking helped him retreat from harm's way, but in return, he started to write a journal with agitation about the navy's shoddy workmanship and placed blame on his friends in high places. A trip around the eastern cape of Hawaii met him with unfavorable winds and adverse currents. The *Discovery* and *Resolution* became separated and did not find each other for several weeks. Finally, with men frazzled and the ship leaking, Cook was forced to find anchorage halfway up the coast of Hawaii.

"It was Master William Bligh who found a dent in the lava-draped coastline. Entering Kealakekua Bay, both ships were escorted by an eminent fleet of canoes, numbering about eight hundred. The Hawaiians greeted the Englishmen with curiosity, cordiality, and enthusiasm.

"The frazzled crew had cruised off the islands for nearly two months. With solid land under their feet, food in their bellies, and lovers in their arms, the time of frustration and anger was soon forgotten. Cook became so immersed in island affairs that he couldn't even find time to keep his own journal up to date.

"His latest entry on January 17, 1779, penned the overwhelming welcome: 'I have nowhere in this sea seen such a number of people assembled at one place. Besides the ones in canoes, all the shore of the bay was covered with people, and hundreds were swimming about the ships shoaling fish.'

"So many Hawaiians clambered aboard the *Discovery* heeled sharply. Finally, in all the confusion, two chieftains cleared the decks. They introduced an old priest by the name of Koa, who approached the captain, offering him two coconuts and a small pig. Koa draped Cook with a red cloth and repeated a long incantation.

"That afternoon, Cook went ashore on a small beach. The Pali loomed above the bay, and the ritual engulfed him. Except for the priest, the Hawaiians prostrated themselves before him. In a dignified procession, Koa guided Cook and his party to a large platform of stone. As they walked, they heard over and over again, '*Erono, erono.*' Cook entered the sacred area, bedecked with human skulls and six-foot images carved in wood. Before one statue was an altar containing a decaying hog. After prayer, Koa escorted the captain onto a rickety scaffold. Cook was adorned with another red sash, and then, with a young priest, voiced a kind of litany. Koa led Cook down to a circuit of images and seemed to berate them, all but one. Koa prostrated himself, kissed it, and desired the captain to do the same. Cook was quite passive and bid Koa to do with him as he chose.

"Cook's men were then taken to a central area where the captain was seated between images. A procession of islanders brought them offerings of food. Then speeches or prayers were said by the young priest while the crowd repeated over and over, '*Erono.*'

"Then Cook arose and distributed a few trinkets that were for the god, and the strangers were escorted out with great solemnity. King reported that two men with wands went before the captain saying the same as before, and all prostrated themselves."

I said, "In looking at this ritual, you have to understand the Hawaiians worshipped a god as they repeated 'Erono.' Their god was a white god, and they believed he would one day come from the sea. Looking at the ritual site, the chair reserved for the god was the tall chair where the high priest sat Cook. It had a tall back with a cross arm attached like a cross. A special material was wrapped around the cross.

"So here, in the middle of a religious event, Captain Cook sails in. He is White, and his ships' masts and yardarms are covered with sails that look like the ritual chair of the islanders. I presume that in the middle of things, the islanders thought that the white god had come from the sea.

"Cook could never know that his arrival coincided with a religious belief. He could not understand that the islanders saw him as the reincarnation of Lono. He arrived in the midst of Makahiki, the season of a great gathering of islanders to pay tribute to their rulers.

It was a season that ran from October and November into February. Dancing, games, and feasts were all underway, and Cook anchored in the midst of it. Thus, Cook was greeted with honors. Tapu honored him by draping a carpet of bird feathers around Cook, and in return, Cook offered ironwork made on the ship's forges.

"A constant exchange of goods then prevailed with long, happy days of peace with the islanders. Once a mutinous crew, now a happy crew, as restrictions were reduced. Cook was even forced to rescind his order of no women on the ship. The ship became overrun with the women.

"Even so, this relaxation kept the pilfering down due to ritual respect. The king was inquisitive about Cook's departure. Cook planned to explore the rest of the islands and then go north for another summer in the Arctic.

"On February 4, the *Discovery* and *Resolution* were seen off by a throng of canoes. They were now sailing north in unsettled weather. On the night of the 7th, strong gales sprang the foremast on the *Resolution*, leaving only the rest of her sails barely sailable. Searching for a reasonable harbor free of treacherous winds, he limped on for days until Kealakekua Bay. No sooner had they anchored than the ship's carpenters began working on the mast.

"They were watched by inquisitive Hawaiians, who boarded the ships out of curiosity about this sudden return. The Hawaiians were much displeased by it. The weary attitude escalated into darkness and scorn. Then it became epidemic when Captain Clerke ordered forty lashes to the individual who had stolen the armorer's tongs.

"Then trying to get water, they were threatened by Hawaiians wielding stones. Cook ordered his men to load their weapons. Then again, the armorer's tongs were stolen from the *Discovery*. In the ensuing chase, Cook pursued the wrong man for miles in the wrong direction. Then two of the crew in pursuit were stoned.

"Cook expressed his sorrow that the Indians had at last obligated him to use force, for they must not ever think they had the advantage over the crew. He was shocked and baffled by the Hawaiians' scorn, indignant about the treatment of his men, and humiliated by his wild goose chase the day before.

"Gentle breezes brushed the ships through the night. Before dawn, some Hawaiians stole the ship's cutter, which was essential for inshore exploration and necessary as a lifeboat. Cook was determined to secure its return, even if he had to resort to kidnapping a chieftain and demanding the return of the boat.

"Cook decided on a show of force, taking a small boat in with nine of his marines, all armed. He had other boats guarding the bay to prevent any canoes from leaving. He posted a guard on the beach at a camp. Then he went to find the priest, Koa, assuring him that Cook would not let anyone be hurt. Cook marched into the village where the priest was staying, asked for directions, and went straight to his hut. The priest woke up, obviously not knowing anything about the missing cutter. He accepted Cook's invitation to the *Resolution*.

"As they started out, one of Kalei'opu'u's wives and two minor chiefs rushed up to detain him. Phillips appeared dejected and frightened, sitting on the ground. A group of agitated Hawaiians had gathered, numbering two to three thousand, armed with war mats, stones, spears, and daggers. With Cook's approval, Phillips ordered his marines to form a line at the water's edge. Facing the crowd, Cook remarked to Phillips, 'We can never compel him to go onboard without killing some of these people.'

"During this episode, musket fire came from an officer who killed a chief trying to leave the bay. A companion of the victim tried to report this to Cook, without success. Cook was making his way toward the water. Suddenly, a man jumped in front of him wielding a stone and a dagger. Cook swung the nozzle of his gun toward the man and fired, discharging the barrel with a shot. The man's war mat absorbed the shot, leaving the warrior unharmed.

"Phillips then blocked a dagger blow with the barrel of his musket. Stones started to rain down on the shore party. A marine fell. Cook fired and killed a man. Cook's voice rang out amid the screams of the crowd, shouting to the marines to open fire and retreat to the boats.

"In the confusion, Phillips was knocked down by a stone and then stabbed. He managed to swim to the pinnace. The men in boats opened fire, checking the crowd. Five marines escaped; four lay dead on the rocks. The *Resolution*'s cannons were firing toward the distant turmoil. Cook, his gun empty, signaled for the boats to come in.

"As he waved, a Hawaiian clubbed him, and another brought a knife down to the back of his neck. Stunned, he fell into the water. A crowd descended upon him and held him under the water. With repeated blows, they killed the man they worshipped as a god.

"Captain Clerke of the *Resolution* was Captain Cook's best friend. A younger man but an excellent captain, Clerke shared a close bond with Cook. Earlier in the journey, Clerke had been struck down with consumption and almost died. Clerke had gone to sea at twelve years old and rose in rank strictly on his merit. Courageous, open-hearted, and good-humored, he became one of the few of Cook's intimate friends, as well as a trusted subordinate officer. Fatally ill with tuberculosis, Clerke took command of the expedition at Hawaii when tragedy struck. His responsibility was now to take command of the *Discovery* and *Resolution*, completing the stated orders. But first, there was the issue of his friend Captain Cook. Clerke appealed to the elders of the island to return Cook's body they had carried off, but they would not. It was their custom if a fallen warrior died in battle, the body would be burned. Then each bone would be gifted to leaders around the island as a tribute. Cook was awarded this tribute.

"Clerke learned this on the night of the fifteenth when Keli'ikea came secretly at night, risking his own life, bringing remains from the pyre. For a week after the killing, a procession came down to Kealakekua Bay, bringing offerings of food and a small bundle wrapped in tapa cloth.

"In the *Resolution*'s great cabin, Clerke unwrapped the cloth to reveal his revered friend's remains. The skull and other bones were there. The hands were preserved in salt to prove that the remains belonged to Captain Cook. The surgeon was also standing by during the inspection.

"On the evening of the next day, Clerke consigned the remains of James Cook to the waters of Kealakekua Bay, with all the dignity and honor that could be rendered in this part of the world. The following day, the *Resolution* and *Discovery* departed the bay, and, I must say, with a universal gloom, melancholy, and grief from leaving without their revered Captain Cook.

"Professionally but with great sorrow, Clerke guided his men through the Hawaiian Islands, then north again to search for the Northwest Passage. Conditions were harsh, and despite devoted effort, the mission was to be abandoned. The first stop was on the Alaskan peninsula.

"Before the long voyage home, the benevolent and personal Captain Charles Clerke died from his consumption. Lts. John Gore and James King finally brought the ships home to anchor on August 22, 1780.

"Four weary years after departure, London had already learned of Cook's death from a letter forwarded from Petropoulos. The great blow of his death was now history, and Britain was involved in war with American independence. All memories were slipping into the past now. So many awards, medals, and presentations. So many tears shed by all—society, the Admiralty, and even King George shed tears over the death of their hero.

"More appropriately, the government gave Elizabeth Cook a handsome pension. Of her sixteen years of marriage to James Cook, she had been with him less than five. She had lost six children and now her husband. A stalwart woman, Mrs. Cook lived to the age of ninety-three. What she said in her judgment was apt: if not a man of boundless vision, he was a man of boundless success. He mapped tens of millions of square miles. He discovered new, intriguing people. He vastly expanded the horizon of the British Empire.

"In Kealakekua Bay, there is a bronze plaque marking the place where Captain James Cook met his death. How I wish that during an evening tide and golden setting sun, I could just sit and gaze at this plaque, the Pacific tide gently moving back and forth, and the golden sun illuminating the black into gold. I would like to stand at attention and salute my hero. I would say, 'Rest well, my friend, in your beloved Pacific.'"

After I said this, I looked at the crew, all with tears in their eyes, as well as tears in mine. I then said to the crew, "There, my friends, I have not only given you the story of Captain James Cook's three journeys, but I have given you part of his life." A moment of silence followed and then an enthusiastic round of thank-yous.

It was time to get back to the ship's duties and relieve Helm, who was still at the wheel. Cookie hustled off to prepare us a meal. Captain took the wheel, and I stayed on with him. Later in the evening, when it was time to turn in, Helm came and again took the watch. Captain turned the wheel over to him and went to retire. I think we all slipped into a sound sleep; the day's activities were long.

In the middle of the night, a huge sea storm began to brew. Soon, the *Sheila II* was tossing and turning in the surf. Big waves thundered across the bow. Water surged down the deck, the rigging creaked, and the lights went dark. Water spilled into our compartments. In our shorts, the wind and rain hit us in full-force.

Then Helm was not at the wheel—he was gone! Captain ran to the wheel, and all in one motion, strapped himself to the wheel, turned on the diesel engine, and shouted, "Man overboard! Man overboard! Turn to! Man, the lifeboat! I want four hands on deck and four hands in the boat! Lower away!"

Before we could act, the captain had the ship in a 180-degree turn, water almost lapping over the starboard side. We ran for the boat. I jumped in with three of the crew, leaving one extra on deck. Then he quickly lowered us down the davit.

Captain was in retreat. He slowed, and with his glasses, he spotted an orange spot on the water. Helm had been smart enough to don his orange life vest before he got swept off. Captain headed for him, bringing the ship slowly behind us. We got Helm onboard, and at the same time, Captain was pulling another 180 and coming to our side. The crew onboard was ready with lines down.

We pulled alongside. Lines were tied, and the lifeboat was pulled up in place. Everyone pitched in then, and Helm was carried below, somewhat in a daze. We stripped him, put him under a hot shower, dried him, and got him in bed. I said I would stay, as the crew had to get topside again for whatever was needed.

The ship was starting to settle down now, so I knew we were in the storm or the storm itself had passed. Helm went into violent shakes. Cookie came in with three cups of brandy: a double for Helm and one shot for us. He winked at me and said, "An old Swedish recipe like you said in your story." Then he chuckled.

The brandy soon brought Helm out of the shakes and into a peaceful sleep. I'm not a drinking man, but I didn't have any trouble getting mine down. I went back on deck, and the sea had settled. The crew was finishing the last of things, in their shorts, and ready to secure. I was in mine and Captain in his.

I couldn't help but laugh. The big man was there in his shorts, tied to the wheel. He said, "James, go get dressed, and bring me my clothes," which I did. I stayed on with him, though he protested, and we stood watch until dawn. He said, "James, take the wheel 'til I can take a bearing where we are." He did and came back. We were lucky we were still on course, coming through the Tonga Islands and heading for Samoa. We will not make it this morning. He picked up the remote radio and tried to raise Hawk, Curt, or the island. Curt came on. "Curt, we are still around Tonga, so we will not get to Samoa 'til late afternoon or evening. Everything okay?"

Curt replied, "Aye, Captain. I'll keep the girls entertained until you arrive."

Captain chuckled. "Okay, Curt. I bet you will like that!" Then he disconnected. "Well, James," he said with a chuckle, "I guess barring all the ups and downs on this trip, we are finally back on track. Samoa, then home!"

I smiled. I knew he, too, was getting anxious like the rest. He continued, "I guess Curt and Hawk will realize that because of circumstances, there will be no party tonight?" Half question, half statement.

I said, "Well, Captain, that's understandable. Many homecomings to reflect back on in the past."

Now past Tonga, which would have been a nice stop, but time dictated that it was time to get in. Soon, the beautiful island came into view, closer and closer. Captain pulled into the harbor and proceeded to the docking area reserved for him. All hands were there. Once secure, everyone came aboard for a short reunion. Satisfied, Captain Mobley was ready to get underway for Sydney before nightfall.

As the ship pulled out, Leilani and I watched as it approached the horizon and would soon disappear. The setting sun went down, putting a red glow on the *Sheila II*'s sails. It reminded me of the old song, "Red sails in the sunset, way out on the sea. Oh, carry my loved one home safely to me!"

I turned to Leilani and took her in my arms. I embraced her tightly, kissing her lips, her cheeks, her eyes, her lips again, murmuring, "Oh, Lei, I love you so very much."

She returned my love. She looked into my eyes with a question. "James, do you think Captain Mobley will go again?"

I was quiet for a long moment, then answered, "I don't know."

She asked, "James, will you go again?"

After a long pause, I again said, "Lei, I don't know!" Then I turned and embraced her again. I said, "Lei, let's go to the house. We need quiet time together." We started our walk back up the hill to our place. Cocoa moved in beside us and went along.

After a light snack, we went out to sit on the porch on the veranda. In our backyard, there is a large hammock tied between two large tropical trees. The trees were in bloom now, and the fragrance in the balmy breeze was at its fullest peak.

Leilani said, "James, let's go to the hammock!" Cocoa, always knowing what we said, ran ahead and took his position underneath. We climbed in, stretched out, and Lei scooted as close to me as she could and placed a soft kiss on my lips. Oh, how I love this woman.

She said, "I want to tell you about my love!"

I said, "Oh gosh, you mean there's another?"

She laughed and playfully punched me in the ribs. "No! Silly, there is only you and always will be only you. Now don't talk, and let me tell my story. The first time we met, you were on your flight back to LA. I was on duty, a flight attendant. You were on return from a cruise with Captain Mobley, a three-masted ship in Sydney Bay. He called attention, so I leaned across you to see and was in awe of the sight. I turned to you and looked into your eyes, and I thought, *This is the man I want in my life!*

"Well, that night on break, I asked you if it would be alright if I took my late-night break in the empty seat beside you. You nodded.

Sometime in the night, it was a little chilly, so I got a blanket and covered us up! The fragrance of your body was warm and wonderful. When I woke, I found that I was tucked into your side and sleeping with my head on your shoulder. I felt secure.

"I contacted Captain Mobley. I guess despite myself, I asked about you and told him about our encounter. With a chuckle, he said, 'Good for you! James needs that. On future trips, I will tip you off as to his return. Book on the flight with him!'

"So, honey, I did. I volunteered on each flight of your return to LA, and we became even closer and closer. Then on your last flight, I had some free flight time coming, and I was planning to resign from my job. We had never talked seriously about our connection, and I was scared. Scared of losing you!

"Captain Mobley had warned me about your thoughts when you and he talked. You felt you were too old and two worlds apart to address a romance! When the plane set down in LA, you were preparing to go. I watched in despair. I started to cry, tears streaming down my cheeks. With a sad look, you said, 'I'm sorry. This is it, kid.' Then you reached out and took your thumbs and gently brushed the tears away and kissed me passionately on the lips."

"That's where I poured everything out. I love you, and age and worlds did not matter. I want you. Come to Samoa. I love you. And you did! My love for you is stronger now than it's ever been! I don't want to be apart from you!" Leilani turned and kissed me full on the lips.

I was silent for a moment, and then, with the balmy breeze and the fragrance of the air, but mostly the fragrant smell of Leilani by my side, I turned to her. "Now it is my turn to tell my side of the story!

"On the first flight when you leaned over me, and I smelled your scent, it hit me like a rocket. Wow. This lady is a fantastic woman, and I wanted you! But I had to pull in my horns because of my thinking. Surely she wouldn't want an old duffer like me? On each flight back to LA, during our nights together, you sleeping on my shoulder, I found myself falling deeper and deeper in love with you!

"But how could I justify this? But when we connected, I felt every fiber of my body drawn to you. I was so in love. Could I love again? Yes! And I did and still do, sweetheart. And yes, I want to be with you forever!"

Lei wrapped her arms around me in a long, sweet embrace.

"Maybe now is the time to answer what I should have answered earlier. 'Will you go?' Yes, Lei, Captain Mobley is dear to my heart, as a man. I am his chosen first mate. If another journey is in store, I will go, but I am reluctant to leave you! Captain Mobley will bring me back safe, even if his life depends on it.

"Our separation will be short, but our love will be stronger than ever!" I took her in my arms then and said, "I need you, Lei. I need your scent, I need your touch, I need your embraces, many! Please don't ever leave me. You are my life, my reason to go on! Hold me. Love me."

Lei passionately kissed me. She asked, "Will you always love me, even to the hereafter?"

I said, "Yes, even to the hereafter!"

We held each other while the balmy breeze gently moved us to and fro. The fragrance was from the gods! We slipped into a deep sleep in each other's arms. A loving couple never left that hammock that night—two lovers in paradise!

Words from the Author

Ship's Captain
(Anita Sutherland Gardner)

There's a pleasure in living by rivers and oceans
As well as hard work, sadness, and strife.
While we carefully maneuver our ship out to sea,
We hear the lullaby at sunset from the music of life.

There are pioneer sailors who rode the waves.
They carried the map while sailing away,
Prepared the mast for the storm,
Keeping fellow workers from danger and harm.

We each face that journey as sailors,
Advancing to the captain as life's walls of water rage.
Standing on the rudder, wisely taking control,
Turning the wheel, safely guiding our ship home.

Words well written by my skipper!
    The journey in life, as well as in my imagination, has a beginning and an end. What is important in this journey is what you achieve in the middle. In my journey's middle, I strived to achieve. My middle has dealt me inspiration and fond memories for the end, but also the inspiration to go on!

James

Pacific Mist to Fogs of England

Acknowledgments

I wish to thank Candace Johnson, Printshop, for assistance on the book cover. Thank you!

I wish to thank Leigh Protuvnak for her assistance as contact lady, and Newman Springs Publishing for all her patience and assistance in guiding me through the book process.

James

Odyssey Down Under VII

From Pacific Mist to Fogs of England

About This Book

In this adventure, Captain Mobley encourages James to come aboard for another fantastic journey! James knew that Captain Mobley always had this dream of following Captain James Cook's journey back to England during his three voyages. Even though this journey could be long and dangerous, James threw caution to the wind and decided to support his mate, Captain Mobley.

This journey would take the *Sheila II* and her crew to the north of England. The search would be for Captain James Cook's boyhood routes and notable British sites in his successful naval career. Many adventures awaited on this journey, so come aboard for this fantastic voyage. Our quest followed in the waters of a man of unparalleled success!

Beginning

Sunday afternoon, the morning was time for worship, and the afternoon was for all good people to work in their nap! Leilani and I were in the big hammock attempting to get ours. Cocoa lay down by the side where I could reach down and give him a pat once in a while. He was already into his nap, four feet stretched out straight. Lei was on my other side, as close as she could get.

Nap wasn't coming easy because our minds were wandering, thinking about the past—past life, past trips, etc., the usual stuff that creeps up out of the subconscious at times. Lei asked, "James, why do you call Cocoa 'Buck' sometimes?"

"I don't know, Lei. I guess I just think it is appropriate. I don't really have any reason. Maybe because if I had him from the start, I would have named him Buck! Strong name for a dog instead of a *cutie pie* name. My past dogs in life were Tom, Gus, Ticket, and Jerry."

"Why did you do that?" she asked. I saw right then that the nap was out!

"I don't know, Lei. I guess I just loved them."

"Is that why you call me Lei for short instead of Leilani?"

"Naw, I call you that because you are cute!" I got a light punch in the ribs. I groaned like I was in pain. Lei rubbed my side and showered me with kisses, and I soaked all that up! Then I said, "That's why I call you Lei! Because I love you."

She gripped me closer and said, "I like it when you call me Lei. It's special!"

"You are special, Lei."

The phone rang! Well, there went the nap and this moment! Lei picked up the call. She handed me the phone, "Guess who?"

I heard chuckling on the other end, and I told Leilani, "I don't need to guess who!" I answered, "Hello, mate, what's turned your crank today?"

Captain Mobley roared with laughter. "Well, James, I'm trying to plan another cruise, and it would be nice if my first mate would join me!"

"Well, where to this time, my friend?" I replied.

There was a pause, then, "I've been hankering to know more about Captain James Cook's early childhood home since you so graciously gave all the history of his life!" Then quiet for a moment.

I responded, "Why, you old fox, you! I knew it would be sooner or later you would want to trace Cook's waters all the way to England!"

He roared with laughter, "Well, James, isn't that a good go?"

"I don't know, Captain. That's a long Atlantic journey plus the South Pacific."

"I know, James, but that never hampered James Cook!"

I said, "Yes, but you, clear to England, or should I say we?"

He chuckled. "James, you forgot I have been to Newfoundland and up into the Great Lakes where I met you?"

I knew I didn't need to respond to that because when Captain Mobley got a mindset, that was it! All or nothing! So I asked, "Go by way of the Panama Canal?"

"Oh no!" He laughed. "Around the caps of South America! I want to see what they called Madeira, you know where he picked up a supply of fine wine!" then chuckled.

I said, "Well, that's a go. I may need a few battles on this trip, and I'm not a drinking man!" He roared with laughter!

"Well, James, I knew you would come around!"

"Of course, but with the same request as our Canadian journey, that Leilani is with me all the way!"

"Request granted, James. That was in the planning. I have some study to do on our course, then I'll contact you!"

"Follow Captain Cook's!"

"Okay, Captain, we will have some planning to do on this end. When ready, call back. We will have Curt and Hawk fly us to Sydney. Looks like Tahiti is out of the question this time?"

"Right," said Captain. "We will come by Tahiti on the return trip! As much as I hate the canal, we will come back through! My plans now are to leave Sydney, sail to the north tip of New Zealand, pick up a few things, then proceed to the Cape."

"Aye, Captain. Good plan. Cook's waters!" then laughed! I could almost see the twinkle in Captain Mobley's eyes! I hung up the phone and said, "Well, Lei, looks like we packed our ditty bags again! But we have time. Let's lay back and resume where we left off!"

Lei giggled and gave me a big hug! "I'm excited, James, and happy that I can come with you! I'm not happy when you sail away." Cocoa looked up in question. I stroked Lei's hair and pulled her close.

A few days later, Captain Mobley placed another call. "James, I'm working on charts for our journey north. Some highlights I want to see are Madeira Island, which I know is near Rio de Janeiro. When we reach England, I'd like to see where James Cook grew up and was born, in fact. There are no heirs because all his children died before their mother, and she was in her nineties when she passed. Next, I would like, if possible, to visit the Admiralty in London to see where his fame started to generate. Lastly, I would like to go to the shipyards in Portsmouth to see where he set out on his journeys. That's a big order, James. I'm good with charts and graphs for any sea travel in the world, but for research from agencies, I'm at a loss. You are the expert on story history!"

"No problem, Captain. Let me contact the American Embassy Group in Samoa and see if they can give me input."

I contacted the embassy, and they were cordial and more than willing to help with this endeavor. They would contact the British Embassy and put in a request for Captain Cook's boyhood home location and clearance for the Admiralty in London and the shipyards in Plymouth. "Wow," I said. "That was an easy go! Let them do the research since most of it is in their archives."

In a few days, I received a packet in the mail. It was the answer to all my requests! Included was a note stating, "Greetings, James. Give me the date of your departure, and I will negotiate clearance for your ports of call with the British Embassy!"

"Hey, this is getting better yet."

The information read: "James Cook was born in October 1728 to James and Grace Cook in Northern England. His father and mother lived in a small thatched cottage, tending a small farm. James was named after his father. He was baptized and belonged to the Church of Saint Cuthbert in a small hamlet of Marton-in-Cleveland. James, if you find the maritime service there, also the church, I am sure you can find directions to the land where the farm once stood. Understand that this was the 1700s. There may not be remains of the farm or home now unless the historical society has preserved part. London and Portsmouth are on any major map, so they are easy to find. I will have clearance in place when you give me the departure date. Thank you! American Samoa Embassy."

Again, I must say I was thrilled. I relayed the information to Captain Mobley, who was also thrilled.

The day before Captain Mobley was to depart, I gave the Samoa Embassy the green light. Curt and Hawk were flying us to Sydney. I had discussed with Captain Mobley that a trip up to Samoa would put him off course, so we would start from Captain Cook's dock where the *Sheila II* was berthed.

With Hawk at the controls, we lightly set down in Sydney Harbor like a big goose coming in for a landing. Hawk taxied into the usual dock he used when he brought passengers in. We all walked to the ship, Lei and I toting our ditty bags. Other necessary gear was always available on the *Sheila II*. We had to pass the vendor's area where the Aboriginal folks were selling their crafts. Once again, they stared at this swarthy-colored man in buckskin strolling by. I wondered what went through their minds.

Approaching the ship, Captain Mobley was coming down the gangway, hand extended. "Come aboard," he said with a chuckle. "Glad to see all of you, mates!" The crew was all ready to lend a hand, smiles on their faces.

Captain asked, "Curt and Hawk, do you want to go along? Secure your plane and come aboard again, like our Canada journey."

"Not this time, Captain," Curt replied. "Curt and I have several passenger bookings, but we will take a rain check for another time. Besides, my little heartthrob, *Little Flower*, says she needs me around to get ready for our flight to see my Uncle Magnus."

Captain said, "What about you, Curt?"

Curt said, "Naw, I have to hang around with this Indian to keep him out of trouble!" We all laughed at that.

Cookie, listening in the background, banged his ladle against his pot. "I said Cookie must have come down from the Marx Brothers!" We all laughed, and Cookie gave us a thumbs-up. After goodbyes, we watched Curt and Hawk start for the plane. Hawk hesitated, then came back.

"Captain, I just wanted you to know that I can track you off the plane, no matter how far. If I think you are heading into harm's way, I will give you a shout."

"Thanks," said the captain. They turned again and were off. We stood watching for takeoff. Curt taxied out, then slowly pushed the throttle forward as the big De Havilland scooted across the water and was airborne, away into the horizon. Then we boarded the ship and settled in. Breakfast in the morning, and we would get underway!

In the morning, after breakfast, we pulled in our lines and departed the dock. As we were leaving the bay, some cannons went off! Then firecrackers, followed by a band striking up the Australian national anthem. Shouting and waving ensued, along with more cannons. A large group on the shore was giving us a grand send-off! Patriots they were! They had gotten knowledge that Captain Mobley was going to follow Captain Cook's waters to England. Captain Cook, their hero! And they were going to give us a big send-off!

Lei, in amazement, hugged me. Captain Mobley, with misty eyes, turned to shore and saluted them. The crew also followed suit, standing at attention in a quick lineup and saluting. I looked at Lei and said, "This is going to be a good journey. We are starting off with a bang." She hung on to me tightly and watched in awe.

Captain Mobley came and stood with us to watch the beauty of the harbor as we left. He had asked Helm to take the wheel until we cleared the harbor and entered the Pacific. He told Helm to set a southeast course until he got back to relieve him. Knowing Helm, being relieved would not be that important to him. He would stand at that wheel all night. He simply loved the sea and guiding the ship.

Captain Mobley said, "James, come with me to my cabin. I have the charts out and want to show you what I have in mind. You come too, Lei. You have never seen the captain's cabin, though it's similar to the cabin for you and James."

As we entered the captain's quarters, Lei was impressed by the surroundings. His bunk, stands, and solid wood desk and table were all securely fastened down to be immovable on rough seas. Her eyes went to his display on the bulkhead (wall)—the arrangement of muskets surrounding pistols that looked like old armament from the old sailing days.

Captain Mobley chuckled at her fascination, then he said, "James, should I tell Lei about these?"

I said, "No harm, Captain. Lei respects anything," so Captain Mobley said, "Lei, since you are so fascinated by my display, I will tell you about them. They are real!"

Lei looked back in shock. "Real?"

"Yes," Captain Mobley went on. "The muskets are single shot. They have to be reloaded after every shot, high caliber! Also the same with the pistols—they are two-barrel, one side loaded with small shot, the other side with a round!"

Lei looked in fascination and then asked, "But why?"

Captain Mobley said, "For protection from anyone that wants to put us in harm's way!"

Lei shook her head in agreement, although she was not fond of firearms. She then asked, "Why not have rifles?"

Captain Mobley explained, "Australia prohibits firearms, but every bloke has one! As well as some law-abiding citizens, so this is a disguise for us to stay out of question!"

"I see," said Lei. "Thank you for sharing. I didn't have to know."

"Yes, I know," said Captain Mobley. "But we want to be above board and share everything with each other. Now James and Lei, let's look at these charts. This is what I propose on this journey, although subject to change where change is needed. First stop, I would like to be north of New Zealand at the Bay of Plenty. I know the Maoris there and have been there before—they are very cordial. Next, across the Pacific to South America and the Cape. Swinging north, we will go to the Island of Madeira, one of Cook's favorites. We can shop a little and purchase some fine wine. Might need a few gifts on the way!" And he chuckled. "Rio de Janeiro is close, maybe we want to give the boys a little fling! The seas in the Caribbean should be calm and warm. Then pushing north in the Atlantic, I would like to set course closer to Africa, instead of America. It will be a long journey. When we see England, I would like to continue up the coast to the north in search of James Cook's birthplace. James, you have that information. Then backtrack down to London, then down to Portsmouth, Ship Harbor, then the long, long journey home! Maybe we can come up with a stop along the way? American side? Bahamas? I sure would like to avoid the Canal if possible!"

We all looked at each other. Lei was impressed but had never seen the other part of the world! She didn't realize the magnitude! I also was impressed but knew the journey could take months and avoiding the Canal would be even more challenging. I knew if you, old fox, we were tracking James Cook's waters, the ones you missed on the last journey!"

Captain Mobley just looked at me and chuckled. I knew he hated the canal crossing in Panama, so I was willing to indulge him. That was okay because he wanted this trip to be the way Cook would have undertaken it, plus he was not going to venture into the Arctic Circle!

"How does this *grab* you, mate?" Captain Mobley said.

"Well, if we get bored on the way back, we can always make a pass through the Galápagos again. Maybe we will meet up with the Duchess of Vienna!" Captain Mobley rolled his eyes and said nothing.

Lei said, "Who is the Duchess?"

I replied, "It's a long story. I'll tell you about it someday!"

With everything in place, I said to Lei, "I think I will take the first watch and relieve Helm. You want to come and stand with me? Then we will have the evening to ourselves."

Lei replied, "I'm with you!" I could feel in my bones a long series of watches coming up on this trip. Even though the crew would take turns, it really wouldn't matter much. Now I had Lei with me. Also, Captain Mobley and I kept each other company when either of us was on watch. If Lei got too tired, she had a nice bed.

Captain Mobley chuckled and asked, "James, do you have any good stories to tell on this trip?"

"I don't know, Captain. We had a lot of stories to tell on our previous cruises. I had not thought about story time since the last go. I'll have to put my thinking hat on and see what can develop before the end of the journey. Give me a little time. I think I can generate another story about a Canadian trip. But this journey is new yet, and we have only inched into the beginning."

"Yes, James, we have only just begun, and I hope it does not become never-ending, so to speak!" I looked at Captain Mobley for a moment, then replied, "No, Captain, never unending with you! We seem to move into one adventure after another, and you know, Captain, it seems like when we are on one journey, we are thinking about another!"

"Yes, James," he chuckled. "I guess there is a lot of world out there for a fella to see, and we have covered a lot of the South Pacific so far. That's what I like—to stay somewhat near to home and not venture out too far and get into harm's way. Now old James Cook did not look at things that way. He was prone to sail into the unknown and take what comes along! Not me, mate. I want to stay within the bounds of safety if possible, and sometimes you can still buy trouble!"

"Well, Captain Cook came to his end the way he did. He was a man ahead of his time and had so much more to offer the world. He was only in his forties and just getting started in life!"

"Aye to that, mate."

Leilani was standing by, wide-eyed and intense. I looked at her and said, "What?" She smiled sweetly, put her arm through mine, and said, "I become enthralled with the talk and stories out of you two! I'm starting to understand now what makes you two click!"

Captain Mobley laughed and said, "And there's a lot more to come, sissy. Just hang on!" Captain Mobley kept chuckling, and Lei smiled. She just loved it when Captain Mobley called her *sissy* because she felt included.

Then trying to generate a story, the captain said, "What drew you to the sea, James?"

"Well, I'll tell you. Not a great story though. When I was a boy, my friend and I went to the river every day. That was our playground. It was not a clean river at the time—cleanup had not been ordered—but that did not deter us. We skinny-dipped when we wanted to, and we explored the surrounding hills and woods. We were fascinated by the tide moving in and out. One time, when the tide was shifting, we found a military pack floating in. When we unwrapped it from its watertight seal and opened the flap, we found a treasure, at least to young boys it was. There were K-rations, canned meat, crackers, malted milk tablets, and cigarettes! We rationed out the goods and ate a little each day. We had a smoke now and then, knowing that was a 'do not.'

"We would find lumber floating in that was suitable for a clubhouse, so we built one! We always had a campfire on the beach, careful to extinguish it before we left. Another time, we took two logs and spliced them with driftwood, found two poles, and we thought we had a pretty good boat. We stayed close to shore as long as the poles would reach, so as not to get caught in the outgoing current. We were poling along thinking we were smart until a water moccasin crawled on and squiggled the length of the logs. We bailed off and 'let her go!' That was the end of our seamanship.

"One day, when we arrived, a stranger was sitting on the seawall. The seawall was the remains of old Fort Billings from the Revolutionary War. He turned out to be a man who lived by himself just off the river, and he did what we two boys did—checked the river for *treasures*. He was carrying his .22 rifle. He said, 'Come here, boys, and I'll let you take a shot. Just one or two because ammo is low.' It was a thrill for two boys. Then he gave me a penny and told me to carry it yonder and place it on a log. I'd say the log was one hundred to two hundred feet away. He raised his gun, sighted in, and pulled off the shot. Then he told us to retrieve the penny. It was embossed dead center. Later in life, I named him 'Neil' and put him in one of my stories for a memory."

Captain Mobley said, "James, that was a good story. I knew I'd get you started!" Then he roared with laughter. Helm was on the wheel, and Captain Mobley got up and went to relieve him. Helm said, "Any more stories before I leave?"

Captain laughed. "You can stay as long as you want to, mate. I know you like games and stories."

Helm said, "Sure do, Captain. Don't want to miss out either!"

Captain said, "James, did you tell all about Canada?"

I said, "No. Jagile Feather told most about me, but not about how I met Glen."

Captain yelled, "Helm, come back here! Helm came back." and Captain said, "James has another story!"

I said, "Yeah, well, I wasn't going to tell it. It might not be all that interesting!"

Captain chuckled. "James, you have not had a tale yet that was not interesting!"

Captain was on the wheel, listening. Helm took a seat, and Lei scooted closer to me. I looked at her and said, "This, with you closer, makes a story better!"

She squeezed me. "Okay, this story is about when I first went to Canada and how I came to meet Glen. First of all, I went to see a camp where a friend of mine from Fort Wayne was looking for a doctor. It was on the bay end where the water became shallow, and the bottom was all white sand. The water was pristine—so good in quality that the cabins around the lake only had to put a pipe in the lake with a pump to have fresh, drinkable water! The lake was huge. You could not see from end to end. The depth ranged up to five hundred feet where it was sounded; in some places, the bottom was not found. Big lake trout could be fished in the winter using copper wire for fishing lines. The Jardian name for the lake was Wawacodie, to residents, it was Big Basswood.

"My friend Jim Johnston took me and another Canadian friend to another lake to fish. Several lakes in the area were owned by a timber company. Jim took us to a lake called Lake Reception. It was four miles in by four-wheel-drive truck, then a four-mile hike through the woods to the lake. All gear was packed in! Jim took the outboard on his back. Allen and I had to carry the rest of the gear. This lake had a sandy bottom, and the only fish species was Walleye Pike. A portage from the upper lake flowed down, but the fish never mixed! In that lake, there were Brown Trout and Rainbow Trout. They inter-bred and were called 'Splacks' by the Canadians. Many good trips to Reception, many good dinners on the shore, and many good fish fries back at camp.

"One night, this one Canadian came by my trailer acting drunk but wasn't. In the morning, I found bear poop on my step! This is how Glen and I first met. We were instantly friends, and the friend-ship lasted many happy years of our visits to Mountain Ash Lake— hunting, fishing, and camping. Sometimes we never got far out but stayed at Glen's home on the Little Rapids, just enjoying time with Glen and his wife, Ive. Our friendship was always full of adventure. A lot of our adventures I wrote in my log, *Return of the White Wolf.* It was a sad time for me when, on our last journey together, the Great Creator took Glen up."

So here my story ended with all eyes upon me. Helm then said to me, "I can read into your stories, James, even when you don't go into detail, that had to be a very special time of your life—that nine years with your friend!"

I said, "Thank you, Helm." Helm had become a special friend to me, so different from the rest. He was always quiet, attentive, and eager to please. Unlike the rest of the crew, Helm would step up for work! There was no need to assign or order. When time off the ship came, many times Helm would stay behind. The partying was not for him. He was duty-bound, and his work was his life. His life had always been the sea. Being on board was when he was in his element!

Leilani reached over to me with a soft hug, and I hugged her back. There is always something about a woman's touch! I whispered in her ear, "I love you!" Her eyes were misty, and she nodded her head in reply. Captain Mobley softly chuckled. "Well, James, that was a wonderful story. I'm glad I got you off and running. Maybe you have some more good stories to tell before we accomplish this quest!"

"Maybe so, Captain, maybe so."

Then Cookie said, "Supper is stewing in the pot! Time to get up, boys, chow time!"

Supper in the pot turned out to be a gourmet meal, leave it to Cookie. During supper, Captain Mobley announced, "I haven't checked the compass yet, folks, but my guess is we will see the coast of New Zealand come dawn!"

Everyone retired to their watch and duties. It was free time for me, so I took Leilani up on deck. The sea was calm, and the breeze was easy, although enough to keep us tacking at eight knots and sometimes pushing a little harder. Lei and I sat close together and told our own stories until late in the night before we headed to bed.

Dawn came, and we could smell good things from the galley! All hands were up and going. The man on watch would get relieved last to come to breakfast, and he would probably get extra! Cookie liked to spoil the crew.

On deck with the morning sun coming up, New Zealand's north promontory was in sight. Captain Mobley said we would pull in on the north tip, the beautiful island spot that Captain James Cook had named the Bay of Plenty. Down through the centuries, the name had never changed. In fact, most places in the South Pacific carrying his name never changed. It seems like every place he touched, his name stuck, and that to me is a wonderful legacy.

As we approached the island, Captain Mobley, at the wheel, asked Helm to see if he could raise Hawk in his seaplane, maybe in the area. "96 on Padaram, weather channel, and see if there is any disturbance around the Cape of Good Hope. The Cape can be tricky at times, blowing up a storm that will turn you back or even catch you with ice in the middle."

Helm came back a little later and reported, "Hawk is just now headed for Fiji. He has a full ship of tourists. He says the Cape is clear now, but storms are expected in five days."

Captain Mobley got a frown on his face and was deep in thought. His expression eased off, and he said, "We've got a window, close, but open!" This was like talking to himself and not an announcement. We all pondered this but felt secure with any decision that Captain would come up with, for he was a man of safety, keeping his ship out of harm's way!

We pulled into the Bay of Plenty and were relieved to get a little rest. Already at the dock was a small group of Maori Indians with their elder chief, waiting for us to dock. When secure, Captain Mobley waved for them to come aboard. Captain and the old chief hugged.

"Back again, old friend?" said the chief.

"Yes," said Captain. "But the visit will be short, storms are coming on the Cape."

The chief frowned, "But you can have a meal!"

Captain Mobley laughed. "Yes, quick stay. You would have a meal if the island was freezing over!" We all laughed.

The chief said, "Better to go down with a full belly!" then laughed.

Leilani just looked from one to the other. I said, "These Maoris are friends of Captain Mobley's. Through the years, he has always stopped here and also took care of any of their needs. Also, they always want to put on a hog roast!"

The Maoris couldn't take their eyes off Lei, a pretty island girl from a different world. We disembarked, and the festivities were on! We settled into the feast, and then later, Lei and I wandered through the village, looking at crafts they had for sale. At the feast, a little Maori boy, about twelve, latched on to Lei, held her hand, and went everywhere she went. As we were wrapping up our shopping, a Maori woman asked the little boy who the woman was in their language. The little boy answered, still hanging tight to Lei. I asked her what the little boy said.

She said, "The little boy says that this is the most beautiful girl in the world!" So the hand-holding went on until departure. When we were boarding, Lei and I went on last. Lei stooped down and gave the little boy a long hug while he sobbed, tears running down his face. She told him that she loved him, and he seemed to understand. Then we boarded, and everybody was a little misty-eyed. We waved goodbye. His mama took him by the hand and was leading him off while he kept looking back and waving.

Later I said, "Gosh, Lei, I almost lost my love!"

She looked at me seriously and said, "He meant well! I remember a time when I stood in front of you, tears streaming down my face. I thought you were going out of my life."

I stared at her and then lost it! She grabbed me in a big hug. I said, "I am so sorry, Lei. I love you and will never leave you!"

She said, "I know. We are as one and always will be!"

I didn't care if anyone was watching or hearing. Never take for granted your love! We were underway again, leaving the Bay of Plenty and setting course for the Cape.

When we were well on the Cape, I called Lei by my side. I said, "This is where two worlds meet. The traveled Atlantic met the unknown worlds of the Pacific. I am so glad that Cook took his chances to explore. I am glad he found Samoa. I am glad I found you! You are so special, and this is a special time for us. You are with me, and that's what counts. I love you! Now we will turn the tables. You will come from the world as you know it, and I will take you into the Atlantic, a world you never knew. We will even explore a world here that I never even knew!" We hugged tight. Nothing more needed to be said.

The weather around the Cape was cold and put a chill in your bones. Soon enough, we felt the warm air of the Caribbean! Then tropics again. The sea was an azure blue and very calm that day. We could look deep, seeing sea life. Captain Mobley was on the wheel, a relieved look on his face. Helm was standing by. Up the east coast, we would stop at the island of Madeira to shop for fine wine, as James Cook did.

When we arrived there and found docking service, the crew took an excursion boat over to Rio de Janeiro for a festive day. Captain Mobley, with Cookie's assistance, shopped for the finest of wines. Helm stayed aboard as security, by choice. Leilani and I went ashore and looked through the shops. There were many local crafts to offer visitors. Lei shopped for treasures to take home, and I tagged along, satisfied to look and see the environment around me—the structures, the chatter of Spanish, the dress, and the vendors hawking. It was a good day out.

Then Captain Mobley asked the crew, "What do you think about moving out into the bay and anchoring for the night? It will tighten security since we don't know everything about this busy place."

The decision was answered with "Aye, aye" from all. Lei and I sat on deck for a long time that night, watching the lights, noise, and activity on the shore. It went on late into the night! It was peaceful out in the bay.

After breakfast, Captain Mobley had a plan. "It's a long sea voyage from here to England. We could face up to twenty-some days at sea, with continual watches. It's too early to stop at any local islands. Let's go to Corpus Christi, Texas, for a fuel stop. We are a little low anyhow. If we have to resort to diesel power, we want to be assured of plenty. That will break up the long haul a bit. I know it will pull us off Captain Cook's course, but he didn't have a diesel engine on board!" There was laughter all around. "I might dump you men off on Key West for a look around!" The cheer went up.

Helm, the history buff, spoke up, "Yeah, that's where Humphrey Bogart made the movie *Key Largo*!"

All hands just looked at Helm in question. They didn't know who Bogart was!

So with our parcel of fine wine, we pulled anchor and moved out into the Atlantic. From here on, we would have to use the standard weather check. Hawk was out of sight now.

As we headed north into the Atlantic, the journey around the east side of South America was going to be a hard run. Once before, Captain Mobley had taken this challenge when he was following Bligh's waters. But it seemed like any challenge was not too big for Captain Mobley to undertake!

For a few days, we were pulling around the crown of Brazil. A course of the northwest was set until we could head north again past the Isthmus of Panama, setting our course again for the Florida Keys. It was a long stretch, and to think Cook made the journey from England to Madeira in one segment of the journey. We were glad that Captain Mobley had made the decision for a fuel stop at Corpus Christi! Not a long rest but at least off the big Atlantic for a breather.

When the Keys came in sight, Captain entered the bay from the side close to shore. As we tracked the shoreline, when we passed Key Largo, Captain yelled out in jest, "Anybody want to stop to see Bogart?" There was silence in the crew. Captain pushed on with a grin and chuckling. We tacked around the gulf as we did once before and went into the naval docks at Corpus Christi. We went straight to a fueling dock and made the connection. A crew of naval personnel was right on it and was getting the *Sheila II* secure.

We saw a jeep speeding down to the dock, and a uniformed officer jumped out. It was the same officer we had dealt with last time. He trotted up the gangway, stopped, saluted the flags, then asked permission to come aboard! Permission was granted. He came on deck with his hand extended. "Captain Mobley, how are you? What brings you here this time? Going or coming?" The questions came fast without a breath.

Captain Mobley extended a hand with a firm handshake. "Commander, I'm glad to see you are still holding command of this operation. We want to take on a little diesel to top off the tanks. Long trip coming up." Then the two commenced a long conversation, and Captain Mobley reviewed our trip with him. He was duly impressed. Leilani and I were standing by, and he kept staring.

Captain said, "You remember Officer James, my first mate?"

"I sure do," said the commander. "Looks like he's come up in the world!"

Captain said, "Yes, he has! This is Leilani, his first mate!" Then he roared with laughter. They went on with their stories like old buddies.

A seaman nearby asked me, "Boy, this is some ship, sir. Are you recruiting any hands?"

I said, "No, son, sorry. We are full up!"

After fueling was secure, Captain Mobley said, "I didn't pull in here for a free fill. Last time, you would not charge me?"

"Sorry," said the commander. "Regulations say we do not charge any American ship or allies of America! The bill goes to the president, just like with Captain Cook. The bill went to King George!" There was laughter all around. "Really, Captain," the commander said. "I am so glad to once more get in contact with you! Sometimes you must plan to stay over, and we will tell sea stories!"

Captain said, "I would like that and will make a point of it. Sometimes we put it in the plans. Right now, I'm booked up. Have to take the crew over to Key Largo. They have a date with Lauren Bacall!" Then he roared with laughter! All the crew members from both worlds looked at each other in puzzlement.

The commander laughed. "Oh, I get you! *Key Largo*, an old Humphrey Bogart film! Now there was one great. I watch the oldies on TV."

So when we pulled away over to the other side of the gulf, Captain did drop anchor off Key Largo for the night. Don't know if it was intended or not, but Helm was impressed. When we rounded the Keys and headed north, Captain looked to the east.

"James, on the way back, we might stop at the Grand Bahama! We will show those islanders what a real island beauty looks like!" Then he roared with laughter.

Lei looked at me and just shook her head. When we got abreast of the Outer Banks off the coast of the Carolinas, Captain was intrigued by how they lay off the coast.

"James, do you know anything about the Outer Banks?"

"Never been there, Captain, but I would have liked to go for a stay some time. There is a herd of wild horses that run those islands, nowhere else. I guess it's quite a sight when they herd together and run the dunes. They are protected by the government now. The horses are left over from the landing of the conquistadors and have reproduced over the years. Also, if I can get my story right, a rich man from up in the New England area had purchased the USS *Constitution*, all restored. He planned a cruise with a group of folks down the east coast. Just before departure, he was warned about a big sea storm brewing up. He ignored the warnings and set sail anyhow. The ship got caught in a massive storm and could not be rescued. It went down, and all hands perished. I never heard whether any salvage crews tried to bring her up or not."

"Interesting, James. Any more stories, bring them up. Long run ahead of us. When you crossed the Atlantic, how long did it take?"

"Sixteen days one way, sixteen days back! We maybe averaged eight knots, maybe less in bad weather!"

"Well, James, I think we can maintain eight knots easy, maybe even ten at times."

"But remember, Captain. We are going farther north to England."

"Good point, James! We will retake watches among us all, and duty will be light."

A long journey lay ahead. But the sea could also be entertaining, provided it didn't turn into rough seas. As we sailed, we sometimes saw other ships passing. There were days when we spotted schools of flying fish heading north. Occasionally, porpoises going in our direction would swim by the ship, entertaining us for a spell. Sometimes, whales were on the move north to their feeding grounds.

On the downside, sometimes problems arose, which we didn't want to encounter. But if you were lucky, you could experience a calm sea. A calm sea, where you could look clear to the horizon and see a flat expanse, made you think you were on a giant mirror—the most beautiful thing you had ever seen. However, a calm sea required running the diesel to keep pace since there was no wind. The old seamen had to sit it out or put out the longboat and start rowing! Also, if it was time for recaulking the seams, it could be a challenge. On their journeys, they would have to make periodic stops just to recaulk the ship's seams.

But the *Sheila II* was well-built, with no seams to worry about, and if there was no wind, the diesel engine would push us up to speed, as long as the fuel held out. Our small diesel engine also provided battery power to run our utilities. So with a good ship and a good Captain, we kept the edge!

Eighteen days later, we sighted the British Isles. As we drew closer, Captain Mobley headed for the mouth of the English Channel, approaching from the Atlantic Ocean. We had plenty of daylight left, but dear old England always seemed to be clouded in mist. Captain Mobley wanted to get into the Channel, if possible, and go north to the old towns of Whitby and Marton. There, we could get directions from Whitby to the restored Aireyholme Farm, which was once the farm where Cook was raised. His records of birth are still in the church in Marton, right on the banks of the North Sea, which must have influenced a young boy's mind with the calling of the sea. We planned to find the maritime service where he steadily moved up in success before deciding to join the British navy.

Reaching the channel, we proceeded north until we just moved into the channel and then continued north until we broke out into the North Sea. We found the maritime service docks and pulled in. Hands came running to secure the ship. Two officials approached, and Captain Mobley directed them aboard.

"Good day, mates! The tele has been ringing all day. London was informed of your arrival. We can assist you. You want to find the Honorable James Cook's boyhood farm, right? We will take you right there. It's Aireyholme Farm now, restored, but it's still the ground of the seventeen hundreds! Ole James Cook grew up there, and worked for us, you know! Bloody good seaman, on his way up too before he switched to the navy."

Captain Mobley stared at them until they caught their breath. Most excitement around here for a long time. Captain Mobley laughed. "Well, mates, slow down a bit before you blow a fuse! Yes, I am Captain Mobley from Australia. You've been notified that we were to show up! And yes, we would be much obliged if you folks would take us on the tour—his home place, his church, and a little information on how he worked for you. We have come a long way to get our feet on the ground James Cook had grown up on. See his church, see records. You know, mates, he is our hero too! Australia is what it is today since James Cook put us on the charts. Yes, he was a 'bloody good' seaman and an outstanding man, a visionary before his time. So now, gentlemen, this is my first mate, James, from the States, Leilani, his better half from Samoa, my executive officer, Mr. Helmsman, and my crew, who you will get to know on the tour. Let's say, late in the day as it is, we will sleep on board here and you meet with us in the morning for a great day of adventure!" It was not a question but a firm request.

The maritime officers were more than happy to oblige. They got to receive us first before any other agency in England. That gave them something to expound on! Bright and early in the morning, the maritime folks were there with a bus waiting to load us all for a tour of the farmland that young James Cook grew up on. Captain Mobley requested this first, then to the church to see his baptismal records. To see these records was not for proof but for a closer spiritual connection with James Cook.

The farm was well-kept, restored, and contained many artifacts left down through the ages. Everyone was excited and outgoing. I looked over at Captain Mobley and knew he was satisfied with all this, but something was missing—some small thing that would pull it all together.

I nodded at Captain Mobley and said, "How about a walk to the bluff?"

He nodded yes. I took Lei by the hand, and with the captain, we walked out to the Bluff that overlooked the North Sea. Immediately, the memory of a small boy came to mind, looking out to sea, ships passing by—the contour of bluffs and beach. A little boy dreaming dreams of adventure and all that life can bring!

We three stood there staring out, not talking, each in our own minds forming thoughts of the past. Each, in his own way, looked back to the past, and the picture in our minds revealed that what Captain Cook had achieved had now set a pattern in our lives. As the group started to break up and return to the bus, we realized that this small plot of earth was where James Cook grew up, came from, and moved up to the station of life he earned until he was cut down to his death in the South Pacific—the lands that he discovered and loved.

It was time to move on, and the maritime supervisor asked Captain Mobley, "Sir, do you wish to go on to the church at Marton to view James Cook's baptism records? That was his church, you know. If so, we will go, but we have copies of those at the maritime office. Also, we have many artifacts of James Cook and records of his exploits during his rise while in our employ. He was a rising star with us, you know. A bloody good captain with passion and concern for his crew. Then he left all that to serve his country in the Royal Navy. Now that the maritime questions his decisions, his exploits have become the answer for us, and yes, he has become our hero as well!"

Captain Mobley said, "Your choice will be fine, sir. Going to the ancient church was not all that important, although I did wish to see his baptismal certificate. But you have a copy, so that should do. The most important thing you have provided! I wanted to stand on the ground that James Cook grew up on, wanted that under my feet. I wanted to stand on that bluff looking over the North Sea and try to capture what was in a young boy's mind—his dreams, his adventures to be, his goals, and what he thought he wanted to do with his life! This I have now, and more of the journey to pursue."

When we returned to the dock and the maritime offices, we were escorted through to see all the memorabilia, objects, and personal effects that they had saved and acquired. Near the end, Captain Mobley whispered to Cookie, who returned to the ship to retrieve a case of wine. When he returned, we were about to go into our departure goodbyes. Captain Mobley placed the case in the supervisor's hands and said, "This is a gift for you from the Island of Madeira, a major stop for Captain Cook on each journey. Please accept this as if it were from the good Captain himself!" Needless to say, the supervisor was reduced to tears and expressed gratitude for this gift.

As we got underway back down the English Channel, we were told that the Admiralty was on pins and needles awaiting our arrival. "Captain Mobley, you are the talk of London! We have been tracking your course ever since you left Sydney! It's almost like welcoming Captain James Cook himself!"

Captain Mobley felt pretty proud of himself. This was sure a good go to be received like this, especially since Australia and England had been at odds in the past.

The admiral had several limousines parked nearby to transport all the crew to the offices inside. As we were loading, Cookie did not need prompting to run below and retrieve two cases of fine wine. As he ran to get into the limo, a guard stopped him, looking at the parcel. Cookie quickly said, "It's okay. This is a gift for the admiral." The guard nodded and pulled his hand back, not wanting to cause an eruption.

Inside, before the tour could start, Captain Mobley turned to Cookie, took the wine, and turned back to the admiral. "Sir, before we start our tour, I have a gift from Captain Cook for you! This wine is from Madeira, where Captain Cook stopped to load up on three journeys! If alive, he would present this himself."

The admiral was deeply moved. He said, "Orderly, retrieve some glasses, enough for all around, this requires a toast." Very quickly, the orderly returned with enough glasses, exactly, for all present. The admiral started removing corks and pouring a measure into each glass. The room was silent, then he nodded to the orderly to serve. When all the glasses were in hand, the admiral raised his glass in the air, and all glasses went up. He yelled, "Hey, hey! I toast to the memory of Captain James Cook, the most bloody powerful captain that ever sailed the seas. I toast to him and his service to his country!"

Toast over, the admiral shook Captain Mobley's hand vigorously and said, "Mate, I can't thank you enough!" Captain Mobley did not have words, so he said nothing. Thus, the tour began. There were so many charts, graphs, and artifacts about Captain Cook that it boggled your mind.

After the tour, the admiral said, "Don't forget, mate, they are anxious for your arrival down at Plymouth. A lot to see there! And if you are ever this way again, I expect a visit! Now don't forget Plymouth, mate. That would be a bloody disappointment if you did not show!"

"Not to worry, sir. By your leave, we wish to stay dockside tonight, then get underway for Plymouth in the morning."

"Permission granted, mate, and we will keep a good watch over you tonight!"

"Thank you, sir."

We all loaded back into the limousines and were driven back to the ship. Lei was quiet for a spell. I asked, "What's on your mind?"

She said, "Why is everything in England *bloody*? You know, 'bloody well this' and 'bloody well that'?"

I grinned and said, "It's just an expression among the people." I paused, then asked with a grin, "What's your expression in Samoa?"

She paused for a moment, then said, "Bongo! Bongo!"

That cracked me up so bad I started laughing, then Lei started laughing. We got hysterical! Captain Mobley turned around and said, "What's into you back there?"

I said, "Oh, nothing, Captain. We are just having a bloody good time!" Still laughing, that started the captain laughing. Then the other crew members in the limo started laughing. The intercom in the limo sent it all back to the other limo, and they started laughing. Then the British drivers started laughing. And you talk about the relief of tension on a stressful day!

The next morning, after a good breakfast by Cookie, the lines were dropped with the help of the British mates. Sails were unfurled, everything was shipshape, and with a good breeze, we pulled away from the dock. We were Plymouth bound!

When we arrived at Plymouth, we sailed into the docks with a huge welcome group standing by. The Supervisor of Operations and employees, mostly shipbuilders, asked Captain Mobley for permission to come aboard—they wanted to "look her over." Everyone was excited and impressed by how the Sheila was built. They remarked about the craftsmanship and asked who the builder was.

Captain Mobley said, "She was built to scale by an old shipbuilder I contacted from Australia. He was located in New England in a place called Portsmouth!" They all raised their eyes. "He was descended from a long line of shipbuilders, all professional and all craftsmen. He was excited to build the replica of the HMS *Vanguard*. I stayed with him for many hours in the shop and many days in New England to go over all the details of the build. It was exciting to share work with him! It took several flights from Sydney to get this project complete! The crew you see here was my selection of mates who would bring her back! We all flew to Portsmouth to take delivery and went back home by sea. The maiden voyage of the *Sheila* was known then, but later the II was added to her name. That was not to designate a name for a second ship but to avoid any misconception between my ship and my wife!" The builders all roared with laughter. "Now I might add that James here made this name change for me! And he has become first mate!" They all cheered. "Also, the crewmen you see here in full uniform are my mates who took the maiden voyage home, plus many more, and many more cruises since. We are all mates and are bonded by the love of the sea!"

The builders all clapped their hands. What came into my mind then was that Captain Mobley was such a good storyteller, that he should write the log! Also, we were to take the tour here, and Captain Mobley had traveled across oceans to come here and entertain the folks who were to give us a tour! I chuckled to myself and thought, *It's funny how the world turns!* The boat builders took their tour and were amazed at the craftsmanship. Of course, they claimed that the builder who had constructed this fine ship just had to be a descendant from England!

The superintendent stepped forward and said he would now take us on our tour of the shipyards of Plymouth. Cookie had been standing by with two cases of wine, and his arms hurt! Captain Mobley took them off his hands and said to the superintendent, "These are a gift from Captain Cook, posthumously! He always made a stop at Madeira to procure a supply of fine wine for his voyages. There is enough here to present to your whole crew!"

The *super* accepted the gift with humility and many thank-yous. Then he put on his hat as tour guide, and we all were off. We went through the office, then the various shops that specialized in different parts of a ship's requirements, and finally to the build area. At dry dock were two frigates (warships) of the iron variety, of course, and along the tour, we saw many artifacts of the old sailing ships, some even from Captain Cook's *Endeavour*.

At the end, he showed us a big bay where an old ship was being restored. He said, "We are almost complete with this now, all but the caulking—half finished! Any questions?"

Lei, glancing at me, asked, "Is it necessary for the bloody caulking to be completely clear to the top?"

He replied, "You are bloody well right, ma'am! Without it, the bloody ship may take the deed!" Lei looked back at me and snickered. I was in pain trying to hold my laughter back.

The tour was a fine go, and we had a firsthand education on the building of Captain Cook's ships, which were four. We got underway late in the afternoon with all the folks working at the Plymouth shipyards waving us farewell. Now we were on a long journey down the Atlantic with continual watches and events.

It wasn't so bad, really, because some days the Atlantic Ocean could put on a show for you. We were out on the third day when the radio started to crackle.

Helm intercepted the call and brought in the caller. It was Hawk! He said, "I don't know how long I can stay on this frequency, but I'll give it a go. Sounds like it's loud and clear, so maybe I've got time. I ran a vector on the Cape! Large storms coming in within five days! Big winds, rough seas, and ice! Gather everyone around to hear this!"

Helm said, "We are all here, go on!"

"Well," Hawk said, "that's the bad news. Captain may have to take the Panama Canal back this time. I know he doesn't want to!"

Helm asked, "Where are you? I know you are in the air."

Hawk came back. "I'm on flight over Ontario!" He laughed. "While you guys were gone, Curt and I decided not to put off the trip any longer to get back to Mountain Ash Lake and see Eagle Feather!"

Helm said, "Wow, and how did you go?"

Hawk said, "Well, Curt, Little Flower, and I flew from Samoa to Hilo, Hawaii, then over to Victoria Island. We checked in, went up in the air again, and stopped at Thunder Bay. From there, we went into Ontario and Mountain Ash Lake. I am sure glad that James took us to that paradise! Here I was locked in a reservation with that part of the north woods above me and never knew about it!"

Helm said, "What's your purpose?"

Hawk replied, "Remember? Eagle Feather never knew about Little Flower and me getting together!"

"Okay," Helm said, "how did you contact Eagle Feather?"

There was silence, and then Hawk laughed. "That's an Indian thing! We communicate!"

Helm said, "Huh?"

Hawk said, "Give me a reading on your channel strength! I have an Indian story!"

Helm said, "Go for it, we are all gathered around!"

Hawk began his story, "Well, you all know that I wanted to take Little Flower back to Canada to show her off to Eagle Feather. So Curt said, 'Why not now?' and we did. It was beautiful! When I got over Mountain Ash Lake, I made two passes around. I saw Eagle Feather standing on the pier, and someone was with him in buckskin, so I knew things were okay. I made a pass at him and waved! He waved back. I did a one-eighty and came in for a smooth landing, taxiing to the pier. We jumped out, and Eagle Feather was standing there with a very beautiful young Indian maiden. Curt was so struck he just stood there and stared. He didn't even help me secure the plane! As I turned, Eagle Feather was grinning and said, 'This is Little Fawn. She is my adopted granddaughter!' I helped Little Flower out of the plane and said, 'Okay, Grandpa. This is Little Flower from Samoa. The native girl you told me I should get!' Eagle Feather gave a big smile, his plan coming together. Little Fawn hooked her arm in Curt's and said, 'I am glad to meet you, Curt. Eagle Feather has told me so much about you! Come, let us walk the trail and you tell me all about your story!'"

Hawk laughed. "So Curt stumbled on down the trail with beautiful Little Fawn! As things progressed, Eagle Feather came to know Little Flower, and they bonded right away. Curt and Little Fawn became inseparable! We were there for fifteen days! When it was time to go, Curt asked Little Fawn to go too. He just could not live without her! She wanted to go with Curt, but the tradition was somewhat holding her back. Eagle Feather stepped in and said, 'Curt, do you want this woman?' No need to ask that! Then he turned to Little Fawn and asked, 'Little Fawn, do you want to go with this man and stay forever?' Of course, Little Fawn did! So Eagle Feather said, 'Okay, I will fix all things! I am Eagle Feather, Elder of the Ojibwe Tribe. You four come to me!' I looked in question, 'Yes, you too!' Eagle Feather had us two couples stand together, then raise each of our arms at the elbow, and then each clasp the hand of his mate. Then Eagle Feather closed his eyes and began to chant in Ojibwe. Then he opened his eyes and looked to the sky! He said, 'Oh Great Creator, with your blessing I bond these four together, two in marriage, and two in friendship forever. Put your blessing on this and me!' Then he closed his eyes and began to chant again in Ojibwe. Shortly, he opened his eyes and smiled. He hugged Curt and said, 'Curt, you are now my brother,' to Little Fawn, 'Little Fawn, you are my spiritual granddaughter,' to Little Flower, 'Little Flower, you are also my spiritual granddaughter,' and to me, 'You will always be my spiritual grandson!'" Everything went quiet.

Hawk said, "Helm, am I still on station?"

Helm said, "Yes, Hawk, and we—the whole crew—are mesmerized! We are so happy for the two of you and your women. It was so wonderful that Eagle Feather made you legal and approved! And all without a legal Canadian paper that doesn't mean squat! Anything you want to add?"

"No," said Hawk. "Just wanted to share with you a little of our lives. I'm a little misty-eyed right now, and I have three others who are misty-eyed also!"

"You folks can't take us as two anymore. You have to take us as four!"

Helm said, "Thanks, Hawk! Good news means a lot! Bless you!"

"Okay, Helm, thank you. And one more thing before I get off the air: we flew out overjoyed. I took flight and made another pass around the lake. Eagle Feather was waiting on the pier with Wolf Dog. He knew he would get a last wave goodbye. I hope he can still keep going in the north woods with his wolf, enjoying the life he chose. And James was right, sharing with him about the Great Creator and the spirit animals of the woods. He talks to them directly now! Signing off, my friends!" Hawk's story ended.

It was strange to hear current events off the coast of England from the Canadian northland, especially as clearly as it was being transmitted from the radio in Hawk's plane.

Moving out to sea, leaving the coast of England, and passing the coast of France, we were making good time under fair conditions. I could see deep thought on the face of Captain Mobley. He looked at the Cape of Good Hope and into the Indian Ocean.

"If we backtrack up the Atlantic to the Canal, we eat up a lot of distance that we could have used to go back east. I would say, make the passage around the Cape of Good Hope now and set the course at that. Also, we eliminate crossing a good distance from the Pacific. Besides, you will have Capt. James Cook's journey in your pocket!"

Captain Mobley started laughing. "James, I always knew you would be the best for first mate!"

"Yes, I know you think that, but I signed on as a tourist!"

Captain roared with laughter. "Okay, Captain," I said. "We are going on a journey through the Indian Ocean. Now you say over the top of Australia? Across the bottom of Australia to the tip of Tasmania could be shorter? Then up to Sydney?"

Captain said, "Yes, so it is, but I was trying to get you back to Samoa, just north of Fiji."

"Well, Captain, we can go the south route and up to Sydney. I can contact Hawk and Curt for an air flight up to Samoa."

"Okay, James, but what if they are on a tourist flight?"

With Leilani standing by, I made no effort to say we needed a private talk. Leilani was one of us now, and Captain Mobley shared as he would honor any other crew member.

"James, I've had some serious thoughts about our return trip. The most sensible option would be to take the Panama Canal again, but doing so goes against my grain. However, Hawk's predictions of storms brewing around the South American Cape put serious concerns in my mind. It could lead us head-on into harm's way! Before I make any course changes or notify the crew, as crazy as it may seem, I feel I want to take the same course that the good Captain James Cook was forced to take on his venture—down the coast of Africa, around the Cape of Good Hope. Onward then to the east and into the Indian Ocean. We can then either bear north and head up toward the north tip of Australia or go across the top and head straight east for the Fiji Islands, then to Samoa. What do you think, James?"

"Well, Captain, like you, I dread the challenge of beating the storm around the Cape. If we are turned back, the only chance to find safe waters is to head for the Panama Canal. If Leilani doesn't want to sign on for another tour, we can wait or get a flight on Qantas." I chuckled.

That brought Lei up now. She said, "Oh no, James. Once together, always together. No more flight attendant for me! Took me what? Six or seven flights to get you!"

Captain Mobley roared with laughter. "Okay, James, I'll set course for the South Atlantic. Down the African coastline, we'll make a rest stop at Cape Town! I've never seen the place before, anyhow. If the crew notices the shift in course, we can explain, or otherwise, share the plan with them at breakfast."

All things resolved, we settled in for our new adventure.

After breakfast in the morning, Captain Mobley called the crew to attention. "Now hear this!" he started. "Watches will be set according to need. We are changing course today and will track Captain Cook's journey around the Cape of Good Hope. We will sail the Indian Ocean to gain our entrance into the South Pacific. Hawk's radio contact confirmed serious storms brewing around the Cape of South America. This can also spawn hurricane activity in the Bahamas."

He then looked at Leilani and said, "Sorry, sissy, I promised you a look-see at the Bahamas, but conditions call for different measures."

Lei squeezed my arm and replied to Captain Mobley, "Sir, you are the master of this ship, and where you go, I go also without question."

Cookie banged his pan and said, "Well said, young lady! You have become one of the crew, and I am honored, mate!"

The crew all banged their cups, yelling, "Aye aye, bloody well said!" and all roared with laughter. I didn't know who had the red face, me or Lei, but anyway, I was proud.

Everyone then turned to check their duty stations. Helm, without request, went to the wheel. He knew the course! That freed up Captain Mobley, Lei, and me to have a break and watch the coastlines of beauty. We were moving across the mouth of the Mediterranean Sea.

Captain Mobley said, "James, we are getting close to one of your old haunts! Morocco!" then laughed. "That was quite a story, James! Do you want to slip in and down the river to meet with old friends?" Then he roared with laughter. Lei gave him a strange look.

"No, Captain, I think one visit there was all I needed!" I paused for a moment, looking at Lei before I spoke. "Captain, this is a long journey, and I know that upon our return to Sydney, we will all be dog-tired and frazzled. But right now, I can't keep my mind still. You know, if we were to come this way again, a trip to the Mediterranean Sea could be an exciting adventure. Just visiting the seaports would be so exciting!" I looked at Lei. She had a pouty face. Then I continued, "That is if Lei approved and was, of course, an honored guest!" She smiled and took my arm.

Captain Mobley got a faraway look in his eyes and was quiet. Then he said, "You know, James, that is food for thought! That would be a major go, mate! I think I'll store that back in my agile little brain for a while. It deserves at least some thought."

I said, "Well, Captain, I hope I didn't disturb your thinking! Sometimes my little imagination gets in the way of sound thought—reality, so to speak!"

Captain paused, then looked at me and said, "James, sometimes it takes the dreamers to make the world! If Captain James Cook had not been a big dreamer, things would not have come into reality!" Lei squeezed my arm. It was quiet time now as we moved down the coast of Africa, each of us in our own thoughts, pondering what had happened along these shores in times past. I looked over at Captain Mobley and could see the waves of the Mediterranean washing around in his brain. Lei ducked her head and giggled.

In a day or two, after some round-the-clock watches, the next big event would be coming up. As we moved south along the coast, Lei, Captain Mobley, and I were lost in our thoughts. Even Helm at the wheel seemed to be in his own world. I looked at the faraway look in Lei's eyes and wondered what an island girl would be dreaming about right now. Maybe she was thinking about how the Samoans traveled the seas in large sail canoes from different parts of the world, and how the Polynesian people blended on the islands. Could the Melanesian Islands have evolved from Africa centuries back, traveling the Indian Ocean down into the Pacific? So many interesting facts, never to be known.

It can be traced that our Indian tribes evolved by native migration crossing the landmass of the Aleutians from Siberia. But where did the giant sea canoes that could master the oceans come from? When James Cook searched for the Northwest Passage in the Bering Sea, he encountered Indian people. When he explored the Arctic Circle, there was never a log of inhabitants. Through the ages, we have met descendants of the First People, but the First People of the islands have remained a mystery.

It seems like in all of our travels, one thought stays locked in our minds: Where did these people come from, and who are they? Now as we traveled down the coast of Africa, we were about to come upon another group of islands, just away from the first mainland cape we were approaching. These islands were called the Verde Islands. Captain Mobley was making a sail-through so we could visualize closer what the group looked like, but he kept moving toward his next destination, Cape Town. There was no record of a stop here for Captain Cook either. He traveled farther out in the Atlantic with no apparent reason to stop at the Verde Islands. They were already mapped and inhabited with sea traffic coming and going. Yet it made my mind wonder: What kind of people lived there, with their multinational background, culture, and association with the mainland of Africa? Their placement seemed to be like the Galapagos off the coast of South America. Lei and I watched in wonderment as Captain Mobley made a thoughtful and complete pass-through, so all could be observed.

We were grateful for Captain Mobley making this off-course venture; otherwise, we would not have seen the Verde Islands at all. Moving down the coastline of Africa again, it seemed almost a reminder of our trip from the Galapagos, moving south off the coast of South America. In contrast, the Verde Islands were a group of ten to twelve islands. On one pass-through, we were close enough to the islands to see a lot of activity—heavily populated, with small boats moving here and there, taking off or delivering supplies and goods. To stop would have been good, but our next stop coming up would be Cape Town. We intended to stop there and stay overnight, or two days if necessary, to take on water and needed supplies.

Since Cookie was calling down for supper, we realized that no one had lunch. We were so occupied that no one mentioned or even cared. Cookie made up for it at supper, and it was very special.

Later, up on deck, Helm was at the wheel. His watch would end, and Captain Mobley was to take the eight to twelve. I volunteered for the twelve to four, but Helm said he was already prepared to take that. This man was so good. He was always going out of his way to make things better for people. Once, it almost cost him his life in a big sea storm when he got washed overboard! But here he was, back on his feet, doing what he always did.

The sea was smooth now in the evening, and the wind was not strong but steady enough to keep us moving on at about eight knots. Normal for this ship, we could still outrun most ships if necessary, but not a navy destroyer or an English frigate! I guess I must have clicked into one of my thought modes, which I do quite often. I was silent for a very long time when Captain Mobley jarred me back to reality. "James! What's on your mind?" I looked at him and then Lei and apologized.

Captain chuckled, then said, "I don't want all that's in your mind to get wasted, so tell me and Lei what's in your thoughts!" Then he chuckled again.

"Well, Captain, if I tell you what's in my mind, it might turn into another long log!" Captain roared with laughter.

"Go ahead, mate, we have plenty of time! I'm sure Leilani will enjoy hearing what makes you tick!" Then he laughed again.

I said, "Okay, so I'm committed! Actually, it's several things rolling around up there. We are tracking Captain Cook's journey. On this one journey, he came around the Cape, no stop! He proceeded into the Indian Ocean and made his way to the Pacific, past Jakarta. Jakarta was at that time the Dutch East Indies, a large shipping port controlled by the Dutch. Stops were made here for supplies and shipping for many ships, both British and foreign. He passed Jakarta to the Pacific, and his deployment was to sail north to the Aleutian Islands and search for the Northwest Passage across Canada. Not successful, he started to return home, stopping by Hawaii, where he met his death."

"And you have that in one of your logs?"

"Yes, Captain, I do, and much more!"

"That sure was a good cruise, James, clear north. The talk with the Siberian Indian and such!"

"Yes, Captain, all of our journeys have been the best. Now this one allows you to follow Captain Cook's waters clear to England and back, through the Indian Ocean."

"Yes, James, a dream come true, and thanks to you and the crew for exercising extreme patience with me!"

"Well, we wouldn't entertain any thoughts of mutiny!" Captain smiled at that. Lei looked at me funny. "Just kidding, folks. More of my quiet thinking was about Captain Bligh as well! I guess going by Jakarta on this trip conjured up thoughts!"

"Well, James, we will make a stop at Jakarta on the way through for a look around. The Dutch are no longer governing Jakarta. In fact, there's a name change, but I think they still run shipping operations out of there. So go on with Captain Bligh, your thoughts?"

"Well, Captain, as you know, Bligh's mission on several trips was to take on a load of breadfruit and edible plants from the islanders and transport them back to the Caribbean Islands for food for the slaves working on the plantations. Bligh not only had a full crew but dignitaries on board for study—botanists, scientists, explorers. When Fletcher Christian decided to pull a mutiny on the *Bounty*, they had left New Zealand and were halfway to Tonga. Bligh, with dignitaries and some crew, was put off the *Bounty* in a longboat with a week's food, a compass, and a spyglass.

"Somehow, Bligh made that journey to the safety of Jakarta, six hundred miles away, stopping at islands along the way to forage for food and water. On one stop, an islander killed one man trying to beach the boat. They left immediately and pushed on. Once in Jakarta, he secured passage from the Dutch back to England. He would have traveled this same route back, through the Indian Ocean into the Atlantic. It has been said that as they approached England, a British warship stopped them, thus retrieving Captain Bligh and taking him back to England to the Admiralty. Then the search began for the mutineers, and the Pandora set sail for the Pacific.

"In the meantime, Fletcher Christian took the *Bounty* to Tahiti. Knowing that would be a search prospect, he moved on to a small nearby island which was uncharted and thus unknown. He and the remaining crew buried the *Bounty* to avoid detection.

"Fletcher sealed his own fate because he had to live out his life with their supplies running out, depending on the island for food. In time, they died off one by one, and Fletcher was never found. I guess it was that or go to England and dangle at the end of a rope!

"This was strange, though, Captain. Fletcher Christian was a good friend as well as a crew member to Bligh. In fact, it has been said that Captain Bligh was loaning money to Fletcher as a friend that Fletcher never paid back! You would wonder why a mate would set his friend adrift in the middle of the Pacific, hoping he wouldn't make it. If Bligh did not make it, there is no telling what story Fletcher and his crew would come up with about what happened to half the crew. Also, I might relate that Captain Bligh was dispatched on Cook's last journey as ship's master."

Captain chuckled. "I knew there was a good story in there, James! Thank you!"

By then it was growing dark, the sunset slipping down on the shoreline. Helm was arriving for the watch. He said, "You folks better hit your bunks, dawn comes early!" We obliged.

As we retired to our little stateroom—and I say ours because Captain Mobley had always kept it open for us and never allowed anyone else to use it—Cookie, Helm, and the crew had a spacious compartment below the first deck, all equipped, and it was like a second home to them. They acted like it was a big sleep-in with all the antics they went through.

Maybe I failed to mention that the two hatch covers on deck are not storage holds in the ship at all but are two concealed, small staterooms, similar to the one Leilani and I stayed in. They have never been used to my knowledge but are a good asset if another traveler were aboard with his wife. Then it would be open for their private domain. Captain's cabin is a little more plush but not much larger. After all, it should be; he is captain and master of this ship! But he is a man of kind nature and would give up his space if need be!

Lei and I settled down for the night. We looked at each other, and I said, "What on earth are we doing here, girl? Off the coast of Africa!"

She giggled and said, "We are here, honey, because you wanted to share some of the travels you have had in the world with me."

I nodded and said, "And you are the icing on the cake!" She was in my arms then, and we were both in our own thoughts as we drifted into a long sleep.

In the early morning hours, we heard a loud call: "Land ho!" We hustled out of bed. Did we oversleep? No, the clock said it was going on four in the morning. Cookie was already on deck, banging his pan. He called out, "Go to it, mates! Breakfast will be served when we reach dockside!"

Although we passed the islands at Cape Verde, there wasn't much disappointment because Captain Mobley had more up his sleeve than we could guess, and he wasn't revealing anything at the moment. Captain Mobley was at the wheel, and the "Land ho!" call was the sighting of the South Cape of Africa. Cape Town would be our next port of call.

Wow! After the long sea voyage down from Plymouth, England, all the crew would love to get some earth under their feet. Lei and I too! But patience is a virtue until Captain Mobley decides it's time to reveal the plan of the day. We stayed behaved and waited; no one was going to push against Captain Mobley. He is the captain of this ship, the best at that, and this crew knows it. Like Captain Cook, he looks after the welfare of his men and keeps them out of harm's way.

The sight of the land was refreshing, knowing this would be a stop. The sight of Cape Town was not only refreshing but seemed unbelievable to us all as we had traveled almost halfway around the world. Cape Town would be another exciting venture for us, following the seaways of Captain Cook!

The first glimpse of Cape Town revealed the flat-topped mountains behind the city. One could stand on the flat top and have a panoramic view of the Atlantic, following around the Cape into the Indian Ocean. This was the crossroads of the world in the spice trade as far back as the 1400s. The Dutch had already populated this area from the Sahara Desert down and had also populated much of Africa with farms, etc. Portugal was also a rival country in the settlement of lands.

Seeing this, it was not hard to understand how Bligh could find a safe haven and passage back to England. The Dutch East Indies was a well-established business at the time, and ships of many nationalities traveled the waters of the Atlantic and Indian Ocean chasing the wealth of the spice trade. Sadly, slave ships also traveled this route, bringing slaves from Africa to different island plantations in the Caribbean Islands. America had abolished slavery, and plantation owners were searching offshore for sites to recover their plantations and buy free labor.

At the risk of repeating myself, we saw that the Dutch had control of most of Africa and also most of the islands in Indonesia. There was heavy Dutch trading in Jakarta, which was the port Bligh had set his compass on because the Dutch East Indies were operating big there in the 1700s. Bligh knew it was a safe harbor, with financial help and passage back to England, all at the expense of King George!

Captain Cook's journey through the Great Barrier Reef also provided a safe harbor for much-needed repairs, allowing him to return to England.

Before Captain Cook explored, charted, and surveyed the Pacific islands, the route around the Horn of Africa was the one taken to points in the Atlantic Ocean and then to points through the Indian Ocean to the Pacific, as far as New Zealand. Later, when the Pacific became a way of travel around the Cape of South America, there were times when ships were turned back because of strong and freezing storms that could blow in from the Arctic Circle. Then ships were turned back across the Atlantic to sail around the Cape of Africa, into the Indian Ocean, and then out to the Pacific. It made me think how devastating that would feel to the crews on those ships! Most captains were deployed on a mission, so it was necessary.

Well, back to Cape Town. It was a beautiful sight all the way in. The funny thing about oceans, you can't tell where the Atlantic meets the Indian, probably only by a geographic point! Duh!

When we docked, the Sheila was secured, and the next step in order was to get checked by security. A Dutch officer stomped up the gangway, uninvited! That was not supposed to happen! The dock was his domain, and the ship's deck was Captain Mobley's. Captain Mobley gave him a hard look, and the security officer took a chance of being tossed over the side and "deep-sixed." But the captain, being a gentleman, addressed the security officer. "Maybe we will have our check on the dock, mate! I believe you are outside of your security!" Security looked around, apologized, and he and Captain Mobley walked off to the dock. Apologies were made, and security was cleared. We were able to proceed.

Returning to the deck, he said, "I remember Cookie saying breakfast would be at dockside?" and then chuckled.

Cookie responded, "Coming right up, Captain."

As we gathered around the galley table, Captain Mobley said a short thank-you for our food. Sitting, he said, "After breakfast, I will give you the 'Plan of the Day.'" No business while we eat. This was a hard rule with the captain but a good rule.

After breakfast, Captain Mobley looked around at everyone in anticipation. "His plan! Mates, I am declaring a field day! We are low on water and supplies. Cookie is in charge of replenishing needed supplies. There is fresh water dockside to fill our tanks. Helm will assist Cookie in securing needed goods. The crew will assist in transporting to the ship and stowing away in proper areas. When Cookie is satisfied that field day is complete, he will secure, and then he can release you to your leisure. And *no*, to answer your question, James and Leilani will not be assisting you on this venture! When complete, mates, and upon Cookie's release, I'm granting two days' leave in Cape Town, more if needed!"

The cheer went up! As soon as Cookie had the galley all ship-shape, with the crew excitedly helping, it was a dash to the water hydrant and the markets. As the crew filed free of the gangway, the captain said to the crew, "Don't get caught up with any little *Dutch dumplings*," then roared with laughter. I snickered, and Lei just rolled her eyes.

For the next two days, Captain Mobley, Leilani, and I had our time touring the great town. Surprisingly, the captain even wanted the boat trip out to the island where Nelson Mandela was held in jail for so many years.

After the tour, before we loaded on the boat to return, Captain Mobley looked at us and said, "Nelson Mandela is another great man dear to my heart. What he did for his country should never be forgotten." We solemnly nodded in agreement.

On the second day, at supper's end, Captain Mobley looked around and said, "What do you think of having one more day here?" The cheer went up, and Cookie banged his pan! As everyone scattered, the captain, Lei, and I stayed on for another cup of coffee. I said, "That was a *good go*, Captain!"

Captain Mobley replied, "Yes, and it has been a long journey up to now, and we have a long way yet. I don't want any apathy to set in."

"I don't think that would happen, Captain. There has been plenty to see and do on this journey!"

When everyone was back the next night, Captain Mobley said, "Mates, we will get underway after breakfast in the morning. We will be tracing Captain Cook's route into the Indian Ocean. We are heading for the Indonesian Islands. I like to call them the *Dutch East Indies*, even though that has been past history! James and I have not fully charted the course into the Pacific, but we will soon."

Smiles were all around. The crew was refreshed and ready for the next venture! They wanted to take in all they could, because soon the bay of Sydney, Australia, would be in sight!

So underway from Cape Town, we were heading for the Indian Ocean and Jakarta, our next port of call. Lei and I were on deck with the captain at the wheel. "James, I know you were doing a lot of poking around in Cape Town. The Dutch East Indies captured your attention. Share with me what you found out. I know that they were a rich company and were the salvation of both Bligh and Cook. How did the Dutch come to be here?"

"Well, Captain, they had been established here since the 1400s. Not only Cape Town but most of Africa. They colonized much of the country, which gave them a good return on their efforts. The biggest draw for Cape Town and the Indonesian Islands was the spice trade and slave trade. The spice trade was the biggest draw, and when established, the Dutch East Indies began to grow! The spice trade was captivated by the company, and they more or less became the leader in this enterprise. Spices used to come to them overland through Muslim operators. The journey overland was slow and tedious, also expensive. Spices were coming out of the Orient and these islands in the Indian Ocean. The company was formed and established sources here and more or less captured the trade. Wealth came from the spice trade and the slave trade, and the company grew powerful. They even sold stock at that time! Can you believe that? Many investors! They traded slaves and spices as far as the Caribbean! They even established colonies in the New World, America. At one time, New York was really New Amsterdam. Even though other countries were involved here—Spain, France, Portugal—the Dutch took over and won them out.

"I never knew that the Dutch East India Company was so large and covered the trade in the Atlantic as well as most of the Indian Ocean islands and maybe into the Pacific. It was a safe harbor for seamen and a source of communication to other parts of the world. No wonder Bligh and Cook struck out for Jakarta when in trouble. To them, it was safety and a source of rescue. And also, good old King George was paying the bill!"

Captain chuckled at that. "Probably in those days, good old King George had big payouts! After all, he wanted to tap into the business with his *breadfruit enterprise*, shipping from the Pacific to the slave barons in the Caribbean. Also, we are fortunate he had a keen interest in the exploration of the Pacific."

"Right at that, Captain. Those times helped to mold the world," I replied.

Then Lei said, "Yes, and after all that history and discovery, this little island girl would not have advanced in life, become a flight attendant for Qantas, and discovered you!" Captain Mobley just roared with laughter.

Captain then said, "You know, James, talking about coloniza-tion, the Dutch East Indies not only controlled all the islands of Indonesia but they also, in history, colonized parts of Australia and even down as far as Tasmania and New Zealand." Then he chuckled. "How would you like to have a little stock in that company, James?"

"Yes, I would, Captain. You know the Dutch are tight and not about to put their money in a risky venture!" He roared with laughter.

We had a quiet spell, then the captain spoke up again. I had wondered if he was staying on watch too long, but he wanted time to talk.

"James, my course is set to head for the lower tip of Sumatra across from the island of Java. A pass-through there, and we can go on down to Jakarta. I definitely want a stop there. This was the safe port that both Bligh and Cook went to for help. The Dutch are still active there. Jakarta is the capital of the islands and surely a busy place. I bet if we can find a past position of the Dutch East Indies center, we may pick up a little history. Just a chance. Even so, I want to make that stop just to see where our old heroes stood out for!" He was grinning as he spoke.

"Captain, I think it is a *good go* that we stop there!" I agreed.

Then the surprise came out! "You know, mate, Singapore lies just to the north. I think we should show Lei the botanical gardens while we are here." Before I could answer, he turned to the crew on deck and yelled, "Who wants to go to Singapore?" The cheer went up from the crew, and Cookie rushed on deck to bang his pan! Captain roared with laughter. "I guess that confirms it, mates!"

Captain then called for Helm and said, "Take over, Helm, set course for Singapore." We were stunned! I never thought we would ever make a return trip there. When we found a good port and docked, Captain said, "Okay, boys, tour the city for the rest of the day! Tomorrow, we go to the gardens, and the next morning we get underway for Jakarta. A short stop, and then on!"

That night, Lei and I sat on deck, and she wanted to know what this was all about. She was so excited that all this was being done on her behalf. Lei and I stayed up a little late to enjoy the moonlight on the sea and the balmy breezes of the Indian Ocean.

By morning, Helm had found proper docking and called the crew out to secure. All we had to do was come out to breakfast that Cookie had already prepared. Wow! Captain arranged for security. The crew took off for the city. Captain, Lei, and I found a tour bus for our outing for the day, stopping at special sites and also good shops for looking and buying. You know how it is when you are having fun! The day ended too quickly. After an excellent meal, we returned to the ship. Tomorrow was the big event! Captain retired early, and everyone else was doing their own thing. Lei and I had the deck to ourselves. We listened to the sounds and sights of the city.

After a long silence, Lei said to me, "James, what are these gardens all about?"

I said, "They are rated to be the most beautiful gardens in the world. So peaceful, so relaxing, so beautiful. Most are so moved by the tour that they say it is like a glimpse of Eden."

Lei was in deep thought, then she asked, "Is it like Samoa?"

I asked, "Why do you want to know that?"

"Well, James, Samoa is Eden!"

I realized where she was coming from, so extreme care was in order. "What makes you say that, Lei?"

She responded, "Well, people from Samoa think they have always been there. Not from anywhere else. Samoa is the Garden of Eden!"

Carefully, I said, "Can you tell me how the Samoan people came to believe that?"

"Yes, James. It happened at the beginning of time when the missionaries came to the island. They taught us that we were all from the Garden of Eden!"

I said, "Okay. Let me say how I feel about this, Lei. Bear with me because I don't want to upset you or let anything come between our love!"

Lei said, "Go on, James. Tell me what your feelings are. If you believe differently, I will never let that come between us. I love you! Is this something about your two worlds you talked about?"

"No." I chuckled. "It is kind of like the real world!"

She said, "Go on."

"Well, Lei, when the missionaries came, that was long ago, so it's obvious that time had already begun, eons ago! I think what they meant to say was that all of us had come from Eden. That was the garden where the Great Creator made the first man and woman. So that is what the missionaries meant: you and I have all come from Eden. Through the centuries, we came down from the people that He made, Adam and Eve, and yes, it was a beautiful garden!"

Lei went into deep thought. Then she said, "James, the Samoans have said this for centuries. I can see how this can be. They all wanted to believe they were from Eden. But now?"

"But now, Lei, yes, they are from Eden. The missionaries were right. But Samoa is not Eden, only the people."

"Oh, James, I do see now. I understand! So we should say Samoa is not Eden?"

I thought for a moment and said, "Well, let's say that the people of Samoa are from the first couple that lived in Eden, so the people are, yes, in reality, from Eden, descended down. Also, Samoa is such a beautiful place that maybe we can say the beautiful gardens of Samoa are like the Gardens of Eden! But a little east of Eden!"

Lei laughed and jumped into my arms. "Oh, James, you make everything alright!"

I said, "When you see the gardens tomorrow, you will see what I mean, but they are man-made, Lei, and can't hold a candle to the gardens in Samoa that have come up from creation."

The garden tour the next day was spectacular for all, as usual—very impressive and very thought-provoking. To me, the second time around, they seemed more beautiful, more meaningful, and with Lei by my side, that was probably the reason why! After a hearty breakfast in the morning, we got underway for Jakarta. In these two days, we had crossed the equator twice. The equator is almost the center point, parallel across the group of islands.

Leaving Cape Town and going east, Captain set a course around and up the east coast of Africa. He asked Helm to take over for a while. Helm said, "Yes, sir, Captain, and I can take you right into Singapore!" Lei and I listened with interest to the discussions. Talk of the course was sometimes over our heads unless I had hands-on experience.

Helm asked, "Tacking up the east side of Africa, do you want to go as far north as Cambodia, then bear southeast down to Malaysia to Singapore?"

The captain studied the map for a moment, gauging the distance. "That would be likely, Helm. The distance is a little greater than heading for the channel between Sumatra and Java. But then we would have to backtrack north and west to reach Singapore. I think your suggestion is proper. A little longer run, but no backtracking, and it gives us a chance to see Sumatra on both sides, pending the run next day down to Jakarta in Java."

So after all the jargon, we were on course, and Lei, the rest of the crew, and I were ready for sightseeing. Captain said, "James, is there anything more you would like to see in Africa?"

"No, sir, what I would want to see is too far inland."

"What is it you want to see?"

"Well, Captain, I thought Timbuktu was on the coast, but it's quite farther inland!"

Captain had a questioning look and asked, "Why there?"

I said, "Well, in my lifetime, I have had a few people tell me that they would like to *send me* to Timbuktu!" Captain roared with laughter! Lei looked quizzical, and I refrained from explaining.

By evening, we had passed the tip of Sumatra, heading down the Malaysian waters toward Singapore. Captain said, "Perfect, Helm! Time enough for docking, going ashore for a good oriental supper, and tomorrow gives us ample time to take the Garden Tour. After the tour, mates, we can lay back and rest and meditate until the morning dawn. After one of Cookie's hearty breakfasts, we will get underway to Jakarta!"

I thought to myself, "Yes, this has been the longest trip that this crew has ventured upon, and Captain is smart to have some rest stops, even with the excitement of new and interesting places."

As soon as we pulled into Singapore harbor, the majesty of the city was exciting to view. Singapore was no longer a typical island but a modern hub of state-of-the-art activity. It seemed like all the countries in the world had come to Singapore's shores for technology and subcontracting of many sophisticated products to be manufactured and purchased. So it seemed Singapore had built these large majestic gardens to add some presence of peace and beauty, maybe also solitude, for the people of the island. It also drew people from offshore to come and see what the island garden could offer them, for a peaceful mind, away for a while from the business of the world.

The next morning, Helm and Cookie decided to *hang out* with Captain, Lei, and me. We welcomed that, for many times on shore leave they grouped with the crew or traveled alone. The trip through the garden was a long one, but somehow it seemed to end before we were ready. Everyone was awestruck, even we, who had been there once before. Lei was quiet the whole time and could not believe that man could produce such a thing of natural beauty. Of course, he did not create it but placed what was created in such a manner that the beauty of the creation could be shown in all its splendor. Not a word was spoken the whole trip. I looked at Lei many times, and she seemed to be totally captivated.

That evening, after the tour and ample shares of the Singapore cuisine, that became the talk of the evening. Even Cookie was impressed by the chefs' oriental preparations and had conversations with the chefs he liked most. I'm sure he came away with recipes he would later try and introduce to his chefs' cooking school that he and Simone had started in Sydney.

In the morning, after breakfast, we secured everything and started moving away from the dockside. Captain set the course to swing north around the island and take the pass between the islands. This way, we were not backtracking but sailing on the opposite side of the island to see the sights on down. The island itself was Borneo, and Jakarta was on the island of Java, down under. I must say that Jakarta is now the capital of these Indonesian islands. In the 1400s, it was the central place of the Dutch East Indies, sort of like Cape Town in Africa.

We found a docking facility that was still part of the Dutch East Indies company. Once we secured the ship, we stepped off for a look. As we stood on the dock, memories came flooding back of what we had learned. We had to marvel at the exploits of Captain William Bligh and Captain James Cook. Captain Bligh's ship, HMS *Bounty*, was mutinied by Fletcher Christian north of the island of Tonga and west of Tahiti. Bligh was set adrift in a longboat with twenty-some passengers and crew. Twelve who were loyal to Bligh were retained on the ship; there was no room in the boat. With only one week of food and water, a watch, and a looking glass, he had to decide where to go. The only safe port was Jakarta, six hundred miles to the west. He made it with the loss of only one man.

Then came Cook, who was exploring New Zealand, Tasmania, and Australia. He ran aground in the Great Barrier Reef. This reef had never been surveyed, but Cook dumped all he could to lighten the ship and slowly pressed on with a damaged and leaking vessel. When the reef stopped him again, he put the crew in two longboats and, with much effort, towed the HMS *Endeavour* through channels found in that reef. Once back into the Pacific again, he rounded the north coast of Australia and also headed for Jakarta for rescue and repair. The Dutch East Indies, the powerful Dutch trading company, helped Cook make repairs and get the *Endeavour* seaworthy enough to limp back to England. All this kindness was not without a bill! The expenses encountered by both ships were billed to the Crown, which meant good old King George.

The sign for the Dutch East Indies was still there, along with some artifacts and history inside. We marveled at the conversation between Captain Mobley and the store manager—Aussie talk to Dutch talk! When all was seen, the Dutchman said we were more than welcome to use the dock and his facilities. We planned to leave in the morning. It was nice to be tied off to a safe dock for the night. When we got underway in the morning, we would head out to the Pacific, round the Great Barrier Reef, packed with so many memories, and return to Sydney and Captain Cook's dock!

On deck that night, taking in the beauty of the islands, everyone had gone to their own quarters, and things were at peace. No watches, no wheel, no responsibilities. Lei, the captain, and I talked about places we had been and about places unseen. I said, "Captain, when we reach Sydney, we will have somewhat gone around the world!"

Captain looked at me, surprised. "I hadn't really thought about that, James, but I think you are right! What's our next course?" I asked.

"Well, when we leave Jakarta and head east and past Timor, I'll take a shift north for a last look at the other islands, then east out into the Pacific. You know, James, we could set course for Samoa for you and Lei?"

I said, "Everyone is travel-weary and may not like the extra travel."

The captain responded, "Well, James, I would like to do that. No sense in calling Hawk and Curt in when we are closer here. Besides, the crew already told me not to have the homecoming party this time. Save it for later. Too much activity after this long trip. I agree with them; everyone is super tired after this journey. We all got in what you might say is what I wanted to do, and it was a big success at that!"

I said, "I will leave that up to you, Captain. I don't want to make a call on that."

Captain chuckled. "I was hoping you would agree, and I know Lei would feel much more comfortable with that arrangement. So that's the plan. When we clear these islands, we have a straight shot to Samoa. The trip from their home is quick and easy!"

I said, "Well, Captain, I can't thank you enough, so I will tell you beforehand, this has been the most exciting trip of a lifetime, more than any we have done yet! I don't think you need to top it, sir!"

Captain roared with laughter. "No, mate, I think this will be the biggie! But I feel good about all I could hear about Captain Cook! I know you have it all down, and I will enjoy reading it in my old age!"

I said, "What do you mean old age? We are not old, Captain!" and he just roared with laughter.

Lei spoke then, "You men may think you are old, but leave me out! I'm not old yet!"

Again, Captain laughed!

We were making good headway through the Indian Ocean and very quickly entering the Pacific Ocean. The course was set for Samoa. I was anxious in a way. It had been a very long trip, and I was sure everyone wanted to see home. I was glad Captain had postponed a homecoming reception. That would be stressful at this time.

We stood there at the wheel with the captain, and things became quiet. Captain seemed to be in deep thought. He looked at us and then called for Helm, who came quickly. Captain said, "Okay, mate, how would you like to take us into Samoa?"

Helm beamed and smiled. He always loved it when the captain turned over full control to him. Captain motioned to Lei and me to follow him to the back of the ship, on the fantail aft.

He then had a really serious look on his face. I thought he looked rather melancholy. He put his arms around us and said, "Sissey, mate, have you ever watched the wake the ship makes behind her? Not the iron ones with a propeller beating, but an old wooden ship like the *Sheila II* breaking a smooth wake behind her?"

Lei and I watched as we moved along, and the smooth, beautiful wake broke behind us. Captain went on, "As you watch the wake behind, it is a beautiful sight that soon comes to an end." He paused, then said with a very serious face, "James, you are my best mate, and I know that whatever I say to James stays with James."

Captain looked at me. I said nothing. He went on very seriously, "You know when Helm was washed overboard, he was watching this wake with the ship moving away from him, maybe never to see her again. Thank God for our quick discovery of our loss! We turned about quickly and were able to keep him in sight, lowered the longboat into the water, and rescued him. I came near losing my good friend, and that always grieves me. But good fortune smiled that dark and treacherous night, and we brought him home."

Captain's face went soft then as he continued his story, "You were here, James. You had to live through that terror also. You were right in the thick of it with my mates!" Then he went on, "You know after Helm warmed up and got back to normal, I took him to my cabin for a shot of brandy to subside his shivers and to bring about a little calmness. Helm shared something with me I did not know!

Prior to that journey, our old bachelor Helm had found the love of his life and gotten married! And you know what? Through all this, his wife, Sandy, was pregnant. That shocked me pretty badly! Almost losing a good man like Helm, but for him to be married and with a baby on the way!"

We said nothing, just hurt for the captain. Then he smiled and said, "But here is the good part." He chuckled. "Helm has confided in me to keep this in the family. Sandy and Helm have decided to name the boy Jason, after his father. Jason Helms!" Then he smiled. "You know, for as long as I've known Helm and even the crew, we never knew his name was Jason! It was always just Helm!"

We were happy for the captain and also happy for Helm. And also, *Mum* is the word.

It seemed like no time after entering the Pacific that we heard the cry, "Land ho!" In the distance, the beautiful island of Samoa was beginning to take form! Lei couldn't wait. She hurried to our cabin to get our few things in order. Later in the day, we docked. The gangway was set, and two passengers were ready to disembark.

We said our goodbyes all around, with Captain Mobley being the last. He gave Lei and me a big bear hug and said, "I will keep in touch with you two!" We left the ship and stayed on the dock to see the *Sheila II* ship out. She moved full sail out of the bay in all her glory. I had a lump in my throat, and Lei had tears in her eyes. We hugged each other. I said, "Welcome home." She didn't answer, just reached up and planted a big, passionate kiss on my lips. I liked that kind of answer!

Just then, a jeep rolled up, and lo and behold, it was Hawk. Cocoa was riding in the front seat. Hawk opened the side door, and Cocoa was out in a flash, between us, tail wagging and his nose nudging my hand and then Lei's. Hawk said, "I wasn't busy today, saw the ship on the horizon, picked up Cocoa from the caregiver, and hustled down. Need a ride up to home?"

"No thanks, Hawk. We and the old dog will hike up. Need to get our land legs back! How is it with you, Curt, and the lovely ladies?"

"All good!" said Hawk. "When you get settled in and rested, we all will stop by and listen to sea stories!"

I laughed. "Sounds good, my friend!" Hawk roared off in the jeep for another *go* at the day.

We hiked to the house and tossed our things onto the porch veranda. We looked at the low-slung hammock. Cocoa had already taken his position, half under and half out from under the hammock. He let out a happy bark. Lei looked at me and laughed. We piled into the hammock for a good rest before undertaking anything. We settled in. Cocoa's tail was thumping underneath. He always lay half under, half out, so he could roll his head back and check on us. Cocoa always liked to know where we were at all times.

Lei and I were holding hands. She was tight against my side, her head on my shoulder, just like on the plane flights. I had my right hand resting down on Cocoa's body so he knew I was there. Silence for a while, thoughts on our minds, just settling in. "Kicking back," like a friend of mine used to say. We were bone tired.

Lei spoke, "Honey, after such a long trip, do you think Captain Mobley will ever want to venture out again?"

I said, "Sweety, I can't answer that. I guess that will be up to Captain Mobley."

Lei said, "If he decides on another cruise someday, will you go?"

I said, "Maybe."

Lei asked, "Will you go alone?"

"No, Lei, never, ever." She rolled into me and kissed me with passion, then settled back. "So you are promising me that you will never go without me?"

I said, "Never without you, babe, never ever." She scooted in as close as she could get, and that was fine with me. I listened to her soft breathing as she went into a beautiful sleep. As sleep moved into me, my arm was around my beautiful woman, and my other arm was hanging over the hammock with my hand resting on Cocoa's body, my best mate. As I drifted off, I said, "Never ever."

Author's Note

When I was near the end of this story, my mind was thinking about the conclusion. My departed wife was always the *lady* in the story, so I needed to work that in. I also worked in Cocoa, my Labrador, to add a little tribute.

On January 24, Cocoa died in my arms. That stopped the writing. It was hard to resume, but I managed to keep Anita and Cocoa in the story, alive, as a final tribute.

My point, dear readers, is to appeal to your own circumstances. If you have a good woman in your arms and a very faithful pet, love them and never forsake them. Never ever.

Thank you!

About the Author

James left the East at seventeen to join the US Navy and serve his country. He picked up the pen and put it to paper. Now at ninety, he says, "At ninety, I keep saying, 'Just one more!' But my imagination will not let me quit! I guess we go on until we can't. Twilight will arrive!"

I give you another story from my imagination combined with real-life experiences.

Other titles by James A. Gardner

- *Odyssey Down Under*
- *Odyssey Down Under: Parts II and III*
- *Odyssey Down Under: Parts IV and V*
- *Odyssey Down Under: Captain Bligh and Captain Cook*
- *Odyssey Down Under: Canadian Adventure from the Tropics to the Far Northland*
- *Beyond the Black Gate Volume II, cowritten with Anita Sutherland Gardner*

Printed in the USA
CPSIA information can be obtained
at www.ICGtesting.com
LVHW092326210924
791611LV00001B/59

9 798893 082517